Skating Through

Jennifer Cosgrove

A NineStar Press Publication

Published by NineStar Press
P.O. Box 91792,
Albuquerque, New Mexico, 87199 USA.
www.ninestarpress.com

Skating Through

"If You Can Play, You Can Play" is the motto of the You Can Play Project.

For more information: www.youcanplayproject.org

Printed in the USA
First Edition
July, 2018

Print ISBN: 978-1-949340-04-4

Also available in eBook, ISBN: 978-1-949340-03-7

Warning: This book contains depictions of homophobia.

There are two things Ben Lewis has convinced himself he can never have at the same time: playing hockey and being openly gay. Hockey is looking to be his only choice. Until now. Being captain of the team and starting his senior year of high school is a lot to handle. Throw in a budding friendship with his crush, Marcus, and Ben is faced with deciding if he's brave enough to take the next step.

Fortunately, courage can come from unexpected places. His BFF Ryan, new friends, and a voice from the past are great assists to his determination to be true to himself and keep playing the game he loves, but will they be enough?

Thank you.

To my husband Stephen, for your unwavering support and love.

To my children. Love you always.

To Melanie and Deborah, without whom this never would have been written.

To Jessica, who tried for years to get me into hockey. I finally made it! #GoDevils

And finally, to student athletes everywhere, you are amazing. "If you can play, you can play."

Chapter One

"THERE YOU ARE."

A murmured meow was Ben's answer as Biscuit settled next to him, curling close to his side. He was wide awake. It was still dark outside, the only light in the room coming through the window from the streetlight on the corner. The alarm hadn't gone off yet, but he'd trained himself to be up at the crack of dawn. He stretched, careful not to disturb the cat, and ran a hand through his hair in an attempt to flatten out the mess. He was in dire need of a haircut. Every year, he decided to grow it out, and every year, he changed his mind as soon as hockey season was on the horizon. It was just too much to deal with under a hockey helmet. Besides, he looked a little ridiculous with long hair.

He stared at the ceiling and let the rare quiet of the house wash over him. Most guys his age would sleep until noon, especially on summer break, but that wasn't going to happen. The alarm started going off and Ben grabbed for the phone, accidentally knocking it off the nightstand along with his *Band of Brothers* DVDs and sending Biscuit scurrying away and out the door. He fumbled over the side of the bed, finally snagged the phone, and swiped across the screen to turn off the cheerful beeping.

Maybe he should just give in and go to the rink, get in some early ice time. He sat up and swung his legs over the side of the bed. His dad would probably get up and give him a ride. Ben rose and took a step toward the door. Or he'd tell him to go back to bed—*it's an off day, for god's sake, Ben.* Probably not, then. He shut the door with a click and got back in bed, scrolling through the texts from last night out of habit.

Ryan: *he was in the shop again*
Ben: ...
Ryan: *I didn't say anything*
Ryan: *I wouldn't do that*
Ben: *I know.*
Ryan: *you're going to have to talk to him eventually*

At that, Ben had put his phone down and gone to bed. Ryan meant well, but he wasn't ready to deal with that. It just didn't work that way. Not for him. Not now.

Ben looked at the time and groaned. When the phone beeped again, he turned it completely off and tossed it back onto the nightstand. He thought about getting up anyway but dragged a pillow over his head instead. Sleep deserved another try.

THE NEXT TIME Ben woke up it was to a pounding on his bedroom door that could only be one person. "Cut it out, Bethy!"

"Quit playing with yourself and get up, Benny!" The giggling that followed was cut short when he heard his mom's voice coming up the stairs, followed by her light footsteps.

"Beth! Leave your brother alone." A pause. "And don't be crude."

Ben rolled his eyes and struggled to sit up. There was a gentle tapping on his door. "Ben, honey?"

"Yeah, Mom."

The door opened and she peeked in cautiously.

"Remember we're going to help Gran today." How could he forget? She'd reminded him every day for the past week. It wasn't like he was going to suddenly develop amnesia or something. "And we need to leave soon, so if you want breakfast, you'd better get a move on."

He definitely wanted breakfast. "I'll be right down."

"Hurry. The vultures are circling," she said with a wink and closed the door behind her.

Ben got up, stretched, and rolled his shoulders. He thought about going through the flexibility routine Coach Jordan recommended, but he just didn't feel like it. It was his day off, and he was going to stick to that. He let his routine slip a bit during the summer, and he'd get enough of a workout moving heavy boxes and furniture, anyway. His grandma was leaving the cold winters of upstate New York to escape to Florida's warmer climate. She'd laughed when he told her she was a walking, talking cliché.

"That might be true, my love, but I'll still be the youngest one down there." It *was* true. She'd taken early retirement when his grandfather had gotten ill, and now that he'd passed, she had the means to make a move closer to her sister. He was going to miss her.

"Ben?" His mom's voice floated up the stairs.

He sighed and picked up the DVDs that had fallen down beside the bed and started pulling clothes out so he could tell her, honestly, that he was getting ready.

"Five seconds!"

"Plate's on the table."

Ugh. He'd better hurry. He could smell bacon, and either Beth or his dad would have no qualms about stealing it right off his plate. Always the bacon. And today it would be real bacon instead of turkey bacon, so that made it even more tempting. Not that turkey bacon ever stopped them.

He felt a twinge of guilt for making his mom fix two different breakfasts most days, but it was something they'd lived with from the time he'd started high school. Ever since he got serious about hockey.

It was all he'd ever wanted to do. He'd known from the first time he stepped out on the ice. He was good at it, and he was lucky to have supportive parents. It hadn't been easy. The equipment and fees were expensive, and the demanding training and game schedules were always a challenge. But he was never late to practice, and they'd never missed a home game. It would be worth it, he thought. The college scholarship would make a huge difference. He didn't want his parents to bear all the burden of putting him and his sister through school, not if he could help it.

He pulled on a faded Flyers T-shirt and opened his door, almost tripping over the ball of fluff waiting right outside. "Dammit, Biscuit!" He received a put-upon meow in return as he scooped the cat up in his arms. Biscuit's rumbling purr was comforting against his chest as he carried him down the stairs. The cat started to squirm as soon as they got to the kitchen, ready to get at the food waiting in his dish.

Ben absently brushed cat hair off his shirt before sitting at the table in front of a plate piled high with eggs, bacon, and fruit. He was just in time because his dad and sister had almost finished their own breakfasts and were already eyeballing his. It was a cheat day, for god's sake, but they were all vicious when it came to bacon. "Morning."

Not quite sociable yet, his dad answered with a grunt. He'd be better after his second cup of coffee.

His mom swooped by and ruffled his hair. "You have ten minutes." Ben ran a hand through his already messy hair and groaned. She narrowed her eyes. "Get a move on."

He took her at her word and dug in. After he finished, he slurped down coffee and juice and took the extra precaution of downing a glass of water. It was already warm outside, even for August, and it'd be a long sweaty day.

"When do you think we'll be getting home?" He'd promised Ryan he would go to a party with him tonight. It was a promise that only a best friend could drag out of him. Ben didn't like parties for the most part, especially ones where there was drinking and other stuff. He knew it made him look like a goody-goody or a stick-in-the-mud or whatever other term Ryan could dream up to tease him with, but he didn't like to take any chances. He couldn't put his future in danger, as dramatic as that sounded in his own head.

His mom was digging through her purse for her keys. He let her look for a few seconds before reaching over and plucking them off the hook. She took them with a lopsided smile. "Sorry, what did you say?"

Ben rolled his eyes with a grin. She knew his practice schedule better than he did, but could never keep up with her keys. "What time do you think we'll be back?"

"Why? Got a hot date or something?"

Ben grimaced behind her back. There was a lot she didn't know about him, especially in that respect. He opened the front door and gestured for her to go ahead.

"Nah. Ryan talked me into going to a thing at someone's house. Holtsy's girlfriend's?" He didn't think she'd have a problem with him going to a party, but he didn't want to have to answer a lot of questions. Plus, she loved Ryan.

She gave him an odd look before unlocking the car. She knew he didn't like parties. "We should be back in plenty of time. You want to drive there or back?"

He'd had his driver's license for only two weeks and was still nervous behind the wheel. It hadn't helped that he'd put off learning how to drive until this summer, right before his senior year. The only reason he finally relented was because he'd be off to college soon, and his dad pointed out they wouldn't be there to drive him to practice or class. So Ben had sucked it up and decided to learn. Driving still scared the hell out of him, though.

"Back." The traffic would be lighter at least.

"All right." They had a brief squabble over the radio that his mom won, before heading out. It was just the two of them, as Beth would be coming later with their dad after running some errands. "But no trying to get out of it this time."

Ben shook his head and smiled out the window. "I won't."

MARGARET LEWIS WAS Ben's biggest fan. Gran had gone to as many of his games as she possibly could, right from the beginning. He loved her for it. She was waiting on the front porch when they pulled up in front of her house, and was down the steps before they even got out of the car, waving the entire time. Ben's grin matched his mom's. Gran's enthusiasm was contagious.

Ben jogged to the front porch and gave her a hug, accepting her kiss on the cheek.

"You've gotten taller since I last saw you." She made it sound accusatory as she wiped a smear of lipstick off his face, as if he hadn't been almost a head taller than her for years.

"You saw me last week."

"Still." She bumped him out of the way to give his mom a hug. "Anne, don't you think he's gotten taller?" The two of them were very close. His mom's parents had both passed away in a car accident when she was a teenager, and over time, Gran had become a second mom to her.

"If you go by the extra groceries I'm buying, then yes."

Ben groaned as they both laughed, but there was truth in what she was saying. It was a constant struggle to keep weight on and build the muscle he needed to be strong and fast on the ice. He'd learned that bulking up as much as he could during the summer helped him maintain that level of fitness longer during the season.

Still, he knew his line here. "I can't help that I'm always hungry."

Gran patted his cheek and nudged him inside. "Work hard, and you'll get to find out what I'm making for lunch. We're doing the attic today."

Ben bit back another groan. It was going to be miserable and cramped, and he'd be the one shoved up there to lower down boxes for them to go through.

The attic was just as hot and stifling as he'd expected. Ben had to be careful not to accidentally drop something while moving the heavy boxes and other things that had been stored up there. He scrubbed a hand across his sweaty face and pushed his hair out of his eyes. His dad had arrived promptly after lunch and offered to take over, but Ben waved him off. He'd made good progress, and it didn't make sense to have someone else suffer from the heat.

He brought a box all the way down the ladder and handed it off. "I'll be right back, just grabbing some water."

"How much more is up there?" His dad peered up into the narrow opening that led up into the small space.

Ben shook his head. "You don't want to know. We've made a dent, but there's still a lot."

"Shit." His dad clapped him on the shoulder, balancing the box in his other arm. "Go take a break. You've earned it."

Ben went down stairs and grabbed a bottle of water out of the fridge. He flopped down on a kitchen chair and restrained himself from pouring the ice-cold water over his head. The combination of heat and physical labor was more tiring than he'd expected. Slumping back in the chair, he gazed at the living room full of the boxes and bags he'd hauled out of the attic. His mom, Beth, and Gran were going through them but kept stopping to show each other things they'd found. It looked like barely controlled chaos to him, but they seemed to know what they were doing.

He pressed the water bottle to the back of his neck for a few seconds before drinking half of it in one go. Closing his eyes, he let the chatter from the next room wash over him. Somehow, he'd managed to avoid thinking about it all day, but Ben hated that Gran was moving. Even though he hadn't said as much to anyone, they could probably tell.

He opened his eyes just in time to see Beth pull a flat wooden box out of a storage container. She held it up—it looked old and worn, but still solid, and the dark grain caught the sunlight that filtered in through the windows. "Gran, what's this?"

Gran looked at the box and gasped. "Oh, heavens. I haven't seen that thing in ages." She took it from Beth and turned it over in her hands. Her eyes seemed to be glowing. Ben leaned forward to hear what she had to say about it, wondering what was causing such a reaction.

"This belonged to my Uncle Will." Gran ran a finger over the lid. "My mum held on to it after he died in the war. Grandmother refused to even look at it. It always reminded her of...well. Will broke her heart, in the end." She shook her head. "There's quite the story here."

"Which war?" That was from Beth, still looking at the box curiously.

"World War Two, love." She gave her a sad smile. "A lot of boys lost in that war."

Beth snorted. "You should let Ben take a look. All he cares about is hockey and history anyway."

Ben stuck his tongue out at her before walking over to take a closer look. Gran handed it to him, and the box was heavier than it looked. There were initials carved into the lid. "WLH?"

"William Leonard Harris." Gran turned and rummaged in the container that the box had come out of and came up with a framed picture. "Here he is." It was a faded sepia-toned portrait of a uniformed young man, a proud smile on his face. "I never knew him, but Mum told me a lot about him. He would have been my godfather if he'd lived. Uncle Eddie stepped up in his place." She put the picture back in the container. "You should take the box home and see what's inside. It's been so long since I've seen it, I'd love for you to bring it back and tell me what you find. Besides, it would be a shame if it got lost in the move."

"Are you sure?" Ben had to admit, he really wanted to know what was inside.

"Sure, honey." Gran patted him on the shoulder. "Just take care of it, okay?"

"Promise."

THEY LEFT A couple of hours later with the assurance they'd come back the next weekend and help finish up. Gran would have plenty to deal with in the meantime. Beth volunteered to ride along just to harass him the entire way home, despite their mom repeatedly telling her to cut it out. Still, Ben managed to drive them back without killing them all.

When they pulled in the driveway, Beth got out of the car and bounced inside. Ben took a few seconds before opening the door, relief flooding through him. His mom spoke before he got out of the car.

"You did good, kid."

"I still hate it." That was putting it mildly. He'd rather take a puck to the face than drive a car. Reaching into the backseat, he grabbed the box and tucked it under his arm.

"I know you do. But you're doing really well, I swear."

Ryan drove up seconds later, pulling into the driveway just before they reached the front door. He must have been watching for them to drive by from his house, only a few doors down.

"Welcome home, Lewises!" Ryan bounded out of his car, grinning at Ben's mom as she gave him a hug. "How's it going, Mom?"

"Good. We're tired and hungry. Grab a snack if you want. I know you two have plans." She looked between them. "You'll be careful, right?"

Ryan threw an arm around Ben's neck. "Don't worry, I'll keep him out of trouble." He gave an exaggerated sniff. "Dude, you stink."

Ben pushed him away. "Yeah, yeah, yeah. I'm going to go take a shower." They all walked into the house, and Ryan made a beeline for the kitchen while Ben went to clean up.

"Wear something besides sweatpants!" Ryan shouted up the stairs after him, and Ben rolled his eyes.

He got to his room and put the box on his dresser, wondering if he had time to give it a quick look.

"Workout shorts count as sweatpants!"

Dammit. Probably not.

"I'll wear what I want!" Ben gave the box a last look before grabbing some boxers out of the drawer. He dug a little more and threw a pair of jeans and a soft, worn V-necked tee on the bed. The tee was a bit snug in the shoulders now, but it was a comfortable favorite.

He could use the comfort; he wasn't particularly looking forward to the party. There would be a lot of people there who he only kind of knew, and nobody who really knew *him*, except for Ryan. He'd much rather go see a movie or hang out at home. Ryan was really going to owe him.

He turned on the water to heat it up and stripped out of his sweaty clothes. The hot water felt good, and he took a minute to let it work on his aching muscles. He'd been careful. It was second nature, taking care with how he moved. He couldn't afford to hurt himself doing something stupid like helping his Gran move boxes.

Ben had just finished drying off when he heard his bedroom door open. He pulled on his boxers and went to see what damage Ryan was doing.

"Nope." Ryan snatched up the shirt from the bed and started to stuff it back in the drawer.

Ben made a grab for it. "There's nothing wrong with it." He yanked it out of Ryan's hand and went looking for socks.

"Come on. At least wear something a little nicer." Ryan was always giving him a hard time about living in old T-shirts and sweats. "It's got *holes* in it, man."

"So?" Ben's voice was muffled as he tugged the shirt over his head. He'd perfected the art of getting dressed around other people a long time ago. The locker room either made you an exhibitionist or very creative. He pulled on his jeans and looked around for the balled up socks he'd tossed on the bed. They hit him on the head, and without looking, he flipped Ryan off.

"Whatever. Wear what you want." Ryan sighed dramatically and fell back on the bed as Ben found his worn red Chucks. Ben flicked him on the ear. "Ow!"

"I thought you were in a hurry." Ben grinned at him as he rolled off the bed and ducked out the door. They clattered down the stairs, pushing and shoving the entire way.

"Boys!"

"Sorry, Mom!" Answering in unison, they waved as they headed out the door. They piled into Ryan's hatchback, and Ryan backed out of the driveway with a confidence Ben envied. After riding in companionable silence for a few minutes, Ryan gave Ben a look out of the corner of his eye.

"So, um. About the party."

Ben was instantly on alert. He should have known something was up from the whole thing with the shirt. "*What* about the party?"

Ryan kept his eyes forward on the road. "Marcus is going to be there."

Ben absolutely did not squeak. "What? Why? Why would you do that?"

"Ben. Benny. We're going to be seniors. It's now or never." Ryan glanced at him again. "You've been pining over him for how long now?"

"I am *not* pining!" Ben's voice rose an octave. He took a deep breath. "I'm not—I don't *pine*." He would have punched Ryan in the shoulder if he wasn't driving. "And who even says that?"

"Fine. You've had this dumb mopey crush on him for years. Happy?" Ryan glared at him. It was an old argument.

"No!" Ben crossed his arms over his chest and slouched in the car seat. "He doesn't even know who I am." He talked louder to drown out Ryan's response. "And even if he did, it's not like I could do anything about it."

Ryan sighed and pulled into a parking lot. He put the car into park and turned toward him with narrowed eyes. "Why?"

Ben glared right back. He was getting a little irritated by the whole conversation. "Why what?"

"Why can't you do anything about it?"

"You know why." Ryan did know why. Ben had started noticing boys when they were younger, but he didn't understand that what he was feeling was attraction until Marcus walked into his freshman English class. He'd seen Marcus around, had had a kind of nodding acquaintance with him through middle school. They were both Ryan's friends, after all.

But on that first day at Westdale High School, it was like someone had flipped a switch. Ben was sure everyone could tell he'd just been hit with a sudden wave of attraction (or lust, or whatever the hell it was), and at the center of it all was a boy with bright-blue hair.

Marcus had changed his style over the summer. Ben would have never guessed in a million years that skinny jeans and ratty T-shirts would do it for him, but on Marcus they worked. He stood out now, and did it with confidence. That epiphany rattled Ben to the point that he couldn't concentrate on anything else for the rest of the day. Ryan was still playing hockey with him at that point, and after watching Ben flub pass after pass in that afternoon's practice, he finally asked him what was going on.

Ben hadn't known what to say. Ryan was his best friend in the entire world, and he was afraid that telling him would push him away. Still, though, he somehow managed to stutter out the words, "I think I like boys," and Ryan just said, "Okay," like he already knew, and threw his arms around him in a hug.

Ben's fourteen-year-old self had been grateful for Ryan's fourteen-year-old self's tight hug. It was exactly what he needed at that moment. Ben's secret hadn't torn them apart; if anything, it had brought them closer together. Last year, he'd let himself think that maybe that was the year he'd do something, that he'd tell his parents or his team mates. But he hadn't been able to bring himself to do it.

Ben shook his head. "Why didn't you tell me?"

Ryan gave him an incredulous look. "It's hard enough to get you to come to stuff like this as it is—god knows I've tried for years. Would you have if I'd told you?" Ben shrugged, but Ryan had a point. He probably would have made up some lame excuse and stayed home. He sank further into the seat.

"I'm sorry."

Ryan worried about him—worried about what would happen when both of them went off to do whatever they were going to do after graduation. They'd both gotten a little buzzed on a few beers (more like two if he was being honest) at Ben's family Memorial Day cookout, and Ryan had kind of spilled his guts a little. He just wanted Ben to be happy and have a life outside of hockey. The alternative was Ben shutting part of himself off because the sport he loved wasn't accepting of who he wanted to date.

"Don't be." Ryan sighed and leaned his head against the window. "I should have told you." He hesitated a little. "Even though I think he kind of likes you, too."

"What?" Ben covered his face with his hands. It was too much to even think about. "Did he say something?"

"Not really. And before you say anything else, I only just figured it out." Ryan's laugh had Ben peeking through his fingers. "But I can tell, you know? And you know that I'd never out you. So talk to him. Okay?"

"I'll—" Ben dropped his hands, knowing his face was bright red. "I'll think about it."

"That's all I'm asking, all right?" Ryan's grin faded. "You know I'd never push you—"

Ben snorted. "But?"

"But I love your dumb ass, and I want you to be happy." Ryan threw up his hands. "And *that* is enough feelings for tonight. You okay with going to the party now? Or—" Ryan hesitated again. "I can take you home since I got you here under false pretenses."

"Only you could make that sound like you lured me into a murder van." Ben shook his head. "Let's go to the party, asshole."

Ryan whooped as they pulled back out of the parking lot.

Chapter Two

"WHOSE HOUSE IS this again?" Ben blinked at the size of the place. It was in a nicer part of town and had a big driveway that was already full of cars.

"Holtsy's girlfriend's. Jenny Smithwick." Ryan found a place to park on the street and turned off the car.

Ben snapped his fingers. "*Oh,* Smithy's house." Ben *should* have remembered her name. She was Taylor Smithwick's sister for crying out loud, and he'd been playing with the huge defenseman for years. And he'd seen her waiting for Holtsy at the locker room door after games.

Ryan opened the car door, and loud music could be heard coming from the house. "Ready?"

"If I say no, can we go somewhere else?" Ben was only half kidding, and Ryan gave him an assessing look. He surrendered. "It's fine."

Ryan led the way around to the back of the house where it looked like the majority of the people were gathered. There were lawn chairs placed around the huge backyard, and groups of three or four people were gathered, sitting in them or on the ground. While there weren't nearly as many as he'd expected, the arrangement would make it a lot harder to find a handy corner to hide in with a soda until it was time to leave.

A wave of shouted greetings rose around them, and Ryan waved as he walked to the back door of the house, Ben close behind him. It was clear Ryan had been there before and was already familiar with the layout. There was beer and soda inside two coolers next to the door, and chips and other snacks spread out on the counter just inside. Ryan grabbed a beer and tossed a soda to Ben.

"You don't mind driving back, do you?"

"I guess not." Ben wasn't thrilled at the prospect, but he still felt bad about their earlier conversation.

Ryan paused in looking for a bottle opener. "Are you sure?"

Ben's struggle with driving was something they'd talked about extensively, and Ben knew Ryan would put the bottle down immediately if he said he wasn't up for it.

"Yeah, I'll be fine. If not, I'll just make you walk."

Ryan laughed and clapped him on the shoulder before wandering back to the crowd. He wasn't going to hover, which Ben appreciated, though he had the urge to stick by Ryan just so he wouldn't have to make awkward conversation with anyone.

Instead, he opened his soda and sipped it slowly, stalling for a few minutes. Finally, he took a deep breath and went back to where the others were hanging out. The music was just as loud, but he shrugged it off and found a chair that was out of the way where he could sit and watch. He didn't mind people watching; it was people interacting he had a problem with.

The downside of being known at school, because of the team, was that people had no problem coming up to him and starting a conversation. Everyone acted very familiar, too much so, and it made him uncomfortable. He didn't mind anyone wanting to say "good game" or talk about a play or whatever, but other types of conversation put him on edge. He'd probably be considered popular if he could relax into these things, but that wasn't something he was interested in. At least, that's what he told himself.

IT'D BEEN OVER an hour, and Ben hadn't moved from his spot. Every now and then someone said hi and asked when training camp started, but no one stopped to talk for any length of time. He'd been playing a game on his phone for a few minutes when he heard the scrape of a chair next to him. He looked up, and his breath caught in his throat.

It was Marcus. Of course it was.

The two of them had never really talked. There'd been nothing more than what Ryan teasingly called Ben's "longing glances," but Marcus never seemed to give him a second look.

The last time he'd interacted with Marcus was over a year ago at Ryan's sixteenth birthday party. Ryan's parents paid for a bunch of them to go to an enclosed go-kart track. Ben felt a little out of place, holding back because he didn't want to chance hurting himself, but he had fun watching the guys race around trying to beat each other's times. Marcus was also invited, and Ryan had teased Ben like crazy the entire week before, but Ben pretended to laugh it off. When the actual day arrived, he was nervous as hell. At the track, Marcus said exactly five words to him, "You want to go next?" and Ben had frozen, barely able to shake his head, sure that Marcus thought he was an idiot. It had been terrible.

"Want some company?"

Marcus was looking at Ben expectantly. His hair was bright red today, still long enough to flop over his dark eyes. His T-shirt looked as worn as Ben's, emblazoned with a faded comic book character Ben didn't recognize. Frayed camo cargo shorts and grey hi-tops—Ben realized he'd been silent a few beats too long (and, oh god, *staring*) and now Marcus's smile was starting to fade. Ben needed to say something.

"Sure!" His voice sounded overloud to his own ears, and he winced. "I mean, um, sure. Go ahead."

Marcus settled into the chair next to him, and Ben's stomach did a slow roll. Marcus was sitting next to him. He had no idea what to do and looked around furtively for Ryan, but he was nowhere to be found. Trying not to be obvious, he scrubbed his instantly sweaty palms on his jeans and leaned back in the chair. It gave a creak, and Ben couldn't help the noise he made, sure the chair was going to dump him on the ground at Marcus's feet.

"You okay?" Marcus put out a hand as if to catch him, and Ben planted his feet, steadying himself, convinced he'd spontaneously combust if Marcus actually touched him.

"Yeah." Ben hoped the fading light hid his red face. He slouched in mortification and waited for the ground to swallow him whole. A silence settled between them, and Ben couldn't tell if it was comfortable or not. Why had Marcus come over in the first place?

Marcus snorted with what sounded like a laugh, and Ben hunched his shoulders, shooting him a glance, trying to figure out what was so funny. "You're captain, right?"

"What?" Ben sat up a little straighter, the change in subject making him forget his awkwardness for a moment.

"Captain? Of the hockey team?"

Ben blinked at him. "Oh. Um, yeah?"

"I was just thinking that it would completely ruin our chances this year if our captain gets taken out by a rogue lawn chair." Marcus grinned at him, and Ben's stomach flipped again, but this time in a non-nausea inducing way. "Sorry, it's a horrible joke."

Ben laughed despite himself. "No, it's funny." He looked over at Marcus, eyes tracing over his profile in the waning sunlight. He wondered what it would be like, if he was brave enough to lean over and touch him. Marcus looked back at him, and Ben took a drink of his soda to cover that he'd been checking him out.

Marcus sat forward with his elbows on his knees. "So, I—"

"There you are!" A girl Ben vaguely recognized approached them and gave Marcus an exasperated look. "I turned my back for one second, and you disappeared." She did a double take when she saw Ben, and then there was the beginning of a sly smile on her face as her eyes darted between him and Marcus. He followed her gaze and was surprised to find a scowl directed at her. She rolled her eyes and poked Marcus in the shoulder. "Scoot back."

Marcus rolled his eyes right back before sliding in his chair to give her access to his lap. Ben looked away, uncomfortable in the face of such easy intimacy. *Was she his girlfriend?* He searched his memory for her name, and was coming up blank when she spoke up again.

"Ben, right?" She made an odd squeaking noise and batted at Marcus's hand where he'd poked her in the side. It took Ben a second to realize the question was actually directed at him. "I think we had a class together."

It finally clicked why she looked familiar. "Yeah. Um, French, I think." He had noticed her because her brightly colored hair reminded him of Marcus. That made him feel kind of stupid now. "I'm sorry, I don't—"

"Rachel." She was looking him over in a way that made him want to check and see if he had something on his shirt or face. "We've never actually met before. Weird, huh? We've gone to school together for *years* and never even talked to each other." She squirmed again, and Ben could swear he saw Marcus *pinch* her.

Ben blinked at her, not sure what she was getting at. "Yeah, I guess?"

Rachel went on like he hadn't said anything. "I mean, everyone knows who you are, right? Nice guy, captain of the hockey team. Hot."

"What?" Ben coughed, choking on his drink. Was she flirting with him? While sitting in her boyfriend's lap? What was happening?

She started giggling, and Marcus stood up, gently dumping her off his lap. "Sorry. I just remembered that I need to—" He trailed off, grabbing Rachel's arm and hauling her behind him, still giggling.

"Bye, Ben! We'll chat later!" She waved at Ben, and he automatically lifted his hand to wave back. He heard her say, just before they left his sight, "Come on, Marc, don't be mad." And then they were gone.

What the hell? Not only had Marcus purposefully sat down and talked to him but his girlfriend (?) had called Ben hot right in front of him. And what was that? He'd never seen himself as overly attractive. He did work hard as hell to keep himself fit, so he supposed it could be said he had a decent body. But seriously, what?

Ryan came over at that moment and pulled him out of his thoughts. He plopped down in the chair that Marcus— and then Marcus *and* Rachel—had been occupying. He had a bottle of water in his hand instead of the expected beer. "You okay?"

"Yeah. I don't need a babysitter, you know."

Ryan snorted at him. "Yeah, I know. I saw Marcus sitting over here and wanted the deets."

"Is he dating Rachel?" Ben blurted out. If anyone would know, it'd be Ryan.

Ryan's eyebrows rose. "I thought he was gay."

"No, he's bi. Remember that pin on his backpack?"

It was one thing to realize he had a crush on someone, a *boy,* but then to see him wearing the bi flag out and proud— This wasn't just some guy he found attractive; this was someone who could possibly—theoretically—be attainable.

He also remembered seeing Marcus with a split lip to match John Richards's black eye, and the story he'd heard from some of his teammates. John had called Marcus a name, and Marcus took a swing at him. It was surreal listening to the other guys talk about the incident. He wondered what they'd say if it had been him in that position. If they'd known.

In the end, he stayed quiet, keeping his secret close. The other guys talked like they didn't approve of what John said, but they didn't do anything about it either. It had left him feeling unsettled for days.

"Oh, right." Ryan took a drink of water. "I don't think she's his girlfriend, though."

"Are you sure? They looked really close." He hesitated, bracing himself for the teasing. "I think she was flirting with me."

Ryan's laugh was so loud people turned to look at him. "Seriously?"

"Shut up."

"How would you even know?"

Ben glared at him, arms crossed. He should have known. "I can tell when someone's flirting with me."

Ryan gave him a sideways look. "Are you sure?"

Ben kicked his chair. He *could* tell when a girl was flirting with him. It happened now and then, especially at away games when they didn't know who he was except for the "C" on his blue and silver jersey and how he filled out his uniform. He was usually able to sidestep them without hurting any feelings. The worst part was enduring the chirping from his teammates afterward. Their teasing was harmless, but it left him feeling like he was lying to the people he was supposed to trust the most.

"How much longer do you want to stay?" Ben held up his hand to head off a sigh of frustration. "I'm just asking. I'm fine hanging out for a while."

Ryan shrugged. "We can leave if you want." He checked the time on his phone. "Wow. You made it over an hour." He reached over to ruffle Ben's hair. "I'm so proud."

Ben batted his hand away. "Ass. I'm fine with whatever."

Ryan looked around at the people in the backyard and then leaned his head back, looking up at the night sky. "Eh. We can go. Want to swing in somewhere and get milkshakes? It's a cheat day, right?"

"Yeah. Let's do that."

As they got up to leave, he saw Marcus standing on the edge of a group of people sitting in a circle of chairs. He was laughing at something, his face bright, and Ben found he couldn't look away. Just then, Marcus glanced his way, and their eyes met for a long moment before Marcus turned away again, his attention back on the group.

Ryan elbowed Ben. "Hello. Earth to Bennie-boy." He held out his keys. "I asked if you were going to drive." He followed the line of Ben's gaze. "Oh." A smile bloomed on his face. "Look, if you want to stay—"

"Nope. Let's go." Ben snatched the keys out of Ryan's hand and led the way back to the car. It was impossible to even think about taking a step like that.

They slipped into the car, and Ben took a few deep breaths before turning the key.

"You sure you're okay?" Ryan was more patient than Ben's actual family when it came to his fear of driving.

"I'm fine." Ben adjusted the mirrors and carefully backed out, probably taking more time than was strictly necessary. But Ryan left him alone, waiting until they were on the main road before saying another word.

"So." Ryan was leaning his head against the window. "Marcus spoke to you, and you survived."

Ben glanced at him. "Do we have to talk about this?" It came out more harshly than he meant it to, but Ryan wasn't fazed in the slightest.

Ryan shrugged. "I think you need to."

Ben drove in silence for a few moments before conceding that Ryan was right. He didn't have anyone else to talk to, and the privacy the car provided wasn't something to be wasted. He drew in a deep breath. "I don't know what to do."

"I know." It was something they'd discussed before. "You know you don't have to *do* anything, right?" Ryan turned to look at him, the glow from the streetlights skimming across his face. "I mean, what are you going to do when you go to college?"

Ben fell silent, concentrating on the road in front of him. "I don't know." College would allow him a fresh start with people who didn't know him. He'd be a much smaller fish in a larger pond and wouldn't draw nearly as much attention. "College might work. Maybe."

"Maybe?" Ryan rolled his eyes when Ben took a chance and glanced at him. "I'm not trying to push you into making a decision right this second, but—" He picked at the hem of his T-shirt, his fidgeting familiar in a way that only came from years of living in each other's pockets.

"But you *are* pushing me to make a decision."

"No. Am I?" Ryan huffed out a sigh of frustration. "The point is, you can't keep this up." He drowned out Ben's irritated growl. "Are you going to just, I don't know, be alone for the rest of your life?" Ryan sounded upset. "I'm sorry, Benny. But as much as I would love to be your for-always platonic life partner—" He took in a shaky breath. "We're not going to live down the street from each other forever."

Ben pulled to a stop at a red light and stared at Ryan. He knew Ryan worried about him because that's what he did. He'd mother-henned Ben when he was sick, or hurt, or whatever. But this was different. And Ben just wasn't ready.

He tightened his hands on the wheel. "You don't have to worry about me."

"That doesn't mean I won't." Ryan scrubbed a hand over his face, and Ben felt a little guilty. He gritted his teeth as the light turned green. He was suddenly on edge from the combination of the conversation and having to drive.

"Can we just not talk until we get back? Please?"

"Fine." Ryan slumped in his seat, pressing his forehead against the glass. They rode in sullen silence the rest of the way, milkshakes forgotten.

HE AND RYAN parted with a shaky truce, but that wasn't going to be the last time they'd have that argument. Once Ryan had an idea in his head, there wasn't anything that could get him to let it go. That left Ben in desperate need of something to get his mind off their pseudo-fight.

It wasn't until Ben was walking home from Ryan's house that he remembered the box Gran had given him.

The house was quiet, with everyone having retreated to their own rooms to watch TV or crash after a long day. He probably should have been tired, but he was weirdly wired and wide-awake as he let himself in. He was also starving.

Ben made himself a sandwich and a glass of milk and went up to his room, ready to settle in for the night. Once inside, he set down the sandwich and closed the door. The box was on his nightstand. He picked it up, running a finger over the initials engraved on the lid. WLH. William Leonard Harris. Biscuit had made himself at home in his usual spot at the end of the bed so Ben sat down carefully, leaning against the headboard.

The box was held shut with a simple old brass latch that took a few seconds of careful effort for Ben to get open. It was only a few inches deep, just enough room for the few items inside. He wrinkled his nose at the musty smell.

A smaller flat case took up a good portion of the space, so he took that out first. It looked like it was in surprisingly good shape, although the tiny hinges creaked when he opened it. It simply said "Purple Heart" on the lid, and the medal, shiny and perfectly preserved, was exactly what was inside. He was afraid to touch it at first, a little bit in awe, but after a minute, he did anyway.

The award case looked like it had never been opened.

The medal had shifted in the box, and Ben carefully moved it with the tip of a finger, turning it over where it read "For Military Merit" on the back. He knew what that meant, of course. The person that had earned the medal had been either wounded or killed in action. And William Leonard Harris had died during the war.

He gingerly straightened the medal, closed its case, and set it to the side. There was more inside the wooden box. A small envelope had been resting under the medal case, and it clinked with the sound of something metallic when he picked it up. He opened it and a chain with a single military dog tag fell out into his palm. The second one that would normally have been attached by a shorter chain was missing.

He looked in the envelope to make sure it hadn't come detached and then checked inside the wooden box to see if it was loose in there. It was definitely missing.

The tag was scratched but clean; someone had obviously taken care of it before putting it into storage. The stamped letters were clear, and he ran his finger over them. William L. Harris. It listed the usual information: serial number, immunizations, blood type, and religion. On impulse, Ben put the chain around his neck, the tag hanging down to the middle of his chest.

At the bottom of the box was a small stack of letters. They were tied together with a frayed piece of twine that looked like it would come apart as soon as he touched it. He picked up the small stack of envelopes, and the twine parted easily under his fingers. Just like with an old book, the smell of musty paper was strong. The envelopes were still sealed, except for one, or at least they had been. The flaps had started to peel up from age, but they oddly still appeared unopened and unread.

He slid the letter out of the open envelope and set the others to the side. The ink had started to fade, but Ben could read the neatly written words easily:

My darling,

It's been two days, and already I miss you terribly. The boys that I've met so far in training are good company, but nothing compared to you. Though I do think McMillan could give you a run for your money.

It was obviously a letter home to a wife or girlfriend. It went on to tell a funny story involving McMillan and a chicken that had wandered on base. The absolute fondness for whoever it was written to was clear in every word. He got to the bottom, and it was signed:

Always,
Your Will

Ben turned it over, but that was it. It was a short little note, taking up only one side of the page. The envelope that he'd taken it from was blank except for a small *E* sketched in the top left corner, so faded he could barely make it out. He flipped through the other sealed envelopes, and they were all the same. No address or postmark, but all of them had a small, neatly written *E* in the corner. Who was "E"?

Ben surprised himself with a jaw-cracking yawn. The day was finally catching up with him, and the mystery of the letters would have to wait for another time. He carefully put everything back, except for the chain that hung around his neck. Gran wouldn't mind if he kept it out, as long as he was careful. It would be cool to show it to Ryan, anyway.

Ben felt a small twinge for getting lost in the contents of the box instead of worrying about their sort-of fight. It was the only important thing they'd ever disagreed on.

The box went back on the dresser for later. He closed his hand around the solitary dog tag for a moment before he pulled the chain over his head and laid it gently on the nightstand in a little pile of clinking chain for safekeeping... right next to the plate with the sandwich he'd forgotten to eat.

He ate his sandwich and drank his milk, turning over the argument in his mind. He and Ryan disagreed all the time, but they never argued about anything important. Ben sighed heavily, and Biscuit raised his head to look at him.

"It's none of his business, right?" Biscuit blinked at him, judging him in the way that only cats could. "I mean, it's my life. If I don't want to come out until after graduation, then that's my choice." Blink, blink. "But I know he worries." Biscuit yawned and curled up so that his tail covered his nose. Ben had to laugh. "Thanks a lot."

His phone pinged from somewhere. Ben looked around, not seeing it, and felt in his pockets. Nothing. It pinged again for an unread text, and he realized he was sitting on it.

Ryan: *sorry*

Ben felt another wave of guilt. He'd made Ryan feel bad, when all he was doing was trying to take care of him the way he always had. But if he apologized now and left it there, they'd go round and round in circles. He had to get them to move on.

Ben: *Make it up to me by getting your lazy ass up for a run tomorrow.*

Ben looked at the time. He still had plenty of time to get a good night's sleep.

Ryan: *FINE*

Ben laughed to himself. He flicked off the light before stripping down to his boxers and crawling into bed. The morning would come soon enough.

Chapter Three

BEN JERKED AWAKE to insistent beeping. Not the alarm—text alerts. He groped for the phone on his nightstand and thumbed it on.

Ryan: *BEN*

Ryan: *BEN*

Ryan: *GET UP ASSHOLE*

Ryan: *BEN*

Ryan: *BEN*

Ryan: *BEN*

He groaned and dropped the phone. It was literally two minutes before his alarm was supposed to go off, and Ryan was actually early for once. He lay back down and closed his eyes, just starting to doze off when his phone pinged again. And again.

Ben: *OMG STOP*

Ryan: *:)*

Ben threw the covers back and got up, yanking open a drawer to dig out some shorts and a shirt. After putting them on, he grabbed his running shoes, and quietly made his way down the stairs. He snatched two bananas from the bowl on the kitchen counter and stopped to tie his shoes. Ryan's silhouette was there, through the frosted glass of the door, pacing back and forth as he waited. Ben took his battered Flyers hat off the hook by the door and let himself out.

The heat of the day was still hours away. Ryan gave him a huge grin, and Ben mock-glared at him. Ryan was probably still feeling guilty about their fight and was going to be overly obnoxious to make up for it. Ben tossed him one of the bananas, and they sat on the porch steps to eat them.

"We okay?" Ryan said it casually between bites, but Ben knew he was really worried.

"We're cool." Ben took the peels and tiptoed back into the kitchen to throw them in the compost bucket. Ryan was waiting at the bottom of the steps when he came back out. "Ready?"

"As I'll ever be." They started out at an easy jog. Ryan was in decent shape, but he didn't have Ben's training or stamina. It didn't help matters that they were both competitive, and he'd do his damnedest to keep up, so Ben would have to take it easy on him without him realizing. That didn't mean he couldn't mess with him first.

Ben turned around, jogging backward. "See ya!" He turned around and sprinted off, ignoring Ryan's shouted curse. He kept it up for a few more seconds, until he could hear Ryan pounding up behind him. Then he slowed down to a more reasonable pace and braced himself for the incoming shoulder check.

"You," Ryan panted, "are a dick, and I hate you."

Ben cackled and kept running.

BY THE TIME they got back, Ben's mom was up and cooking breakfast. While not quite the early bird that Ben was, she was a close second. She snorted at Ryan's dramatic flop onto a kitchen chair and automatically went to the fridge to get bottles of water, handing them both to Ben. He tossed one to Ryan as she went back to the stove.

"What did you do to him?"

Ben shrugged and hopped up on the counter. She gave him a look, and he got back down, rolling his eyes. "It was just a run."

"You call that a run?" Ryan had gulped down some of the water and was looking a little more human. "That was torture."

"Nah. It means you need to do it more." In reality, Ben hoped Ryan might join him more often. No matter how much they joked and teased each other, it was nice having company.

Ryan gave him a sunny grin. "Whatever, man." Ben was relieved that the run and time spent together had put them back on firm ground again.

"You boys stink." Ben's mom checked on the bacon in the oven, doubling up with the addition of another teenage mouth to feed. "Go shower. Ryan, you have plenty of time to run home before breakfast is ready."

Ryan drank the rest of his water and threw the bottle into the recycling bin. "I don't want to hear the word 'run' ever again." He started to throw an arm over her shoulders and she warned him off with a spatula and a wrinkled nose. "All right, all right, I'm going."

"Hurry, before the horde descends." She winked at him. "And by the horde, I mean Ben."

"Thanks a lot, Mom." Ben bumped Ryan's shoulder before heading upstairs. His mom was right; he really did stink.

BEN WAS DRYING his hair with a towel when he saw the dog tag where he'd left it on his nightstand. The slight weight of it dangled from his fingers when he picked it up and put the chain over his head, thinking about the letter he'd read the night before. He thought briefly about sharing it with Ryan but wanted to know more first—wanted to discover more about the man who hadn't come home.

Voices from downstairs proved that his dad and Beth were up, and he quickly pulled on his clothes. Suddenly starving, his stomach grumbled as it tried to turn itself inside out at the smell of bacon. He was reaching for the doorknob when a plaintive meow stopped him in his tracks. Ben opened the door to find Biscuit sitting in the middle of the hallway, staring up at him with hopeful eyes. He swept the cat up, cradling him as he went downstairs, and set him down when he started to squirm. Ryan was just coming in the front door, and that dumb cat loved him for some reason.

"Biscuit!" Ryan's voice was hilariously high-pitched as he greeted the cat, and Ben could hear Biscuit purring from across the room. "Come see me, kitty, come here." The cat practically leapt into Ryan's arms and started rubbing his face against Ryan's chin. Ben stood there, arms crossed, until Ryan noticed him. "What?"

Ben shook his head and started toward the kitchen. "One day I'm going to film that and hold it over your head for the rest of your life."

"Shhh, he doesn't mean it, kitty." Ryan buried his face in Biscuit's fur. "He's just jealous."

"You are the most ridiculous human being I've ever met. Why do I even like you?"

"He's judging us, kitty." Ryan was talking directly to Biscuit, the cat looking at him like he understood every word. Biscuit meowed at Ryan and put a sympathetic paw on his face, and Ben started laughing.

Ben's mom called from the kitchen. "Boys! If you want bacon, get your butts in here."

"Put the damn cat down and come on." Ben turned his back on Ryan and moved quickly to the dining room. There was a thump as Biscuit jumped down, and then Ryan was elbowing him out of the way. Ben bumped him back, and they skidded into the kitchen, almost upsetting a chair.

His mom didn't say anything, only sighed in exasperation. They took their seats and dug in, concentrating on their food while Beth chattered on about something. It gave Ben time to think about their talk the previous night and ponder what, if anything, he wanted to do. Which made him uncomfortable when his mom pushed the subject to forefront with an innocent question to Ryan.

"So, how's your summer been?"

Ryan chewed and swallowed the bite of eggs he'd just shoveled in, before answering. "Good. Hanging out. Mom wasn't able to take any time off to go anywhere this year so—" He shrugged.

"Well, enjoy it while you can. It's your last free summer." She took a sip of her coffee. "You boys went to that party last night. Was it just school friends?"

Ben froze and didn't look at Ryan. She was about to ask the dating question, he could feel it.

Ryan answered easily, unaware of the danger. And why would that even be on his radar? It wasn't uncomfortable for him. He wouldn't have to lie. "Yeah. We pretty much knew everyone there."

"Anyone special?" There it was. "Ben never tells me anything."

Ben was fairly sure he was the only one to catch the quick glance Ryan gave him. "Nah. Enjoying the summer, you know? Especially since it's almost over."

"How about you, Ben?"

It was like the world stopped. Ben had thought about what he'd do the next time his mom or dad asked him something like that. He'd gone back and forth between blurting out that he liked guys or lying outright. He decided to take the middle ground, a tried and true tactic.

"You know I don't have time for anything like that." He tried to ignore the look of worry on her face and the glance she shot his father, who was acting like he was very interested in his own plate. Ben hated when they did that. And that he couldn't just tell them what was really going on. Should he tell them? Get it over with? He looked over at Ryan, who was steadily not making eye contact with anyone, and caught Beth flicking her narrowed eyes between the two of them. If anyone figured it out, it would be her.

Damn it. It wasn't time. He needed to deflect. Beth had been texting more than usual yesterday at Gran's house, so he made a guess. "I heard Beth has a new 'friend,' though."

It was a shot in the dark, but Beth confirmed it with a squeak, and then immediately started coughing as her orange juice went down the wrong way. Ryan kicked his ankle, and Ben kicked back. His mom, on the other hand, sounded delighted.

"A new friend?"

If looks could kill, the dagger-eyes Beth was giving him would have left him dead on the floor. Surprisingly, she turned her wrath on their dad. "What did you say?"

"I didn't say a word."

"I'm done. You?" Ben grabbed Ryan's plate and headed toward the sink. They needed to get out of there, or there'd be hell to pay. Ryan followed him, finishing off his juice before putting the glass in the sink.

"Smooth man, real smooth." Ryan muttered it under his breath and Ben gave him a dirty look, afraid his parents, or worse, Beth, would hear. However, it looked like they were preoccupied with a now pouting Beth, who was convinced their dad had ratted her out. Ben was happy to leave them to it.

"Do you have to go?"

Ryan had started a job at a local bookstore right after school let out, and his schedule had become a little erratic.

He nodded. "In a little bit. I've got to be at work in an hour." They escaped out the door, away from the drama at the kitchen table, and sat on the front steps in their usual spots. "You okay?"

Ben picked at a rough spot on the side of the wooden step where the paint was starting to peel. "Yeah." He blew out a breath and looked out over the yard. "I hate it when that happens."

"I know."

"I probably shouldn't have thrown Beth under the bus."

Ryan grinned at him. "I'd sleep with one eye open for a while if I were you."

Ben sighed. "I should just tell them, shouldn't I?"

"I'm not saying anything. That is totally your decision." Ryan stood and clapped a hand on Ben's shoulder. "But if you decide to do it, I'll hold your hand through the whole thing."

Ben laughed. "You really would, wouldn't you."

Ryan jogged down the steps before turning around and pointing at him. "Anytime, man. Just for you."

LATER THAT DAY, Ben was getting his laundry together (and hiding from Beth) when the box on his dresser drew his attention again. He opened it and took out the letters, wondering how much care he needed to take to open them, or if he should open them at all. He touched the dog tag through his shirt, running his fingers over it in indecision. Gran had trusted him with the box, and she had to have known what was in it. He'd open one letter, he decided. That would be enough.

He took one of the letters out of the box at random and rummaged around in his nightstand drawer for his pocketknife. Biscuit had been keeping him company, sprawled across his bed, and looked at Ben with one eye when he sat on the edge of it.

The flap of the envelope had already started to become unstuck, so it didn't take much to open it the rest of the way, just a gentle shimmy with the flat of the blade. The letter he pulled out looked exactly like the first one. The same neat writing, fading along the edges, and the same greeting:

My darling,

I promise never to complain about our Indiana winters ever again. I have never been so cold in my life. As much as I miss your face, I am so glad that you're not here with me. Your poor lungs wouldn't have been able to take it.

Ben paused. After reading the letter about boot camp, he'd assumed William had been on the front lines. If he was writing home to his sweetheart, there shouldn't be any chance of her being out there in the cold, so why would he say it? That was weird.

He finished that letter, which went on to talk about socks, of all things, but ended the same way as the other one:

Always,
Your Will

He flipped through the remaining letters, fanning them out like playing cards. There weren't that many of them, six in total, all in different states of wear and tear. The one that looked the best must have been the most recent, while the others seemed like they'd been carried around with Will. He wondered why they'd never been sent. Maybe Will had been in an area where he wasn't able to send or receive mail at the time. But the one from boot camp should have been easy to send, it would seem.

He picked up his pocketknife and carefully peeled up the flap on the next one in the small stack, unfolded the letter inside, and began to read.

BEN LAY BACK on his bed, hands behind his head, and stared at the ceiling. Biscuit had curled up beside him, and every so often he'd bump his head against Ben's hip for head scratches, which were absently granted. That final letter...

It had been a goodbye letter. Will apparently wrote one just like it before every major action, but only this one had survived. It was the last thing Will had ever written, and Ben wasn't sure how he felt about reading it.

My darling E

Something had been written and then scratched out, but Ben could still make out the *E*. Will had started to write out the recipient's name, but had marked through it so hard there was a small hole in the thin paper. The edges were smudged with something, probably from dirty hands in a cold forest or a broken-down city. Ben couldn't begin to imagine what it must have been like.

...I want to say these words to you in person, nothing would be better than that. I have loved you since I was twelve years old, darling, from the very moment I knew what that meant...

Ben let out a shaky breath. He'd watched more war documentaries than he could possibly remember, but the letters made it more real than all of them combined. He definitely wanted to know who "E" was and what had happened to her when Will didn't come back.

He thought about texting Gran to ask her what she knew but then decided he'd rather talk to her about it in person. They were supposed to go over to her house to help again before school started, so he could be patient. He sat up, and Biscuit uncurled himself with a baleful look before jumping down off the bed with a thump and stalking to the door. Ben let him out just as his dad was coming up the stairs. Looking back at the papers stacked neatly on his nightstand, Ben suddenly wanted to keep it all private. He stepped out and closed his door, hiding all of it from his dad's eyes. All the longing expressed in the letters had lodged in his chest, and he just wasn't ready to share that with anyone.

"Oh, hey." His dad smiled at him, and Ben made himself return it. "Dinner's ready, it's your turn to set the table."

"What are we having?" His dad had been going through a Julia Child cookbook after watching some movie about her, and it was a crapshoot what he would make. Ben was wary after whatever that gelatin thing was that he'd attempted and—after a family vote and many threats—promised never to make again.

"Ratatouille." He sounded so proud, Ben almost didn't have the heart to tell him that he had no idea what that was. Almost.

"Like that cartoon about the rat?"

His dad shook his head in exasperation. "Unfortunately, yes. It's vegetables. You'll love it." He started back down the stairs, and Ben followed on his heels. "I also made chicken, so don't panic."

"Not panicking." Ben paused with a real grin on his face, the somberness fading with the noise and brightness of the kitchen. "Unless it's that weird Jell-O stuff again."

"You guys are never going to let me live that down, are you?" His dad smiled at him, and Ben felt the remaining uneasiness over that last letter and the mystery of "E" fade away.

He laughed softly. "Not a chance."

Chapter Four

AFTER DINNER, BEN got a text from Ryan asking if he was busy the next day. He wasn't, but he was instantly on alert after the whole "oops Marcus will be at this party" thing.

Ben: *Why?*

Ryan: *POOL*

Ryan: *PARTY*

Ryan: *!!!!!!!!!*

Ben rolled his eyes. Ryan just didn't give up. He was going to make sure Ben interacted with people whether he wanted to or not.

Ben: *???*

Ryan: *T's house*

Ah. That explained a lot. Tyler Hicks. Ryan was good friends with him, and Ben knew him from the hockey team their freshman year. He'd quit about the same time Ryan did, and they'd ended up hanging out together in the stands at games. Tyler lived in a really nice neighborhood and had a pool in his backyard. He threw a big pool party at the end of summer every year. It was kind of a big deal.

Which made Ben immediately not want to go. He sat on the edge of his bed and stared at the screen, waiting for Ryan's next impatient text. It buzzed in his hand.

Ryan: *I can hear your no from here*

Ben: *I'm not saying no.*

Ben's phone started ringing, and Ryan's picture flashed across the screen. Ben looked at his silly cross-eyed face for a second before answering.

"You're not saying yes, either," Ryan said immediately. "I've got tomorrow off. Come on, Ben. Please? For me?" If Ryan had been there, he'd have dramatically dropped to his knees and begged.

"Who's going to be there?"

"Why are you asking?"

"I swear to god—"

"Fine! Fine. Yes, he's going to be there." Ryan rushed on, stumbling over his words to get them out. "He came into the bookstore, and I kind of overheard him and Rachel talking about it."

"You followed them around and listened to them?"

"No!" Silence. "Well, maybe a little. I may have needed to re-sort that area. Several times."

Ben scrubbed his hand over his face. The neat stack of letters caught his eye. He hadn't put them away, and though it wasn't as palpable as before, he could still feel the sorrow the last letter contained. It wasn't that Will knew he was going to die. It was that Will wouldn't ever get to see his "E" again. Ben sighed. What was he doing? *Shit.*

"Okay." Ben closed his eyes. He needed to get out more. God. He was letting the letters get to him, and they were making him freaking sad. He felt lonely, even when he was around other people. Something had to change, so he'd go to the party and see what happened.

"What?" Ryan sounded almost shocked, and Ben grinned to himself.

"I'll go. What time are you picking me up?" He thought for a second. "And no drinking this time."

"Yes! Sure, whatever you want!" Ben held the phone away from his ear as Ryan celebrated, chanting, "Going to a pool party, going to a pool party!" and brought it back to hear, "I'll pick you up at noon. He's going to have food and stuff there." Then, "I'm hanging up now before you change your mind. Bye!"

Ben looked at his screen and shook his head. He threw his phone onto the bed and started putting the letters back into the box.

IT TOOK ABOUT thirty seconds for Ben to realize he'd made a mistake. There were easily three times the number of people that had been at the other party milling around the backyard. He froze.

Ryan turned to him with a smile that dropped as soon as he saw Ben's face. "Nope."

Ben looked at him, startled. "What?"

"You've got your 'get me the hell out of here' face on."

Ben tried his best to look innocent. "Do not."

But Ryan wasn't buying it, and he folded his arms across his chest, giving him a skeptical look. "So you weren't about to turn around and run?"

"No?"

"Whatever, man." Ryan's face softened, and he looked back over to where a ton of people were splashing in the pool. "Look, if you want to go—"

"I'm fine." Ben plastered a huge fake smile on his face. He was going to *try*. "See?"

Ryan grimaced. "That's just fucking scary." Ben kept making the face, leaning closer to him. "Okay, okay, I get it! You can stop now." When Ben grinned for real, Ryan shook his head. "Come on."

Ben was wearing sunglasses so he'd have something to hide behind, but with this many people, it wouldn't matter. Ryan, at least, had already been noticed and was giving his "Cool. What's up?" nod left and right. Ben wished he was half as good with people. It was something he'd have to learn if he wanted to go any further with hockey. College hockey had a much bigger fan base, and the high school fans were already pretty hardcore. It was kind of like high school football in Texas, if you believed the movies.

"Hey, Ben!" Ben looked up in surprise when someone actually spoke to him. It was Rachel. She was sitting by herself on a blanket, having staked out a nice spot in the shade. "Come sit with us?" Ben felt the urge to look behind him to see if there was another Ben that she was talking to. It wasn't like he was the only one.

"Jesus Christ, will you stop staring and just go over there?" Ryan gave him a nudge, and Ben started toward her, with Ryan trailing along after *him* for once. She gave him a big smile, and that feeling was still there, that she was smiling at someone else. She didn't even know him, and now he was going over there to make a fool out of himself. At least he wouldn't be doing it alone.

"Hey, Rach." It was Ryan's flirty voice—amazing how easy he made it sound. Confidence oozed from him when he turned up the charm. Rachel *giggled. How the hell did he do that?* Ryan flung an arm over Ben's shoulders. It looked casual, but it was actually an anchor to keep Ben in place. Ben realized belatedly that Rachel had said "Come sit with *us,*" which meant—

"Ben?" It was Marcus.

Ben was thankful for his sunglasses; he probably had that deer-in-the-headlights look going on.

Marcus had two cups in his hands, clearly having gone to get them drinks. "I didn't know you were going to be here." He cut his eyes toward Rachel, who shrugged and patted the blanket beside her. Marcus sat, handing her one of the drinks.

"I didn't either." Ben was surprised his voice didn't croak. He poked Ryan in the side so he'd let go of him. "It was kind of a last minute thing." His mouth felt inexplicably dry, and his tongue was somehow three sizes too big. *Were those even words?* Marcus smiled at him, and Ben's stomach tried to turn itself inside out.

"You guys want to sit? We have lots of room." Marcus was looking from Ben to Ryan as if he was trying to figure something out. "I mean, if you want to."

"Sure!" Ryan answered for them both, knocking his shoulder against Ben's when he didn't move. "I'm going to go grab us some drinks first, though."

Ben felt something close to panic run through him. Ryan was going to leave him alone with Marcus. And Rachel, of course. But, still. Marcus.

"You need me to come with you?" Ben tried not to sound like he was begging, but the muted giggle from Rachel's direction proved he sucked at that too.

Ryan waved him off and gave him a pointed nudge toward where the other two were sitting. He lowered his voice. "Go and freaking sit down. Play it cool, all right?"

"Fine." Ben gave him a look over the top of his glasses that told him he was *not fine*, and Ryan rolled his eyes. He sat on the other side of Rachel, hoping the tiny bit of distance would allow him to act like a normal human being.

Rachel gave him a smirk as if she knew what he was doing, glancing between him and Marcus, and in the awkward silence that had fallen over them said, "So, how's your summer been?"

Ben was trying to act casual, and almost certainly failing. He wasn't sure what Marcus was doing, because he couldn't even stand to look at him. Rachel, on the other hand, looked like she was having a grand time. They were in the shade, but she leaned back on her elbows as if soaking up the sun, watching Ben for a reaction. Her hair was bright purple today, and it went well with her retro-looking swimsuit. She had great style. Ben thought about looking her up and down, wondering if that was what she expected, and found that he couldn't do it.

"Fine. Just hanging out and stuff." Ben was relieved that his voice didn't crack.

Rachel smirked at him again, but from the other side of the blanket, Marcus caught his eye and gave him a small smile. Ben felt his face heat and was thankful yet again for the sunglasses firmly on his face. He gave Marcus a strained smile in return before looking down at his hands. Someone (probably Rachel) snorted, and there was a whispered word or two. They were probably regretting asking him to join them. God, he was terrible at this. *Where the hell did Ryan go?*

An icy can was suddenly pressed to the back of his neck, making him jump.

"Shit!" Ben swatted behind him, not connecting with any part of Ryan and almost falling over. "You asshole!"

Ryan's unmistakable cackle had Rachel laughing outright and Marcus chuckling a bit. Ben righted himself and glared up at Ryan, barely getting his hands up to catch the can that was tossed at him. Ryan threw himself down, wedging himself in so that Ben had to scoot closer to Marcus. "Aren't you supposed to be some sort of, I don't know, athlete or something?"

"I hate you."

Rachel snorted again, covering her mouth with her hand, eyes shining at their ridiculousness. Ben knew what Ryan was doing, and it was working. He caught Marcus still looking at them with an unreadable expression on his face, and bravely gave him an actual smile. Marcus returned it for a second before turning away, and Ben felt absurdly proud of himself. He'd made eye contact without spontaneously combusting.

He was starting to think that Ryan dragging him along to this thing wasn't such a bad idea after all.

HOW HE'D MANAGED to forget that pool parties actually involved an actual pool and actual swimming was beyond him.

They'd been sitting on the blanket in the shade with Ryan and Rachel dominating the conversation for the most part as the two argued the finer points of a series of books versus the TV show based on it. Ben and Marcus added in opinions, but Ben found himself talking more and more to Marcus, tuning out what the other two were saying. It was a little stilted at first, mostly on his side, but it was good. Marcus was pretty funny once he got going. It took them both a few moments to realize Ryan and Rachel were looking at them curiously, Rachel quirking an eyebrow over her oversized sunglasses.

"What?" Ben was glad he wasn't the only one who hadn't been paying attention. Marcus looked just as startled as Ben felt.

"We're going to get in for a little while, you two coming with?" Rachel was looking at both of them expectantly, a knowing look on her face. "Or are you staying here?"

"Um." That was from Marcus. He shrugged and stood. "Might as well, right?" Ben pushed his sunglasses up on top of his head to squint up at him at the same moment Marcus tugged off his T-shirt. All of Ben's earlier pride over not bursting into flames in the shade went right out the window.

What he felt was a crush. A simple crush. Nothing serious. *Really.*

What was happening at that moment, on the other hand, was very serious.

Locker rooms had made him immune to the sight of bare skin a long time ago. The difference was, he'd never memorized the curve of the jawline of any of those guys while daydreaming in class. Or their dark eyes. Or the way they bit their lip in concentration while writing notes.

It was almost too much.

Ben pried his eyes away from the sight of Marcus's bare chest and looked over to Ryan, pleading and helpless. Making a gesture with the hem of his own T-shirt, Ryan pulled it off and tossed it at Ben's face, giving him a moment to get his shit together. He automatically caught Ryan's shirt and dropped it onto the blanket. Rachel grabbed Marcus's arm and dragged him toward the pool, giving them a bright grin over her shoulder as they went.

Marcus's shoulders looked broader without a shirt. He always seemed so lean with his skinny jeans and boots, but now Ben could see he was actually strong and sturdy. Ben blinked and looked away when a shadow fell over him.

"Dude."

Ben struggled to his feet and tugged off his shirt. "Shut up." When Ryan pointed at the top of his head, he yanked his sunglasses off as well. "Why did I let you talk me into this?"

"Calm down." Ryan stepped closer, and Ben took an automatic step back, not wanting anyone to get the wrong idea. "Ben?"

"I thought we were getting in." Ben pushed past him and walked quickly to the edge of the pool. He caught a glimpse of Rachel and Marcus splashing each other a few feet away as he eased himself in. Luckily, the shock of cold washed away any lasting emotional upheaval from seeing the smooth lines of Marcus's back, the freckles scattered over the width of his shoulders and— Ben closed his eyes and ducked under the water. *Better.* Everyone around him was blurry and distant. He wanted to stay there forever. That would be so much easier.

He rose to the surface with a gasp and raked his hair out of his face. He blinked the water out of his eyes just in time to see Marcus turning away and Rachel looking over at him with a wicked grin. Ben flushed and sank back down into the water until it was up to his shoulders, feeling a little self-conscious. At least there were plenty of people playing around in the pool to take the attention off him.

A splash caught him right in the face. Ben sputtered and stood, looking around for whoever had done it, though he had a good idea. Sure enough, he turned just in time to see Ryan send another wave his way. Ryan snickered and dove away from Ben as he tried to retaliate by pushing him under the water. He finally caught him, and they wrestled, Ben eventually winning and holding Ryan under until he tapped out.

Ryan came up looking like a waterlogged puppy, and Ben started laughing, harder than he had in a while. "That is totally not fair! When the hell did you get so freaking strong?"

Ben shrugged, giving him a wide smile. "I work out. You should try it." He heard a strangled noise behind him and spun around just in time to see Marcus dive under the water while Rachel laughed at something. She looked past Ben at Ryan, and the two of them had some sort of silent conversation, which was really odd because Ryan never did that with anyone but him. Ben felt a tiny stab of jealousy run through him—there and gone again in the flash—that left him feeling a little weird.

He headed toward the side of the pool and heaved himself out, feeling suddenly tired. The blanket was rumpled from their hasty exit, and he straightened it out before grabbing a towel. Tyler's parents must have been used to having large groups of people over, because there were small stacks of towels set around for guests to use. He pulled his shirt back on over his damp skin and sat down on the blanket, his arms folded over his drawn up knees. He wasn't sure how long he sat there, zoning out, before someone came over. To his surprise, it was Marcus.

Marcus didn't bother drying off, just flopped down on the blanket and stretched out in the patch of sun that had crept into their shady spot. Ben automatically averted his eyes so he wouldn't be tempted to stare. He glanced up to check where Ryan was and found him in the deep end of the pool, treading water. Rachel was nearby, her purple hair a beacon. The two seemed to be in deep conversation. As Ben watched, both of them glanced his way and waved, their smirks almost identical. It was more than a little concerning.

"Hey." Marcus moved around next to him, obviously getting comfortable.

"Hi." Ben uncurled and lay back, making sure not to touch Marcus anywhere, not sure if he'd be able to stand it. He groped for his sunglasses, finding refuge again in his mask, and leaned back on his elbows.

"So, what else do you like to do? I mean, besides hockey."

Ben let out a startled laugh. "I don't know. I'm pretty boring."

"Nah." Marcus's eyes were closed, but he had a smile on his face. "I'm sure there's something."

"I like movies, I guess. My favorites are the ones about history and stuff. But I like some of the ones that Ryan makes me watch."

Marcus nodded, eyes still closed. Ben took the opportunity to sneak another look. He let his gaze drift across the bare skin of Marcus's chest as it rose and fell with his breathing and then to his stomach before he skimmed down to just above his inexplicably neon pink swim trunks. A trail of golden hair led down to the waistband pointing toward— Ben jerked his eyes away, face burning.

"So what kind of movies do you guys watch?" Marcus was continuing the conversation, completely oblivious to Ben's examination. Ben cleared his throat and eyed the water, wondering how weird it would be if he flung himself into it again. He sighed.

"Usually action stuff. Ryan's obsessed with superheroes." He carefully kept his eyes on the people in the pool, watching Ryan talking to Rachel. Still. *Interesting.* She was cute and snarky, kind of like Ryan. They'd moved to the shallow end and were leaning against the edge, letting their legs float in the water. It looked like they were going to be there for a while.

"Me too."

An easy silence settled between them. They lay there side by side, enjoying the day. Ben finally started to relax, regardless of not knowing if he wanted Marcus to put his shirt back on or not. He finally settled all the way back, mirroring Marcus, and smiled to himself. He could leave it off.

"YOU GOOD?" BEN'S dad was peering through the driver's side window at him and looked as tired as Ben felt. For entirely different reasons— Ben's head hadn't stopped buzzing since Marcus and the pool party the weekend before.

Ben hoisted his equipment bag onto his shoulder and took a step back from the car. "Yeah. Two hours?"

His dad nodded, and Ben raised a hand in a wave as he pulled away.

The ice rink opened at six a.m., and he was ten minutes early. It was still cool out, making him glad of the hoodie he'd pulled on in preparation for the chill of the rink. Ben dropped his bag and leaned his stick against the low wall near the entrance and settled in to wait.

He was playing a game on his phone and trying to stay awake when he heard the door open.

"Ready for you, Ben." It was Brenda who owned the rink. She'd let him in and then go catch up on paperwork. He'd be alone for a while until a few more early risers showed up to practice. Sometimes, a few of the guys would join him, but it was usually a crapshoot. Especially this late in the summer. His appreciation for keeping up a routine wasn't a widely shared sentiment. He found that he couldn't stay away.

Ben liked having the ice to himself. It was a rare thing after school started and everyone was competing for the morning slots, so he took advantage while he could. He finished tying his skates and stood.

The first step onto the ice was his favorite. It was just a clean sheet in front of him, unmarked by anyone else. It helped him think. Ben started off slow, taking a few laps to warm up before he put on the speed, racing around the rink a few times before stopping with a shower of snow. It helped clear his mind.

He needed that. His mind was full of Marcus in a way he'd been able to avoid previously. It was one thing when he was this person Ben looked at across the lunchroom or passed in the hallway, but in the last few days, Marcus had become a person Ben liked even more than before. Seeing him wet and shirtless might have helped. A little. Or a lot.

Ben made his way over to where he'd left his bag and stick and dug out his gloves and a puck. He tossed the puck out onto the ice and followed it, moving it across the surface, slowly at first and then with speed, carrying it with him back and forth as he moved.

Marcus had a mole on his left shoulder blade; it stood out against his pale skin.

The puck slipped away, and Ben barely caught it before it went skittering out of reach. That was *embarrassing*, and he was glad no one else was there. He needed to get his head back in the game. He started over, moving slowly and then picking up speed.

Marcus also had an appendix scar, the only flaw on his flat stomach.

Ben sent the puck careening against the boards with a bang before leaning over with his stick on his knees to catch his breath. *What the hell was wrong with him?* They'd spoken, had an actual conversation. Big freaking deal. It meant nothing.

He skated over to where he'd sent the puck flying and started over.

He'd managed about half an hour before the bang of a door announced the arrival of more skaters. They pretty much left each other alone, but the distraction helped to pull him out of his head and away from thoughts of Marcus and his bright pink swim trunks.

Chapter Five

"I'M GOING TO the grocery store, you want anything?" Ben's mom called up the stairs to him and Beth, but there was only silence from Beth's side of the hallway. Either she had her headphones on or she was ignoring the question because she didn't want to get roped into going. Ben liked going to the store. He liked being able to pick out his own food, not that he actually cooked or anything, but it was nice having input.

"You want me to go with?" he shouted while trying to find his shoes. Somehow one of them had managed to worm its way under his bed, and he practically stood on his head to get to it. He got up and looked down at himself. It wasn't his rattiest pair of shorts, but it was close. He wondered if he should change but shrugged to himself. It was only the grocery store. He'd worry about what he looked like when school started.

"If you want." His mom's voice floated up the stairs. "I'm leaving now."

Ben stuffed his feet in his shoes, laces flopping, and trotted down the stairs. He started to go out the front door but then turned and went to the kitchen to grab the bags his mom always seemed to forget. He wasn't that concerned with saving the planet, but they were a lot easier to carry than the plastic ones.

"Thanks." She smiled at him as he tossed them onto the floorboard. "I always forget those damn things."

Ben rolled his eyes and folded himself up to tie his shoes. "I know. It's a good thing I'm here, huh?"

"Yeah, yeah. You just want to be in charge of picking out apples."

Ben laughed. "You got me."

IT WAS THE flash of red that caught his attention at the end of the cookie aisle. Ben had avoided the aisle at first but circled back to pick up the chocolate chunk cookies his dad liked. He was supposed to be grabbing the milk. He looked up, cookies in hand, and ducked around the end of the aisle. Marcus. It was the first time he'd seen him since the pool party, which made sense because it had only been about a day and a half, and Ben never saw him outside of school.

He needed to move or Marcus was going to see him. Which was ridiculous, because why was he hiding? Ben glared at the cookies in his hand as if they would tell him the answer. He should just go say hi. Casually. He could do casual. He peeked around the corner and drank in the sight of Marcus standing under the fluorescent lights. He should just go talk to him.

His brain helpfully slotted in the memory of Marcus in the pool, Marcus lying on the blanket in the shade, Marcus... Ben ducked back out of sight, closing his eyes tight. This was stupid. His phone pinged, and he glanced at it to see a series of *???????* from his mom. Milk. He needed to get milk.

"Ben?"

He tightened the grip on his phone to keep from dropping it. Marcus's grin was unsure enough that it somehow made Ben feel a bit more confident. They were on equal footing, at least.

"Hey." He waggled his phone at Marcus. "Mom wants me to get milk."

"To go with the cookies?"

"Um."

Ben looked at the pack in his hand as if he'd never seen it before. Marcus stepped closer to get a better look, and Ben was painfully aware of how close they were to each other. Marcus nudged him with his elbow and grinned. Despite the thrill that zipped through him at the contact, Marcus's small smile put him at ease. He relaxed a little bit more.

"Those are good. My favorite are shortbread." He stepped farther into the aisle and Ben followed him, curious. Marcus picked up a familiar red plaid packet. "These. They're what I was getting, anyway."

"You need milk?" Ben winced at the awkwardness of the question, but he was committed now. "Mom's waiting for me." His phone pinged again. "See?"

Marcus laughed. "Sure. Why not?" They walked toward the dairy aisle in companionable silence. It was kind of nice, if Ben didn't look at it too closely.

"So, what are you up to?" Ben hoped that didn't come off as weird. He wasn't freaking out, but he might if his mom decided to come and find out what was taking him so long.

"A whole lot of nothing." Marcus grabbed a small jug of milk and then, grinning at Ben, grabbed a bottle of chocolate milk as well. "Unless you count catching up on TV shows."

"That totally counts." Ben tucked the cookie pack under his arm and picked up his own choices, flushing a little as he made sure to look at the expiration dates.

"Are you training yet?"

The question took him by surprise, but Marcus seemed genuinely interested.

"Some. Ice time, gym, trying not to sweat to death. The usual." They started toward the front of the store, and Ben wondered how he was going to manage to distract his mom if Marcus followed him to the cash register. "Practice doesn't really start until after tryouts, but I have to work out hard now, to keep up later."

"Oh, wow. That's—that's a lot." Marcus's voice was a little strangled, and Ben looked at him, wondering if he'd said something wrong or rambled too much. But then, the problem of parental embarrassment was neatly solved when Marcus said, "Shit. I forgot something. I'm going to— Um. See you later?"

"Sure. See you later."

The last was said to Marcus's retreating back. Ben gave in to the urge to *look* and jumped when his phone dinged again, as if he'd been doing something wrong. He didn't have a hand free to check it, but he knew who it was. He hurried to the front, a small smile on his face.

IT WAS WEIRD. It was like when his mom and dad had bought a new car and then he saw that kind of car everywhere. Except this was a person. After the grocery store incident, Marcus was everywhere. Ben was on the way to the gym, and he noticed Marcus at the coffee shop down the street as they drove by. Ben had slid down in his seat, enough that his dad noticed and gave him an odd look, and Ben pretended his phone had fallen down beside the seat. He was being an idiot for no reason. It wasn't like Marcus was looking out for him.

But Ben saw *him*.

At the coffee shop again, hanging out with Rachel, laughing over something. At a stoplight, in a car with someone who was probably his mom. Ben noticed the rainbow PFLAG sticker on the back as Marcus's car pulled ahead, and he wondered if his own parents would do that if they knew.

He saw Marcus in places he'd never noticed him in before, but didn't actually make contact with him. Until Ryan kidnapped him one day and dragged him out of the house for milkshakes at the diner. Ben was supposed to grab a table while Ryan went to order. It was faster that way.

Ben spotted a table near the back and claimed it without looking around at who else was there. That was his first mistake. The second was thinking that if he sat there quietly, Marcus wouldn't notice him. Despite his best efforts, Ben failed at turning himself invisible, and Marcus spotted him anyway.

He was sitting with Rachel and a few other people who Ben vaguely recognized from school. Marcus smiled when he saw Ben and said something to Rachel before walking over. He slid into the seat next to Ben like he belonged there. It happened so fast Ben didn't have time to reach his usual level of awkwardness.

"It's you again." Marcus didn't seem uncertain at all this time, his smile wide and bright.

"Yep, it's me." Ben couldn't help but return the grin. "What are you doing here?"

Marcus nodded toward the table full of people who were talking amongst themselves, Rachel the only one looking over their way. "GSA lunch. Just some preplanning for the school year."

"Oh. You're president, right?" Ben knew that for a fact but didn't know what else to say.

"Yeah." Marcus fiddled with the little tray of sugar packets. "They have to elect a new one since I'm graduating." Ben nodded, not sure how to respond. Luckily, Marcus kept talking. "Do they do that for the team? Elect a new captain?"

Ben shrugged. "Kind of. The players pick someone, and then Coach makes the final decision. Usually, it's the same person, so it works out."

"So, the guys picked you last year?" Marcus looked weirdly proud when Ben nodded. "That's awesome."

"I guess." Ben laughed quietly when Marcus raised an eyebrow at him. "Okay, fine. It was awesome, and it's a lot of responsibility."

"Yeah, but they trust you to handle it, right?" Marcus rested his hand on Ben's arm, and Ben tried not to react to the gentle touch. It was at that moment that Ryan showed up with the milkshakes, his face a mix of amused confusion. Marcus snatched his hand back, and Ben slid his own farther away on the table.

"Here's your shake, loser." Ryan didn't miss a beat, setting it in front of him. "Always vanilla. *So* vanilla."

"Shut up." Ben noticed Marcus's glance at Ryan and couldn't tell what it meant. Marcus covered it with a grin, but the look was there.

"I'd better get back." Marcus waved a hand at Rachel's table as he stood. "It was good. Seeing you, I mean."

Ben blinked up at him. "You too."

Marcus turned and headed back to his table, where he sat and was immediately drawn into whatever conversation was going on. Rachel glanced over at Ben once, and he looked away quickly, facing Ryan's smirk instead.

"So," Ryan said, "what was that?"

Ben took a long drink of his shake. "You know what? I have no idea."

THE NEXT FEW weeks went by in a blur and didn't give him much time to ponder Marcus or anything much at all. Any plans Ben had to ask Gran about the letters were put on hold because she'd had to take an unexpected trip to Florida, something to do with the house she was purchasing. He hadn't really been paying attention to that part—mostly he wanted to know more about "E" and what had happened to William.

Then school started, and it was a distraction in itself. Just like he'd seen Marcus everywhere after the grocery store incident, those instances were doubled or tripled once they started school. They didn't have any classes together, but Ben would see him in the hallways, putting up posters for GSA club meetings, or walking by, his head close to Rachel's in conversation.

Ryan had gotten Rachel's number at the pool party and had been talking to her a lot. It was getting to be a little ridiculous, and Ben wondered if that was how Ryan had felt about him, the whole time.

"Why don't you just ask her out?" Ben finally asked when they were taking their desks in Econ. He'd watched Ryan text under his desk, grinning at the screen the entire time. They evidently had a lot to say to each other.

"Why don't you talk to—" Ryan broke off what he was about to say and just made a face. "I mean, you could."

Ben sighed and looked at his hands. "It's not the same and you know it."

"What if it was?"

Ryan had hinted that he knew something, and Ben itched to ask him exactly what, but he held back. He wasn't sure if knowing would make things better or worse. And it wasn't like Marcus hadn't dated anyone before. That had been more painful than he'd expected, to actually see him with someone else.

"Whatever." Ben wasn't trying to be petulant, but he was failing miserably. They only had a few seconds before the teacher started class, and he couldn't help saying, "If it was, he would have said something."

Ryan turned to stare at him, but it was too late, class was starting. Ben was glad he had a clinic that afternoon so he could put Ryan's meddling off for at least a few hours.

WHILE EVERYONE ELSE grumbled about them, Ben actually looked forward to clinics. Most schools in their division didn't do anything like them, but it was good for team building and figuring out what they needed to work on before tryouts and official practices started in late October. It gave them a leg up and it had earned them championships. So the school didn't blink an eye at putting it in the budget.

And the first clinic was definitely kicking his ass like it did every year. No matter how much he tried to prepare, it was never enough. His left shoulder felt like it was one big bruise, and he'd have to break out the ice packs as soon as he got home. He just had to skate through it and do his job.

He winced as the whistle blew. Coach Jordan waved them all over, and they took a knee, ready for the end-of-clinic talk. Ben took his place beside coach, the *C* on his practice jersey making him stand out from the others. They had a good team this year. Most of the guys had stuck it out from junior year, and some of the new guys showed a lot of promise.

Coach stared out at them, hands on his hips, before speaking. "I won't say it was a good practice—because it wasn't. You've got until next week to shake that crap out." The rookies looked around nervously, but Ben just fought the urge to roll his eyes. It was the same speech every year, obviously designed to scare the newbies. "Lines for next week will be announced on Friday. Don't be late. Get out of here."

Ben stood and got his skates under him, tapping his stick on the ice. "Come on, guys. Showers and then go home. Rest up." The others started shuffling off the ice. "And remember to eat!" There were a few laughs at that from the older players. It never failed. They always had someone pass out because they didn't eat enough or drink enough water. He'd done it himself the first year.

Ben watched them all head toward the locker room. Someone skated up behind him, and he knew it had to be Coach Jordan even before he spoke. "You're doing a good job, kiddo." Coach stood next to him on the ice, arms folded across his chest. "They listen to you."

Ben shuffled his feet. He didn't think he'd done all that great. The guys were working hard, and that made the difference. It had nothing to do with him, but it was nice of Coach to say. "Sure, Coach."

Coach gave him a friendly nudge with his elbow. He wouldn't push it. He knew Ben too well. "Go on. Take your own advice."

"See you next week."

Ben headed toward the locker room to see what kind of chaos was ensuing, automatically tapping the sign reading "Home of the Westdale Knights!" by the door with his stick. That many teenage boys together was always a disaster waiting to happen, no matter how exhausted they were. It was very loud when he walked in, as per usual. Shaking his head, he made his way over to his stall to start taking off his gear.

He rolled his shoulder. The ache was definitely getting worse. It was only a bruise, but experience had proved it could have the potential to hold him back if he didn't take care of it. Heat and ice. He slumped on the bench for a few seconds and let the multiple conversations wash over him, grimacing as he picked up on what Smithy and Holtsy were talking about. Smithy made a gesture that Ben was fairly certain wasn't physically possible, and he decided it was time to get a move on.

Ben stripped out of his sweaty undershirt and shorts without a second thought and wrapped a towel around his waist. Casual nudity in a locker room was a given, but with all of the other guys' preoccupation with sex and talking about sex and thinking about sex, he wondered what they'd think if they knew. Would they understand that he didn't think of any of them like that—didn't really pay attention to anything other than what might affect their game? He noticed if someone was limping or if they were moving slowly, but he never saw them as objects of lust. Other than the fleeting thought of "Wow, so-and-so's really been hitting the weights," it wasn't on his radar. Just like coming out to the team wasn't something he'd considered in detail. Only that it was something he couldn't see himself doing. He hadn't even told his parents.

He tried not to dwell on it too much as he grabbed his shower bag and headed to the showers, receiving a few fist bumps on the way. The hot water helped clear his head as he rinsed away the sweat and grime from practice.

Ben turned off the shower and started to dry off. He wasn't sure why the thought of telling his parents made his stomach twist. He was reasonably sure they'd be okay with one of their kids being gay. Hell, one time, his mom had dressed down another parent for using a homophobic slur during a game. But thinking about it and the reality of actually doing it were two different things. Once it was out there, he couldn't take it back.

Not that he would. It was part of who he was— But all of that was too much to think about now, in the locker room, and he was just too tired. He pulled on his comfortable shorts and T-shirt and packed up his gear bag, hoping his mom was already in the parking lot.

BEN HEADED UPSTAIRS to drop his gear in his room and pull out all of the grungy stuff that needed to be washed. He was just wondering why Biscuit hadn't tripped him coming up the stairs, when he shouldered his bedroom door open to find Ryan lying across his bed, playing a game on his phone. Biscuit was curled up next to him, content and seemingly asleep. He roused himself to open one eye to peek at Ben for a second and then went back to his lazy doze.

"Did I know you were coming over and forget?" Ben dropped his bag by the closet door and flopped down on the bed beside Ryan with a groan.

"Nope."

"Then how'd you get in?" He knew the answer before he finished asking the question. His mom and dad had both come to get him, which left Beth at home. He had a sneaking suspicion that Beth had a tiny crush on Ryan, which he supposed was only natural. Ryan was good-looking, if you went for tall, dark, and snarky.

"Bethy," Ryan said, confirming his suspicions. Ryan dropped his phone on his chest and looked over at Ben. "She said you guys would be back soon."

"Yeah." Ben yawned. "Mom and Dad ran to the store to get something for dinner. What's up?"

Instead of answering, Ryan held his hand up and something shiny was hanging from his fingers. "Where'd you get this?"

Ben reached over slowly and took the dog tag from him, fighting the urge to snatch it away. They'd always had free reign over each other's space, never hiding anything away. But the letters and the box, now securely tucked away in a bottom drawer, felt different somehow. He wasn't ready to share them with anyone, at least until he had a chance to talk to Gran about them. "Gran gave it to me. It was her uncle's or something." It felt a little bit like lying, but it wasn't like he wouldn't tell Ryan the whole story later, when he knew everything.

"Oh. Cool." Ryan dropped the subject without blinking. He sat up and looked down at Ben, a huge grin spreading across his face. It made Ben a little nervous. "I came over because one—" He held up one finger. "—I miss your face." Ben tried to bat Ryan's hand away when he moved to pinch his cheek. "And two—" Ryan held up another finger, which Ben met with a single middle finger. "—to tell you what you're doing this weekend."

"Sleeping and watching TV?"

"Nope." Ryan bounced to his feet and rounded the bed to offer a hand to Ben, who sighed deeply and allowed himself to be pulled up to a sitting position. "We are going... bowling!" He made jazz hands, and Ben snorted before catching himself. Ryan was definitely up to something.

He stared at Ryan, deeply suspicious. "What's the catch?"

Ryan looked absurdly proud of himself. "Well, I finally asked Rachel if she wanted to hang out. You know, outside of school." He gave Ben a considering look. "I actually talked to her—with words. Unlike someone else I know."

Ben groaned and fell back down on the bed. He knew where this was going. Biscuit, by this time, had abandoned his nap, and was meowing to be released from the madness. Ryan opened the door for him and then started poking Ben in the ribs where he was the most ticklish.

"Stop it, you shit!" Ben smacked at his hands until Ryan relented. "What else?"

"Look, you were able to talk to him at the pool party like a real boy and—"

"Ryan—"

"—you seem to really get along, like at the diner, and—"

"Ryan—"

"—Rachel is really cute, and I—"

"Ryan!"

"—kind of like her. Come on, please?"

Ben pulled a pillow over his face. "I hate you."

"You love me."

"No, I don't."

Ryan nudged him over and lay back down beside him. "It'll be fun." He took Ben's pillow away. "If you have a horrible time, you can smother me with this, okay?"

Ben rolled his eyes. "Fine. All right?"

"Really?"

"Really." Ben couldn't help feeling a little pleased at being included.

"Yes!" Ryan did a fist pump.

Ben looked over at Ryan's happy face. "So, you really like her?"

Ryan shrugged. "Yeah. I mean, I think so. We've been texting and stuff. It's hard to get a read on her like that. I don't know."

Ben interpreted what Ryan was really saying. In Ryan-speak, it meant he really liked her a lot and was being a dork about it. At least he wasn't a cowardly dork. "So, bowling with Rachel and Marcus. Just the four of us?"

Ryan nodded. "If you don't want to go—"

"No, it sounds like fun." Ben elbowed him when he looked at him out of the corner of his eye. "Really."

"Good. Because I don't know what I would have done if you'd said no." Ryan patted Ben's shoulder and got up. "Aren't you hungry?" Ryan knew his routine as well as he did.

Ben's stomach gave a perfectly timed growl. He sighed with resignation and made himself get up. He'd regret it if he didn't eat something. "Bowling, huh?" He nudged Ryan as they left his room, walking side by side down the stairs.

Ryan shrugged. "I panicked. So sue me."

BEN HAD NEVER been so thankful to have the distraction of his Saturday ice time and the gym. Ever since Ryan had told him about bowling, he'd been tied up in knots. It looked an awful lot like a double date, and it made him wonder if that was what Marcus thought. And that made hot panic run through him because Marcus didn't know, at least not for sure. He was fairly certain he hadn't been completely obvious.

It helped that stepping out onto the ice had always been the place where he felt the most at home. He knew exactly what to do when he was out there, and he was going to do it the best way he knew how. So he gritted his teeth, got down to it, and ran his drills, pushing away the nervousness and the tiny bit of fear that sat in the pit of his stomach. It helped that a few of the guys had shown up to do the same thing.

It worked right up until he got back home and showered. He was drying his hair when he realized it was just a few hours before they were supposed to go out. The gym had done nothing to burn off his nervous energy, and now he was stuck, flip-flopping between hope that the night would turn out well for Ryan and his pursuit of the fair Rachel, and wanting to hide in his room and leave Ryan to his own devices.

Ryan's Ben-is-freaking-out sense must have been working overtime, because he appeared just after lunch. He took one look at Ben, who was loading the dishwasher, and jerked his head toward the front door. "Come on out when you're done."

Ben slowly finished up and pushed the start button, staying to listen to the water run. He leaned against the counter for a few seconds before scrubbing a hand over his face and following Ryan out onto the porch, unsure of what awaited him.

"Take a walk?"

Ben shrugged and followed Ryan off the porch. He had a good idea where they were going: to their bench. There was a small park in the center of the neighborhood that had been their home base when they were younger, and it remained one of Ben's favorite places to go when he needed to get out of the house for a while.

It was where they went when they'd decided to run away from home when they were eight. They'd been friends for about a year at that point. Ben couldn't remember exactly why they'd decided to run away, but he remembered their parents finding them there in the rain, both of them huddled on a bench under some overhanging trees. That had been their bench ever since. It was where Ben had told Ryan his biggest secret.

They walked in comfortable silence for the few minutes it took them to get to the park. It was unusually empty for a Saturday, only a few kids playing in the small playground area. They made straight for their bench, each taking an end and leaning back in the shade.

Ryan broke the silence first. "You know there's nothing to worry about, right?"

"I know."

"It's just a couple of friends. Hanging out. Doing dumb bowling."

"Dumb bowling?"

"Very dumb." Ryan leaned over and punched him lightly on the shoulder. "Knowing you, you'll get overly competitive and forget to be a nervous dork."

Ben blew out a breath. "You're paying—you know that, right?"

IN THE END, it was just easier to let Ryan pick out something for him to wear.

"I'm doing you a favor, man." Ryan was digging through Ben's T-shirts and making a general mess. "Do you only own hockey stuff?" He held up a faded tee that stated "Property of Westdale Knights Hockey Team."

Ben shrugged. He was sitting cross-legged on the bed and trying not to think about who would be there besides Rachel to judge his clothes. "Maybe?"

Ryan made a sound of triumph. "Here you go!" He flung something dark blue at Ben's head. Ben caught it in midair and looked it over—it was a shirt Gran had given him for his birthday that he'd never worn. Not a bad choice, actually, but Ryan wasn't done. "Wear the good jeans." Ben looked down at the jeans he was wearing and raised an eyebrow.

"Not those. The other ones." Ryan dug them out and flung them at him as well. "There."

"Why does it matter what I wear? You're the one that's trying to impress someone."

Ryan gave him a pointed look and sat down next to him, blocking his access to the exit. "I'm not saying that you have to do anything, all right? It's just, I don't know... Practice?"

"*Practice.*"

Ryan rubbed a hand over his face. "Yeah, maybe? Try dressing up a little. It's *not* a date, I swear. Not even for me. It's the four of us hanging out, like I said."

Ben thought for a moment, but one last look at Ryan's hopeful face settled it. He sighed. "Why not?" He stood up and started to pull his T-shirt off. "Are you going to sit there and watch, or are you going to go home and get ready too?"

Ryan whooped and jumped up, ruffling Ben's hair on the way out the door. "Be back in twenty!" he called back as he pulled the door closed behind him. Ben looked at the clothes on the bed. He could do this. It was just bowling. And then maybe somewhere for food or something. Easy.

He got dressed slowly and then finally looked in the mirror. He'd never say it out loud, but he had to admit Ryan really did have an eye for color. The dark blue shirt made his eyes stand out, and it looked good. *He* looked good.

Ben started to leave his room but hesitated and then walked over and took the dog tag from its hiding place in his nightstand drawer. He ran his fingers over the scarred surface that told such a story of courage. Tapping it for a few seconds, he decided Will probably wouldn't mind if he borrowed a little bit of that courage. He slid the chain over his head and tucked the tag securely inside his shirt. It made him feel better somehow, more secure. Grounded. He was ready.

Ben walked downstairs and was putting on his Chucks when his mom caught sight of him. "You look nice!"

"So I look horrible the rest of the time?" He laughed. "Is that what you're saying?"

She reached up and smoothed down a lock of hair that was sticking up. "Of course not. It's just not your usual, you know?"

She had a point. He lived in hockey T-shirts and workout clothes, mixed in with comfortable, faded jeans. He was making an effort, at Ryan's urging, and it felt...good.

He gave her a grin that she gave right back. "Yeah, yeah, yeah." He saw headlights sweep over the front lawn and brushed a kiss to her cheek. "There's Ryan. We shouldn't be out late."

"It's fine. Just text if you are, okay?"

Ben waggled his phone at her before shoving it in his pocket. He eyed his Flyers hat out of habit, but left it hanging on its peg and grabbed a hoodie instead in case it was chilly later. A wolf whistle split the night air as he slipped quickly out the door. Ben rolled his eyes.

"Looking good!" Ryan said, laughing and leering, and Ben flipped him off, jogging over to get in the car before Ryan could embarrass him even more.

Ben fastened his seat belt, looked resolutely forward, and took a deep breath. "Are we meeting them there?" He was secretly pleased his voice sounded normal.

"Yep. Rachel just sent me a text saying they were running a few minutes late. We're supposed to go ahead and get a lane."

Ben breathed a small sigh of relief. It wouldn't be quite so awkward if they were ready to go when the others got there. At least he hoped not. "Sounds good."

Ryan side-eyed him. "You're really okay with this. I'm proud of you, dude."

Ben slumped down into his seat, torn between feeling irritated at himself for making Ryan feel like he needed to coddle him, and annoyed at Ryan for actually coddling him. "'S'not a *thing*."

Ryan nodded. "Of course it's not."

IT WAS TOTALLY a thing.

"Oh my god, would you sit down?" Ryan snapped, and Ben caught the balled up napkin that was tossed in his direction. "They'll be here in a few minutes."

Ben ignored him and went back over to the bowling balls after stripping out of his hoodie. His palms were starting to sweat as he poked through the different weights again. He hadn't been bowling in years. Did he need a heavier ball? *Oh god, oh god, oh god...*

"Hey!"

Without thinking, he snapped around when he heard Rachel's greeting. She and Marcus were headed their way, bowling shoes in their hands. Ben realized he was staring when Marcus caught his eye and smiled, waving. Ben managed to raise his hand in an awkward wave and turned back to the colorful balls. *Not a big deal, not a big deal.*

He took a breath and grabbed a ball at random and carried it back to their lane. Rachel gave Ryan a hug before she smiled over in his direction. She seemed genuinely happy to see him. He'd wondered, vaguely, if he was encroaching on anything, but then she had brought Marcus with her. He was probably in the clear. He was also probably overthinking things, as usual.

Rachel and Marcus leaned down to change their shoes, and Ryan gave him a look over their heads, checking in.

Smiling as he walked past him, Ben put the ball down. "Hey, guys."

Rachel finished tying her shoe and bounced to her feet, looking Ben up and down appraisingly. She shrugged and held her arms out, tilting her head in question. "Hey, yourself."

He laughed and gave her a quick hug. When he nodded to Marcus, Ben found himself wishing he would ask for a hug as well, and then ran a hand through his hair, trying not to blush.

Rachel rubbed her hands together. "All right, everyone is getting a nickname. Let's do this."

They watched the larger screen over their heads as she started typing. Ben rolled his eyes when CAP was put up, but tilted his head in confusion when the names JAMES, DIANA, and STEVE T appeared as well.

He sat in the seat next to her. "Okay, I get Diana and Steve Trevor—we just watched that movie. But James?"

"James Buchanan Barnes? Bucky? Captain America's BFF and, if fandom gets their way, life partner?" She rolled her eyes. "That's Marcus's fave character, anyway."

"Oh. Right." She wasn't quite making fun of him, he didn't think. Was she? He'd just roll with it. "And Cap? Really?"

She looked him up and down again. "You've got this whole"—she waved a hand around—"blond-haired, blue-eyed, all-American thing going on." She gave him a grin. "It works on many levels."

Ben felt a presence behind him and looked up at Marcus standing over them, giving Rachel a pointed look. "Don't mind her. She thinks she's *funny*."

Rachel shrugged. "You know I'm hilarious. Besides, I ship it." Ben looked between them and had the distinct feeling he was missing something, but he wasn't about to ask. Rachel stood up and clapped her hands together. "Let's get this game started. Cap, you're up."

Chapter Six

BEN FOUND HIMSELF relaxing and having fun. Marcus was absurdly bad at bowling, while Rachel was giving them all a run for their money. She was just as competitive as Ben, so Ryan and Marcus were now heckling them both. Loudly. Ben couldn't remember the last time he'd laughed so hard. They finally finished up their first game, and decided to take a break for some bad bowling alley food. Ryan and Rachel volunteered to go and place the order, but Ben was fairly sure they just wanted a chance to talk. The flash of jealousy that he'd had was completely gone, mostly because he was beginning to think they were perfect for each other.

He sat down in one of the plastic seats to wait and was a little surprised when Marcus took the one right next to him. He'd mostly gotten over his initial reaction to having Marcus in close proximity. That didn't mean he hadn't gotten his fill of looking at the way his back and shoulders looked while bowling. Or how Marcus's hair had faded to magenta, and how it somehow suited him. It was okay to look, he reminded himself, just not to stare like an idiot. Especially at how his skinny jeans seemed to cling to his—

Ben flushed and looked away, trying to drive the stray thoughts from his head before facing him again. Marcus glanced at him and looked like he was about to say something but then stopped. Ben turned toward him, and Marcus gave him a shy smile.

"Can I ask you something?" Marcus asked, a little hesitant.

"Sure." Ben's heart started pounding. Marcus looked so intent, his brown eyes warm but serious.

"Um," Marcus looked down, scuffing the toe of his bowling shoe on the floor. "Are you and Ryan a thing?" Ben must have made some kind of face, because Marcus hurried on. "I mean, I didn't think Ryan was bi, but I also didn't want to assume anything, and Rach is—"

"We're not!" Ben's voice sounded loud to his own ears, and he took a deep breath. "Ryan's just a friend. My best friend. And straight." Ben blurted the next words out before he could second-guess himself. "I'm—I'm actually gay." A small, hysterical sounding giggle escaped, and Ben automatically clapped his hand over his mouth. Marcus was staring at him with wide eyes, and Ben didn't know whether to laugh or burst into tears.

Marcus rested a gentle hand on Ben's shoulder. "You want to go outside and talk for a minute?" Ben nodded, not trusting his voice. "Ryan knows, right?" Ben nodded again. "Okay, hang on just a second. Change your shoes so they don't try to tackle us at the front door."

Ben nodded numbly and started to slide off his shoes as Marcus walked over to Ryan and leaned in to speak quietly to him. Ben wouldn't have been able to hear them over the roaring in his head anyway.

Ryan's head whipped around to look at Ben, eyes searching his face for trouble. Ben tried to summon a smile to reassure him, but it was halfhearted at best. Ryan mouthed *Okay?* and Ben shrugged. Frowning, Ryan said something else to Marcus, and Marcus nodded, clapping him on the shoulder before heading back Ben's way. Ryan shot Ben a worried look but gave him a thumbs-up that made Ben smile and shake his head as he laced his shoes up.

Marcus sat down and kicked off his bowling shoes. Ben wordlessly slid Marcus's dark red Doc Martens over with his foot, and Marcus put them on quickly, not bothering to tie the laces. He stood up and jerked his head toward the entrance of the bowling alley, giving Ben an encouraging smile. "Come on."

Ben followed him numbly, the enormity of what he'd done starting to dawn on him. He'd never actually said the words before. Not out loud. And now he'd just come out in a bowling alley to his years-long crush. Why had he done that?

Marcus glanced over and put a hand on his back, guiding him around a corner of the building to a spot where they'd have some privacy. Ben almost fell against the brick wall, his knees suddenly weak. Marcus kept a warm hand on his shoulder, rubbing small circles with his thumb that were both comforting and distracting. Ben took another deep breath and felt a little better.

"You okay?" Marcus's voice was low and soothing.

"Yeah." Ben leaned his head back against the brick. "I'm sorry. I didn't mean to—"

"I won't tell anyone, if that's what you're worried about." Marcus sounded a little hurt, as if Ben thought he was going to announce it over a loudspeaker.

"No!" Ben wrapped a hand around Marcus's wrist, not thinking. "I know you wouldn't do that." He looked down at where their hands were joined and let go, his own falling to his side. "I just—didn't mean to blurt it out like that."

Marcus took his hand away and leaned against the wall next to him, close enough that their shoulders pressed together. "That the first time you've said it out loud?"

Ben huffed out a weak laugh. "How could you tell?"

"Your face. I thought you were going to pass out or something." Marcus ducked his head a bit, looking up at Ben through the fringe of his brightly colored hair. "It's okay to be a little freaked out, you know."

"Thanks." Ben was able to summon up a wan smile. "Look, you don't have to stay out here with me or anything. I'll be okay."

Marcus shook his head. "Nah. I'm good." He bumped Ben's shoulder with his own. "I like hanging out with you." He kicked a piece of gravel with the toe of his boot, laces flapping. Ben glanced over at him, cheeks burning, only to see a similar flush on Marcus's face.

"Anyway." Marcus cleared his throat. "Thanks for trusting me with—" He bumped Ben's shoulder again. "—you know. Everything."

Ben nodded and then laughed softly. "Honestly, it feels weird. Ryan's the only person I ever talk to about anything."

"Give me your phone." Ben looked at Marcus, who was holding his hand out expectantly. He pulled his phone out of his pocket and handed it over. Marcus pulled up his contacts and tapped for a few seconds. "There. Now you have one more person."

Ben took the phone back from him, ignoring the way their fingers brushed slightly. He quickly sent a text, grinning at his own bravery when he heard Marcus's phone ping. "And there's mine. You know, just in case." They smiled at each other for a moment, until Ben's text alert pinged.

Ryan: *everything okay?*

Ryan probably thought that he was having a heart attack or something. Ben felt surprisingly okay at the moment with Marcus there beside him. "I think they're looking for us."

Marcus eyed him carefully, and Ben wondered what he was thinking. Marcus started to say something else before shaking his head and giving Ben another smile that helped any remaining panic recede. "Ready to go back in?"

Ben nodded and pushed off the wall, leading the way and tapping out a quick reply.

Ben: *All fine. Coming back now.*

Ben bumped Marcus's shoulder with his own. "Um, thanks again."

Marcus's reply was quietly spoken but sincere. "Anytime."

RYAN AND RACHEL were sitting at their lane, heads together over a basket of fries. Marcus leaned over to whisper right in Ben's ear. "You see it too, right?" Ben barked out a startled laugh, drawing the attention of both of their friends.

Ryan was wearing his worried face by the time they got there, and Ben offered his knuckles for a fist bump to put him at ease. He smiled at Rachel, who was watching with wide eyes, and deftly reached around Ryan to steal a fry. "Are we playing or what?" Ben sat to change his shoes and smiled to himself when Marcus took the seat next to him to do the same.

Ryan glanced between the two of them and gave Ben another look that promised: *We are so talking about this later.* "Yeah, yeah, yeah. We just can't wait for you and Rachel to kick our butts again."

Ben shrugged and stole another fry before grabbing his bowling ball. "Well, do better then." Then he threw a strike that had Ryan groaning behind him.

The rest of the game went the same way. Ben and Rachel cleaned up, neck and neck in points, leaving Marcus and Ryan far behind. Especially Marcus. At one point, Ben asked him quite seriously if they needed to put the bumpers up. It was amazingly easy between them. There was a flirtatious edge to their bickering, and he could tell Rachel and Ryan were picking up on it. It felt good, and that was a pleasant surprise. It was one thing to say he was gay out loud to someone else, but acting on the chance that Marcus might somehow be interested was another. Add that to the fact that, just because Marcus liked guys, there was no guarantee he actually liked Ben that way. But it would be nice to have a friend who understood.

Ben threw his last ball. It came up short; Rachel had beaten him by a few points. He gave Rachel a fake glare, and she grinned at him and ruffled his hair. Ben liked her. Quite a bit, in fact, and even better, he liked her for Ryan. He almost felt like he needed to have a talk with Ryan about being careful with her. And given the way Marcus was eyeing Ryan, he was probably thinking the same thing about Rachel.

As they changed shoes, Ben realized he wasn't quite ready for the evening to end. He surprised himself by suggesting they go to the diner down the street and get something there. Ryan raised his eyebrows at that but didn't say anything, much to Ben's relief.

The diner was a good idea. They slid into the booth, Rachel and Ryan on one side and Ben and Marcus on the other. If Ben had given any thought earlier to how it would feel to sit that close to Marcus, knees brushing under the table when one of them shifted, he'd have been convinced it would have turned him into a sweaty, inarticulate puddle on the floor. Instead he was laughing, mostly at Rachel picking on Ryan over his terrible bowling skills, and not worrying about being anything other than himself.

It didn't feel awkward until they all walked back to the parking lot where Ryan had left his car. Rachel and Marcus were parked a few spaces over, so they paused at Ryan's car to say goodbye. It had been more like a date for Ryan and Rachel, so Marcus and Ben moved away to give them a few moments alone.

"So, are you practicing yet?"

Ben shook his head. "Not yet. We have a few clinics before tryouts and then practices."

"Wow, that's a lot. You don't really have all that much time to just hang out or whatever, right?"

"Not really." Ben shrugged. "Worth it though. I like playing." He took a chance. "Do you ever come to any of the games?"

"Sometimes." Marcus grinned at him. "I'll make sure to go to more this year for sure."

Ben could feel his face heat for the millionth time that evening. "That'd be cool." He winced internally. He'd been doing so well, why was he being such a dork now? Rachel broke the weird silence that had fallen between them when she finally walked over.

"Ready to go?" Rachel asked Marcus, and Ben nodded to Marcus and stepped away. To his surprise, Rachel stepped in front of him, stopping him in his tracks. She gave him that same appraising look that she had before, but this time it felt like approval, somehow. That was—good. He liked her, and it was nice to think she liked him too.

She wrapped an arm around his waist, giving him a one-armed hug. He squeezed her shoulders in return, hoping it wasn't too awkward. She pulled away and walked around the other side of the car to get in, raising her hand in a wave. "Later, dude."

Ben raised his hand to wave, realized she couldn't see him and lowered it. Marcus laughed quietly at him, and Ben was still trying to come up with a response when Marcus suddenly closed the distance between them and gave him his own hug. Ben was so shocked that he froze. He felt Marcus stiffen and start to pull away before he got it together and wrapped his arms around him. Marcus was a few inches shorter than Ben, and his hair brushed the side of Ben's face. Ben wanted run his fingers through it, just to see if it really was as soft as it looked.

Marcus relaxed into the hug for a few seconds before stepping back. There seemed to be a blush forming on Marcus's face, mirroring Ben's own, but it was really too dark to tell.

Marcus cleared his throat. "If you want to talk or anything, just text. Okay?"

"You too." Ben jumped when Rachel beeped the horn, and Marcus nodded before getting in.

It was easy to ignore Ryan's smug smile through the window as Ben walked over to his car. He got in and put on his seatbelt before facing him, ready to get it over with. "Go ahead. I know you want to."

"That—" Ryan cranked the car and put it into gear. "—was painful to watch."

Ben groaned and slid down into his seat.

"Did you at least get his phone number?"

Ben made another pitiful noise and covered his face. "Yes, but I think it was because he felt sorry for me."

They stopped at a red light, and Ryan gave him an incredulous look. "Are you insane?" He stared until the light turned green, and Ben made a frantic gesture for him to go. "He was *flirting* with you, and you were flirting *back*."

"No, I wasn't. I was just—"

"Nope. Do not take this away from me." Ryan was shaking his head. "I have never been so proud of you in my life."

Ben thought about that for a second. "I'm not sure if I should be offended or not."

"You loosened up and actually *talked* to the guy you like. And—" Ryan pointed at him without taking his eyes off the road. "—he likes you too. Just like I said."

Ben really wanted to change the subject because going further down that road meant thinking about how Marcus had looked at him—like he might think of him like *that*—and Ben just couldn't deal with that. Time to go on the offensive.

"Rachel seems to like *you*, that's for sure."

Ryan's mouth shut with a click. "Okay. Point to you. I'll shut up now."

THE CLINIC AFTER another week of school wasn't any easier than the first, but Ben felt more settled, which made things *feel* easier. He was still tired and sore at the end of the day, but they were coming together as a team. It had been worth it.

Coach called him over as they all cleared the ice after the last set of drills. "They're looking good, Lewis. Some of them might even be keepers." The gruff assessment made Ben grin around his mouthguard. The rookies were still terrified, but that would push them to work harder. They were all bruised and exhausted, but they were done.

Ben had spent the week awash in a wave of homework and going over plays, but something else had been on his mind.

Marcus had been texting him.

And he had been texting him back.

A lot.

Ben retrieved his phone from his bag even before he started stripping his sweaty gear off and scrolled through the missed texts. There were a few from Ryan, of course, but most of them were from Marcus. He'd apparently been watching some sort of cooking competition after school and live-texting it. Ben snorted a laugh, his mouthguard caught between his teeth. He plucked it out of his mouth and tossed it onto his bag.

Ben: *You've been busy :)*

Marcus: *I'm so boooorrreeddd. have fun hitting people all afternoon?*

"Is she cute?" Smithy's voice right next to him startled Ben so badly that he bobbled his phone and almost dropped it.

"What?"

Smithy elbowed him like they were sharing a secret. No matter what people thought, hockey players gossiped like nobody's business. "Your girlfriend." He smirked at Ben. "Or whoever she is."

A wave of sheer panic washed over Ben as he locked his screen so Smithy couldn't catch the peek he was angling for. "Just a friend." His voice was solidly on the right side of steady, but Smithy didn't look like he was buying it.

"Sure. A friend." The larger boy actually pouted because Ben wasn't spilling his guts. "I'm hurt, Cap." Ben gaped at him and Smithy laughed, loud enough that other people were looking over to see what was so funny. He elbowed Ben again, almost knocking him over. "Just kidding. But I'll take any deets you're willing to throw my way."

Ben was sure his face was bright red by then, so he covered by pulling his jersey over his head. He stripped out of his pads in record time and busied himself with his gear bag until Smithy strolled off to the showers only in a towel, apparently done with him. Ben stared at the blank screen of his phone until it lit up again.

Marcus: *when are you done?*

Ben shoved the phone in his bag, pushing it under everything so no one could see it. He clenched his jaw to try to look like he wasn't freaking out, but he was definitely freaking out. And why? Because someone had made an assumption? He hadn't done anything wrong. He hadn't even lied about it. Marcus *was* a friend.

It was just—

Ben pulled his undershirt off with a little more force than necessary. It wasn't anyone's business who he talked to. He could just as easily have been texting with Ryan or even Beth. It was the assumption that pissed him off. And that it immediately made him feel like he had to hide whatever he was doing. Like it was some sort of dirty secret.

Was that what it was always going to be like? He looked around the locker room, really looked, and wondered who would be staring at him if he was talking to a guy like they would talk to a girl. It made him feel a little sick to his stomach.

Smithy had already come back out before Ben finally made himself go take his shower. He grabbed his stuff and bolted before Smithy could make any more comments. He needed to talk this through with someone.

"ARE YOU FEELING okay? You look a little pale." Ben fended off his mom's attempt to feel his forehead when he got in the car. "Did you eat enough today?"

"I'm fine." *God, pass out just one time, and you never heard the end of it.* "Tired, I guess."

His phone buzzed in his shorts pocket. He'd retrieved it from the bowels of his gear bag before packing the last of his stuff away, but he hadn't responded to Marcus yet. He clicked the home button and read the text.

Marcus: *??*

"Is that Ryan?"

Ben jumped and automatically locked the screen. His mom wasn't even looking at him, eyes on the road.

"Um." What had happened in the locker room still had him rattled. "Nope." He tried to make his voice sound normal, and he didn't know if he'd succeeded or not.

"One of the boys, then?" It took him a few seconds to realize she was referring to the guys on the team. She always called them "the boys" or "the hockey boys." She was probably only making conversation.

"Just a friend from school." Ben thumbed on the phone and typed quickly.

Ben: *On the way home now. Talk later?*

Marcus: *:)*

HIS MOM HADN'T pushed, knowing how exhausted he could be at the end of a hard practice, and he was glad to be home. He took his bag upstairs and gave Biscuit a quick scratch behind the ears before sitting down on the edge of his bed and pulling the cat into his arms. Biscuit meowed a bit in protest but finally allowed a cuddle to Ben's chest, settling in with a rumbling purr.

Ben was tired and hungry and a little bit sad. He sighed. At least he could take care of two of those problems. He gently released Biscuit onto the bed and stood, stretching and taking inventory of any places that might need icing. Nothing stood out, but he'd probably be sore in the morning.

He rolled his shoulders and went back downstairs in search of food.

Ben followed his nose to find his dad in the kitchen taking something that smelled really, really good out of the oven. "Lasagna?"

"Yep."

"Need help with anything?"

"Cut the bread?" That was one thing Ben appreciated more than anything about his dad. In the midst of the normal chaos of their household, he was usually the calm one who kept things together in the background. Usually. Ben was getting the bread knife when he spoke up again. "Everything go okay today?"

Ben rolled his eyes. It had been too much to hope that his mom wouldn't be that observant. She must have talked it over with his dad while he was upstairs hugging Biscuit like a teddy bear. He put the bread on the cutting board and carefully started slicing it into Mom-acceptable pieces.

"It was great. The team's really coming together."

His dad made a noise of encouragement and got the salad out of the fridge. "Sounds good. Get the plates?"

Ben nodded and put the bread on the table before getting plates out of the cabinet. He knew this game. His dad never approached things head-on, like his mom did. No, he would bide his time and then pounce when the time was right.

Well, he might as well give him something to work with. "Coach says the new guys are looking good," he said casually. His dad made that noise again, and Ben waited.

"How's being captain working out for you?" And there it was. They probably thought the stress of being in charge of the team was getting to him. They were so wrong that it was almost funny. Almost.

Ben shrugged. "Okay, I think. The new guys are still terrified of Coach Jordan so they come to me instead." He picked a piece of carrot out of the salad bowl and crunched it for a few seconds. "I don't get why they're so afraid of him. He's fair, and he's nice enough when you get to know him."

His dad snorted and batted Ben's hand away when he tried to sneak another carrot. "I think you answered your own question there, son. They don't know him like you do."

"I guess."

His dad set the lasagna dish on the table. "If you need to talk about anything, we're here. Okay?"

Ben stared at his dad's bent head. Did he know? He suddenly felt the urge to blurt everything out, get it over with. Of course, that was when his mom and Beth made an appearance, saving him from his indecision. He met his dad's eyes when he straightened up, giving him a quick smile and a nod that seemed to put him at ease.

Ben grabbed a seat, hip checking his sister before she could sit there. It was the prime spot, or so it seemed to them, and they'd fought over it since they were little. She flicked him on the back of the head and sat in the chair across from him. They glared at each other over the table until his mom sighed.

"Can you two please get along?"

"She started it."

"He started it."

They weren't really mad at each other. It was just a game they played to mess with their mom. Their dad had figured it out a long time ago. Ben jerked his foot back before she could kick him in the ankle. She did something complicated with her eyebrows that made him snort, and the truce was finally made. They both looked innocently at their mom, and Ben could swear he heard a chuckle from the other end of the table, deftly covered with a cough.

"Are you done?" His mom rolled her eyes at both of them before Beth started chatting about something she needed to pick up for school.

He let the sounds of his family push away the remaining edge of anxiety. He wasn't ready, not yet. He'd worry about it later.

Chapter Seven

BEN ESCAPED TO his room after dinner with a slightly damp shirt. It had been Beth's turn to do the dishes, and he'd helped clear the table, putting himself directly in the line of fire. Beth was lethal with the sprayer. He pulled the shirt off and tossed it into his laundry basket, before opening the bottom drawer to grab a sleep shirt. There, hidden in his clean laundry, was the wooden box. He'd been too busy to give it or the letters any thought for a while.

Biscuit chose that moment to interrupt, pushing his way through the not quite closed door and jumping up on the bed to immediately curl up on the pillow. Ben chuckled to himself. "Just make yourself at home." He pulled on his shirt and turned back to the box—and finally took it out of the drawer after a long moment's consideration to set it on the nightstand. It still hadn't been possible to talk to Gran about the letters, and he hadn't taken the time to look at what else was in there.

After closing the door, he sat down on the bed and shifted the cat-laden pillow over to make room, getting a sleepy, one-eyed blink before the cat curled up tighter, closing his eyes.

The dog tag was still in his nightstand drawer, but he'd left everything else where it was. He set the letters and envelopes to the side, not really wanting to look at them again just yet. The Purple Heart in its case was also placed carefully on his nightstand. That left only a few more things in the box.

There was a pocket watch that looked much older than anything else. Ben picked it up and was surprised at how solid and heavy it felt. He turned it over in his hands and tried to open it, but found he couldn't. It didn't open. That wasn't surprising, given how old it seemed to be, but Ben really wanted to see what it looked like. He pressed the release again and felt the cover start to move, but it felt like something was caught in it.

Ben slid his thumbnail along the edge, praying he wasn't causing any damage. It held for another second and then slowly creaked open. There was something between the watch face, which was cracked, and the cover. A picture. Ben put the watch to the side and opened up the folded image, the edges worn and the creases threatening to come apart in his hands.

He recognized one of the two men as William Harris, remembering the portrait Gran had shown him of the smiling young man in uniform. The picture in his hand looked like it had been taken before that one, judging by the clothes and the length of William's hair. The other man he didn't know. The man who had Will's arm flung companionably around his neck, both of them with huge smiles on their faces, their heads tilted together.

Ben turned the picture over. Scribbled in the bottom corner, so faded he had to squint to read it, was "Will & Eddie—May 1939." He looked at the picture again, holding it closer to his face. The two men looked happy, and they were sitting closely together—

"Oh my god." Ben looked over at the letters he'd so carefully stacked on his nightstand. He thought about the little war stories Will had told in them, and how he'd sounded so glad that "E" didn't have to be there with him, too.

"Oh my *god*." He looked at the picture again. "E" was Eddie.

He picked a letter at random and scanned it. It was just like he remembered: addressed to "My Darling," and very careful not to say anything about E's gender. This one talked about how the cold would be so bad for E's (*Eddie's*) lungs. Ben looked at the picture yet again and took in Eddie's smaller stature. He didn't look sickly, not by a long shot, but that didn't mean he didn't have asthma or something similar that wasn't obvious.

Wait. Gran had mentioned an Uncle Eddie once. Hadn't she? He needed to talk to her soon. She'd be back from her trip to Florida next week, so maybe he'd be able to carve out some time to ask some questions. He'd only been curious before, but now he really wanted to know what Gran knew. If he was right in his conclusion, and he was pretty sure he was, then the letters were even more heart-wrenching than he'd originally thought. Because if they'd been in a relationship in that time, not only would it have been seen as a mental illness, it would have been illegal and cause for immediate dishonorable discharge.

He had more questions now than he knew what to do with. He carefully packed everything back into the box and placed it in the drawer so he wouldn't be tempted to obsess over it before he could get some answers.

It was time for bed, and he was tired, but that didn't stop him from grabbing his phone when it buzzed.

Ryan: *guess who has a date this weekend?*

Ben huffed out a laugh. He'd been waiting for the inevitable to happen.

Ben: *Try not to spill anything on her this time.*

Ryan: *that only happened once!*

Ben: *Twice. Remember Tracy's party?*

Ryan: *I hate you*

Ben smiled at his phone and locked the screen. Ryan had a date. That was a good thing. He hesitated, waiting for the bitter taste of jealousy to hit him, but it never did. Rachel was cool. She actually talked to him like a person, without seeing him as some weird kind of competition. He might actually be on his way to being her friend.

It was the same thing he hoped was going on with Marcus. He'd certainly been talking to him a lot, and Ryan and Rachel had been a hot topic of conversation. It was nice to have someone to talk to who was watching the same thing play out. Plus, he just liked talking to Marcus.

He put the phone on his nightstand without setting the alarm, fully intending on sleeping in the next morning. Hopefully, his body would let him.

"YOU CONSTANTLY TELL me that I have no idea how to dress myself, so how the hell am I supposed to be helping right now?" Ben lay on Ryan's bed, head hanging off the edge so he had an upside-down view of Ryan tearing off and then putting on yet another shirt. He'd walked over to Ryan's house after a series of frantic texts that included several blurry mirror selfies that were getting more and more pathetic.

"You can at least tell me if it looks good or not." Ryan's voice was muffled until his head popped through the neck hole. "How about this one?"

"I think you tried that one on already." Ben didn't actually think that, he just wanted to mess with him.

"Seriously?" Ryan frowned down at the shirt, and Ben couldn't keep a straight face. He started laughing. "You dick!"

Ben curled up in a ball before Ryan could pounce on him, just managing to say, "You're going to mess up your hair," between gasps of laughter, which put a stop to their roughhousing. Ryan popped up in front of the mirror again, and Ben resumed his position on the bed, still looking at him upside down. Ryan did look good, objectively speaking.

He'd never really been attracted to Ryan. Ben could appreciate his strong build and that he had nice eyes, but attraction had never played into it. He supposed it was because they'd been friends for so long, but he had no idea how that even worked. Why were some people attracted to dark hair and light eyes, when he found himself drawn to warm dark brown eyes under a shock of brightly colored hair?

He flicked his gaze back up to where Ryan was still staring into the mirror, biting his lip. Ben could feel the insecurity rolling off of him. Ryan was normally the most confident person he knew, diving into social situations without a second thought, but this was different. He must really like her.

"Hey." When Ryan looked at him, Ben made a weird face to make him laugh. "You look good, all right?"

Ryan turned back to the mirror, appearing a little less panicky. "Yeah?"

"Yep." Ben gave him a thumbs-up before checking his phone for the time. He'd missed a text from Marcus.

Marcus: *since Rachel is dumping me and going out, you want to do something?*

Ben didn't notice Ryan reading the text over his shoulder, hadn't even realized he'd crossed the room until he started laughing. "See! I told you he likes you!"

"Shut up." Ben cursed his pale skin, because he knew he was practically glowing. "We've been talking." Ryan cackled, and he raised his voice. "As *friends*, you asshole."

"Good." The sudden about-face made Ben look up. "I mean, I know you like him and all, but it's good that you're friends." It was Ryan's turn to look embarrassed.

"Yeah, yeah. You big softy." Ben tried to turn it into a joke. "Aren't you going to be late?"

Ryan smirked. "Aren't you going to answer that?"

Ben turned his phone over in his hands. "What should I say?"

"Well, what were you planning to do tonight?"

"Watch a movie on my laptop."

Ryan shrugged. "So ask him if he wants to do that. Don't make a big deal out of it, just hang out." He pointed an accusatory finger at Ben, almost touching the tip of his nose. "Gossip about us like I know you want to."

Ben crossed his eyes to look at Ryan's finger and laughed. "I think I can do that." Ryan made an impatient gesture at Ben's phone. "I guess I'll do it now."

Ben: *I was going to watch a movie or something on my laptop.*

Ben: *Want to hang out?*

"Oh god, why do I sound like such a dork?" Ben covered his face with his hand.

Ryan elbowed him. "Because you *are* a dork. Look, he's texting back." Three stupid little dots, and Ben was terrified of them.

Marcus: *sounds good. text me your address.*

Ben stared at his phone until Ryan took it away from him and put in his address. There was an immediate reply.

"You've got like twenty minutes or so. Go home and panic about how the boy you like is about to meet your family." When the blood drained from Ben's face, Ryan looked at him with alarm. "Or, you know, pass out or something. Jesus, man, breathe."

Ben gave him a wide-eyed stare. He'd completely forgotten about his family, who didn't know anything about— "Oh god."

"He's a friend, okay? No matter what else is up here—" He tapped Ben's forehead. "—he's just a friend. It'll be fine. The Lewises are my favorite people. They won't embarrass you or whatever." Ryan gave him an encouraging smile.

Ben tried to return it. "I'm supposed to be the one making you feel better. You're going on a date."

Ryan shrugged. "It'll be fine."

"I hope so."

"Just think of it this way. If he survives meeting Beth, then he's worth keeping around."

Ben laughed. "You might be right."

BEN RAN MOST of the way home.

And made himself slow down one street over so he wouldn't look like a maniac bursting in. He walked very calmly through the door and peeked into the den where his mom and dad were watching TV.

His mom noticed him first. "Hey, kiddo. Thought you were over at Ryan's."

"I was. He had something that he had to do." He didn't dare say date. They always got this *look* when they knew Ryan was seeing someone, and Ben didn't want to go there. It might make him ponder how much they knew. Or suspected, at least. "My friend Marcus is coming over in a little bit. We're going to watch a movie in my room."

"Sure, hon. Just bring down any dishes if you take any snacks up there."

"Okay." Ben breathed a sigh of relief and started to go up the stairs when his dad called him back.

"Marcus. Is he on the team? Plays left wing?"

Dammit. "Nope. He's just a friend from school."

"Oh. Okay." Ben fled up the stairs before he made a fool out of himself.

He burst into his bedroom, opening the door with enough force to send Biscuit looking for cover, and glanced around to make sure there wasn't anything that needed to be put away. He was reasonably neat and believed in laundry hampers, so it wasn't too bad. Ben got his laptop out and put it on the bed, which was the only place for two people to sit besides the floor, and started to panic again. He sent a quick text to Ryan.

Ben: *I can't do this.*

The response was immediate. Ryan must not have left yet, probably still looking at his hair.

Ryan: *yes you can. now go away so I can leave*

Ben rolled his eyes. Ryan had been waiting for him to text, knowing he'd have one last freak-out.

Ben: *FINE*

Ben took one more look around his room and figured it would have to do. At least he'd already taken the smelly hockey gear out. He'd just sat down to start scrolling through Netflix to find something that wasn't completely boring for them to watch when he heard it. How had he forgotten that Marcus rode a freaking motorcycle?

Marcus had gotten it the year before, and Ben hadn't quite known what to do with himself the first time he saw him on it. He liked them in general. And as with most things, *Marcus* on a motorcycle made them seem even cooler.

Ben heard a faint "Who is *that*?" from the living room and pelted down the stairs to get to the door before one of his parents. He stopped and took a breath, making himself wait until Marcus rang the doorbell before yanking open the door and herding him away from prying eyes.

The doorbell rang.

"I've got it!" He said it like no one was aware he was already there, but he was committed. He took another deep breath and opened the door.

"Hey." Marcus's hair was bright purple and sticking up from the helmet. Ben felt an insane urge to smooth it down with his fingers and clenched his hand into a fist at his side.

"Hi. Um, come on in." He stepped to the side to let Marcus in and took a peek outside at the motorcycle. It was a nondescript black, and Ben wouldn't have been able to identify what kind it was if he tried. It was cool because it was Marcus's. Impressive. And kind of hot.

Get it together.

Ben lowered his voice. "Sorry about this in advance." Marcus gave him a confused look before following him into the den, helmet still in hand. "Mom, Dad, this is Marcus. Marcus, these are my parents, Anne and Rich." Marcus stepped forward with his hand out to shake. Ben's dad flicked his eyes up to the purple hair before shaking his hand firmly and grinning.

"It's nice to meet you. We've heard absolutely nothing about you."

Ben willed his parents not to be overly *weird* about anything. He had friends that weren't Ryan, after all. Teammates, people in his classes. He just didn't invite them home with him. Usually.

His mom shook Marcus's hand as well, shooting Ben a look he couldn't quite read. "Don't be like that, Rich. There's snacks and things in the kitchen if you boys want something."

Ben took that as his cue to escape with Marcus in tow. "Um, you want to put that down or...?" He gestured toward the chair that was next to the door. Marcus put the helmet down and ran his fingers through his hair, making it stick up even more. Ben decided it was a good look on him. As were his pink cheeks from the chill outside. "Do you want a drink or anything?"

"Sure." They walked into the kitchen together, and Ben could breathe again. He was not going to be awkward about this. They were going to go watch a movie, and it would all be fine.

Chapter Eight

OF COURSE, IT was the dumb cat that made him relax. Biscuit, for some reason, decided he liked Marcus almost as much as he liked Ryan. He poked his head out from under the bed when they came in, and Ben assumed he'd bolt for the door. Instead, he gave a plaintive little meow, and Marcus sat on the floor, cross-legged, right next to the bed.

"Who's this?" He held out his fingers for Biscuit to sniff, and Ben prayed the cat wouldn't do his patented "sniff, sniff, chomp" on him. He was completely surprised when the cat came out from under the bed and promptly demanded head scritches.

"Wow. I mean—that's Biscuit."

"Biscuit?" Marcus gave him a grin and tugged off his jacket before settling down with his back against the bed.

Ben looked away, embarrassed. "It's another name for a puck."

"Seriously?" Marcus sounded *delighted*. "I never knew that." Biscuit had worked his way almost into Marcus's lap by that time, and Ben couldn't help but laugh.

"Ryan is going to be so jealous." Marcus gave him an odd look. "I mean, sometimes I think he only comes over here for the cat."

Marcus laughed at that and it was like something clicked, and suddenly, Ben was okay. Marcus managed to move Biscuit enough so he could straighten out his legs. He then kicked his boots off and announced that he couldn't possibly disturb the cat, so Ben would just have to come down there with him.

Somehow, Ben found himself sitting next to Marcus on the floor, close enough together that their shoulders touched, his laptop resting across his thighs but angled so they could both see. Marcus picked the movie, and it was something Ben had never heard of, but he was told, in detail, that it was based on a series of comic books he'd be required to read.

Ben was just thinking that the movie had been good so far, and he might give the comics a try, when Biscuit finally decided he'd had enough and wriggled out through the cracked door. Ben adjusted the laptop so that they were sharing it on both of their laps, and Marcus shifted slightly toward him. Ben had been able to mostly ignore his proximity so far, but now he was painfully aware of how closely they were pressed together.

"Watch this part. This is really cool."

It *was* really cool. There was a music battle on the screen with some great animation added, and when Ben turned to say something about it, Marcus was right there, looking at him. Ben's breath caught in his throat. They were sitting so close together, and Marcus's eyes were so dark where his hair had flopped over his forehead—

Marcus leaned over and kissed him.

Ben froze in place, only vaguely realizing that Marcus's lips were soft and dry against his own.

Marcus pulled back. "Oh god, I'm so sorry. I thought—" He looked horrified.

Impulsively, Ben kissed him back, a quick chaste thing, barely a press of lips. It wasn't his first kiss, or his second. But it was the first time with a guy and the first time that it felt right. Marcus looked at him closely, eyes roaming over his face, before bringing a hand up to run fingers down Ben's jaw. That produced a shiver, which awakened nerves that seemed to be connected to *other* things.

"Can I?"

Ben nodded, still a little shocked at what was happening. It was better than anything he'd ever imagined. Ben closed his eyes, and Marcus's lips were on his again, more firmly this time. Ben felt the laptop start to slide sideways and shut it and set it aside without looking. Then he finally got his fingers into Marcus's hair, and it was just as soft as he had thought it would be.

A swipe of Marcus's tongue on his lower lip had Ben making an embarrassing noise in the back of his throat and opening his mouth to let him in. He felt hot all over and wasn't sure what to do with his hands. Marcus rolled toward him, hooking one thigh over Ben's and fisting a hand in his shirt.

Ben heard the footsteps coming up the stairs and reflexively pushed Marcus away, eyes wide. He grabbed the laptop and opened it back up, hitting the spacebar to start the movie again. The steps paused but then went down the hall toward Beth's room. She must have just gotten home.

He listened for a long moment and waited for his racing heart to calm down. Nothing. Except for his own harsh breathing.

"Are you okay?" Marcus's concerned face was very close, and Ben desperately wanted to kiss him again. But then the vision of Beth or his parents walking in and seeing them spiraled into his teammates finding out, and it all made his stomach turn. He made himself take a deep breath and moved farther away. The hurt he saw in Marcus's eyes was almost too much. Ben put the laptop to the side again.

"I'm sorry." Ben's voice was hoarse. "I don't—"

"It's okay."

"It's not okay." He was whispering now. "It's not. I can't—I'm not—"

Marcus sighed, and Ben watched as he clenched his fingers together in his lap so hard his knuckles turned white. He let go and started to put his boots back on. "It's my fault. I shouldn't have." He tied the laces tightly. "I'm going to go."

Ben wanted to tell him to wait. That he really liked him and, god, could they try that again? But his courage failed him. Instead, he got up and reached for Marcus's jacket where he'd tossed it on his bed a million years ago. Ben handed it to him and silently followed Marcus out the bedroom door and down the stairs. His parents were still in the den, and he dimly heard Marcus saying goodbye to them because he was nice and polite, and Ben was an awful person.

Marcus met his eyes again as he picked up his helmet, turning it around in his hands. "I guess I'll see you at school?"

Ben couldn't help but look away. "Yeah. See you."

He closed the front door behind Marcus and waited until he heard the motorcycle start up before he escaped up the stairs, thankful that his parents had gone back to whatever they were watching on TV.

He couldn't decide if he wanted to curl up in bed or hit something. He felt stupid and guilty. Ben grabbed his phone, intent on texting Ryan and asking him what the hell he should do, before he remembered Ryan was still on his date. He dropped the phone on the bed, flopped down face-first, and covered his head with his pillow.

"What's wrong with *you*?"

Ben groaned. Beth. Of course, she'd have to come and stick her nose in. "Nothing."

"Uh-huh. Whose motorcycle was that?" She shoved at him until he moved over enough so that she could sit beside him, propped up against the headboard.

"Friend from school."

"I knew that." He could practically *hear* her eye-roll. "But who? You don't have any friends." She really hadn't meant anything by it, but that cut deep.

"Go away." He should just answer her, which was the quickest way to get rid of her, but he didn't want to.

"Nope." She sounded so cheerful that he wanted to push her off the bed. He didn't. "Come on. Whose was it?"

"Marcus Blake." Saying the name made guilt and shame wash over him. Marcus was probably blaming himself for the whole situation, and Ben was letting him. He felt sudden hot tears prick the corners of his eyes, and he wanted Beth to just *get out*. "Can you go away now?" He swallowed hard, struggling to control his voice. "Please?"

She hesitated like she knew something was very wrong and was deciding whether or not to push. As much as they bickered, they knew how the other worked.

"Fine," she said finally and patted him on the shoulder before leaving the room. As the door closed gently behind her, he took the pillow off his head and rolled over onto his back to stare at the ceiling.

Ben hadn't cried since he fractured his hand two years before. But it felt like his chest was cracking open. A sob caught in his throat, and Ben rolled over to his side, curling in on himself. He scrubbed at his face, fingers coming away wet, and ignored the buzzing phone on his nightstand. It was probably Ryan with good news about his date. Ben just couldn't.

BEN WOKE UP with gritty eyes and a heavy lump in his stomach. He groped for his phone to check the time and was shocked by the number of missed texts, all from Ryan. It was after eight o'clock, which was practically sleeping in for him. He struggled to sit up and started to scroll through his texts.

Ryan: *hope you're having funnnnnnn*

Ryan: *dude i really like her*

Ryan: *she's so funny*

Ryan: *i didn't spill anything yay!*

...

Ryan: *rach just called me really upset*

Ryan: *ben?*

Ryan: *you up?*

Ryan: *ben*

Ryan: *ben*

Ryan: *ben*

Ryan: *i'm coming over in the morning*

Ryan: *omw*

Ben got to the last text just as someone tapped on his door.

He looked up and Ryan, who never knocked, took one look at him and quickly shut the door behind him. "Dude, what happened?"

Ben shook his head. He looked down and realized he was still wearing the same clothes from the night before. "He kissed me." Silence.

Ryan was staring at him. "Wasn't that what you wanted?"

It like a dam broke inside him, and Ben had to let it all out. "Yes. No. God, I don't know. We were sitting there, watching that movie with the evil exes—"

"*Scott Pilgrim*?"

"Yeah. And then he kissed me." Ben hesitated. "And I kissed him back."

Ryan was still staring at him like he'd lost his mind. "It was good?"

"Yeah." Ben sighed and slumped back down on the bed. "And then I told him I can't—That I couldn't—" The bed dipped, and Ryan stretched out beside him. "Everyone would know."

When Ryan spoke, his words were careful, quiet. "Yeah, they would."

"I heard Beth come up the stairs. What if she'd walked in? What would she think?" Ben sniffed, hard, determined not to tear up. "What would Mom and Dad think? My team? You know how those guys can be."

"I think—" Ryan pressed their shoulders together. "—that they would be okay. They know you, all right?"

Ben swallowed past the lump in his throat. "Why is this so hard?"

"Because it's important. Important things are hard."

"You sound like Yoda. What the hell."

Ryan snorted. "Hard important things are."

Ben allowed himself a small laugh. Then, he remembered something. "Rachel knows doesn't she." It wasn't a question. "She hates me now."

Ryan nodded thoughtfully. "She doesn't hate you, but she's not happy with you, that's for sure." Ryan bumped him with his elbow. "You know you're going to have to talk to him, right?"

"I don't want to. He probably hates me too. I'm awful."

It was Ryan's turn to sigh. "He doesn't hate you either, and you're not awful."

"I feel really bad. He looked so hurt, and I just let him leave. I'm such a coward."

Ryan's hand wrapped around his wrist, and that small gentle touch almost pushed him right over the edge and into ugly crying territory. "You are not a bad person." Ben opened his mouth to argue, and Ryan kept going. "And you're not a coward. You wouldn't let huge guys slam you into the boards if you were. That only makes you an idiot."

Ben gave a wet-sounding laugh. "Yeah, I know." He sniffled and was hit in the face with a small wad of tissues that more than likely came from his nightstand. He blew his nose and took a deep breath. "What are you going to tell Rachel?"

"I won't say anything if you don't want me to, okay?"

"Tell her I'm sorry?"

Ryan gave his wrist a squeeze and let go. "I can do that, but you're going to have to see them at school. You do realize that, right?"

Ben groaned and covered his face with both hands. "You think Mom would let me stay home for the next year?"

"Not a chance." Ryan sat up and poked Ben in the side, making him twitch away. "Now are you going to get up and go for a run or not?"

Ben groaned again, but a run would help. Ryan knew him too well. "Fine. Go downstairs and bug Mom." He thought of something as Ryan opened the door. "Oh, and Biscuit likes Marcus better than you."

The over-the-top gasp was totally worth it. And then Ryan was talking to the cat that must have been waiting outside his door, as usual. "Traitor! He could never love you as much as I do." Silence. "Yes, you're very cute and soft." More silence. "Okay, I forgive you. But just this once."

Ben heard him walking down the steps and got up to get ready. He didn't know what the hell he was going to do the next day.

"YOU LOOK LIKE hell." Ryan was already shooting Ben worried looks, and they hadn't even made it to school yet.

"Thanks." Ben glared at him, but it was ruined when he gave a huge yawn along with it. "I couldn't sleep."

He'd picked up his phone a thousand times the previous evening with the intention of apologizing to Marcus, but he'd chickened out every time. He'd ended up spending the time watching the rest of that stupid movie. And then some cooking show that made him think of Marcus and how he'd text him about it when he was bored. And to top it all off, he'd gone through Will and Eddie's letters again, which made him feel even worse. He put a hand to his chest and pressed the hard outline of the dog tag into his skin. He didn't know why he was wearing it, exactly. It reminded him of Will's courage, he supposed. And his love for Eddie and how he sacrificed his life. Ben was a coward and a glutton for punishment. So he wore the tag.

"You going to be okay?" Ben knew Ryan was asking him this on a couple of different levels. Was he going to be okay seeing Marcus at school? That was a hard no. Was he going to be okay wanting something he wouldn't let himself have? Probably not, but he'd have to get used to that. He slumped down in the seat and banged his head against the window.

"Noooo," he said, answering both. Ben felt drained, and he still had to survive a day at school and then go to their first real practice before the season started. He was going to die.

"There's something I have to tell you."

Ben hunkered further down. Those words never preceded something *good*. "Oh god, what now?"

"Um." Ryan shifted in his seat. "Rachel's going to hunt you down today. Fair warning."

"I figured." Ben tried to think of what he'd do if someone had treated Ryan that way. He had a pretty good idea what Ryan would do: the words "scorched earth" came to mind. "She has every reason to hate me."

"Dude, she doesn't hate you, I promise. She's just really, really pissed."

Ben had a sudden thought. "This whole thing didn't mess up anything with— I mean, she wouldn't blame you for *me*, would she?"

He shook his head. "Don't worry about it. We talked it out and we're cool."

Ben breathed a sigh of relief. "Good. That's good."

They pulled into the parking lot and both looked for a spot. It could get a little crazy, sometimes.

Ben pointed. "There's one."

"I see it." Ryan deftly parked and turned off the car. "Seriously, you going to be okay?"

"Seeing as how I don't have a choice, I'll have to be."

Ryan gave him a look. "Ready?"

"Fine." They got of the car, and Ben shouldered his gear bag as they started toward the front door of the school. "I have to go drop this off. See you in second period?"

"Sure, man." Ryan offered him a fist to bump, and they went their separate ways.

PRACTICE WAS BRUTAL. Ben had managed to make it through the day without running into Marcus or Rachel, but he was exhausted. He was making mistakes all over the place, and people were starting to notice. The whistle finally blew, sharp and piercing.

"Lewis! Get over here!" Coach Jordan did not sound happy. Ben skated over to him and braced himself for a dressing down. Coach motioned to the bench, and Ben went through the door, his mouthguard clenched in his teeth.

"Yeah, Coach?" Ben knew exactly what he was going to say. He was screwing up. They had a game in two weeks, their very first game of the season, and their captain was playing like shit.

"What the hell is going on out there?"

Ben wanted to ask him which time. He'd fallen on his ass during drills, and had sent the puck flying over the glass just before Coach yelled at him.

"Sorry, Coach." There was no answer that was safe to give. He was failing at everything.

Coach Jordan gave him a long look. "Don't be sorry. Get it together." He clapped Ben on the shoulder. "Get back out there."

"Got it, Coach." Ben fit his mouthguard in and went back on the ice, ignoring the looks some of the other guys were giving him. He had a job to do; he would have to suck it up and skate through it all.

He managed to make it through the rest of practice without incident. The stinky locker room had never seemed so nice. Ben untied his skates with more force than necessary and resisted the urge to hurl something across the room like a child. He was angry more than anything else. Angry at himself, the situation, the world. Why did everything have to be so stupid?

He ignored the usual dumb conversations going on around him but noticed that all of the guys were staying away from him. Especially when he was broadcasting Do Not Disturb all over the place, so he couldn't blame them. It was also how he only caught the end of a conversation between Smithy and one of their left-wingers, Jordan Roberts.

"—so I told him to quit being such a little fag about it—"

Ben had no idea what they were talking about, but he suddenly saw red. Later, he couldn't remember standing and getting up in Smithy's face. It was like he appeared in front of him, so close their chests bumped together, from one blink to the next.

"No."

Smithy took a step back from him, shock written all over his face. "What—"

"Do not use that word." Suddenly his teammates were all staring at him, but he was too far in to back down. "Say it again, and I'll report it."

They'd all had a sensitivity meeting during camp, and anyone heard saying any homophobic slurs was supposed to get an automatic bench for the next game. Of course, it had never been enforced, but he had it to fall back on. Smithy narrowed his eyes, and Ben felt a second of panic. If Smithy decided to take offense, he had several inches on Ben and about thirty pounds of muscle. He was a D-man for a reason.

Ben put on his best game face and stared him down. There was complete silence in the locker room, tension building and ready to burst.

Smithy finally backed off and ran a hand through his sweaty hair. "Sorry, Cap."

Ben blinked in surprise but recovered quickly. "Just think before you speak, okay?" He clapped Smithy on the shoulder and returned to his stall. Ignoring the extended silence, he pulled his jersey over his head and concentrated on taking off his pads. When tentative conversations started up again, Ben wondered if he'd shown his hand, if they'd be whispering about him, or if they'd just see him doing his job as the captain.

Ben put on his track pants and hoodie, not bothering with a shower for once, and shoved his feet in his sneakers. He needed to get the hell out of there. Ryan didn't have work that night, so he'd offered Ben a ride, and Ben hoped he was already out in the parking lot. Gear bag in hand, he left without saying another word to anyone else.

Ryan was waiting out front, and Ben sighed in relief, practically running to his car. He jumped when Ben yanked the door open and put his seat up from where he'd leaned it back while listening to music. Ben dropped into the passenger seat and slammed the door closed.

"Can we go?"

Ryan stared at him for a second. "What the hell is wrong with you?" He blew out a breath but put the car in gear and pulled out of the lot.

"So many things." Ben didn't even know where to begin.

Ryan wrinkled his nose. "You stink. You didn't shower?"

"No. I kind of almost started a fight with Smithy instead."

"What?" Ryan swerved a little, and Ben felt his heart leap into his throat. "He could eat you for lunch! What for?"

"He said something about calling someone a little *fag*," Ben spat the word out, "and I lost my mind. I don't know what I was thinking." He gave a hysterical little giggle that didn't sound like him at all. "Oh my god, why did I do that."

Ryan didn't answer right away. Ben looked over at him, and he was staring grimly out the window, lips pressed in a hard line that always meant he was pissed. Great. All Ben needed was for Ryan to be mad at him too, and this perfect day would be complete. He jumped when Ryan started to speak.

"I can't imagine what it's like for you. To hear people say shit like that everyday."

So maybe he wasn't mad at him after all. Ben shrugged. "I don't know. I try to ignore it." He looked out the window, unable to meet Ryan's eyes. "It just got to me today."

Ben could see Ryan shake his head out of the corner of his eye. "I'd have punched him. But then he would have wiped the floor with me. What did he do?"

"Said he was sorry."

"Seriously?" Ryan laughed incredulously. "He just said 'Sorry for being an asshole'?"

Ben had to smile at the ridiculousness. "He actually said 'Sorry, Cap.'"

Ryan's startled cackle made Ben laugh a little, and soon they were both giggling. Ben felt the band that had been around his chest all day start to loosen. Ryan's next words made it snap back instantly.

"You didn't see Marcus today?"

"No." Ben couldn't bring himself to tell him he'd looked for a flash of bright purple the entire day. "Did Rachel say something?"

Ryan's silence was telling. "Yeah. She's still kind of pissed."

"Sorry."

"That's not something you should be saying to me. You don't ever have to say that about something like this to me. I've got your back."

"I know you do." Ben glanced at him, and Ryan was biting his lip. He knew that look. Ryan was about to say something he wasn't sure would be received well.

"Um. You should know. They messed up Marcus's Econ, and he's going to be in ours tomorrow."

Ben's heart started to pound. "Oh, shit." His voice was faint, and he wasn't sure if Ryan had heard him until he spoke again. "After all this time?"

"Yeah. Something about consolidating classes, I don't know. So, we need a game plan."

"We?" Ben's head snapped up. "What?"

"Look"—Ryan smoothly turned the car into their neighborhood, deliberately driving more slowly to give them more time—"I know how you work. If you don't have a plan, then the likelihood of Rachel punching you in the face goes way, way up."

"I'd let her."

Ryan rolled his eyes, coming to a stop just down the street from Ben's house. "But I don't want that to happen, and I'm fairly certain *Marcus* doesn't want that to happen, so we need a plan."

"So, what's the plan?" Ben sighed heavily and turned in his seat to give Ryan his full attention.

"First of all, you have to quit being so down on yourself." Ryan punched him lightly in the shoulder. "Yeah, it was a shitty thing to do, but you have to move on and fix it, you know?"

"You really are embracing this whole Yoda thing, aren't you."

"Shut up and listen to Yoda." Ryan poked a finger at him. "Second, you need to talk to Marcus." He grew more serious. "He knew you weren't out, right?" Ben nodded. "And he seems like a pretty good guy?" Ben nodded again. "Then he's not going to be a giant dick about this. Trust me."

"He probably hates me." Ben flinched when Ryan poked at him again.

"Stop saying that." Ryan went to poke him again, and Ben swatted his hand away.

"Cut it out!"

"I mean, you're probably not his favorite person right now, but he doesn't hate you."

"Thanks. You're very helpful."

Ryan made a wounded face. "I am the *most* helpful." He put the car back in gear and pulled up into Ben's driveway. "Now get your stink out of my car and try to get some sleep tonight."

"Fine." Ben grabbed his gear bag and backpack out of the backseat. He closed the door but stood there for so long Ryan rolled down the window. "Are you sure?" Ben asked quietly.

"Sure what?"

"That he doesn't hate me."

"Yeah, dude. I'm sure." Ryan offered him a fist, and Ben bumped it. "See you tomorrow?"

"If I have to."

Chapter Nine

"COURTYARD. NOW."

Ben clutched his lunch tray closer to his chest as if it could protect him from Rachel's glare.

"What?" His voice went up an octave, and he winced.

"You. Me. Courtyard." She took a step forward, and he involuntarily took a step back. He'd faced less terrifying D-men, all taller than his shoulder. His fear must have shown on his face, because she unfolded her arms and sighed. "C'mon, Ben. We're talking this out."

She turned on her heel and headed toward the doors to the courtyard. Ben looked down at his chicken tenders, his appetite suddenly gone. He dumped the tray, picked his backpack up off the table, and headed in the same direction like he was facing his own execution. Honestly, he didn't know what to expect from Rachel, so he was going to have to trust Ryan's judgment.

Ben took a deep breath and pushed through the doors, leaving the safety of the cafeteria behind. Looking around, he blinked in the sudden sunlight until he spotted Rachel sitting on top of one of the picnic tables that were scattered throughout the courtyard. Even though he was glad to see she'd picked one over in the corner, so they'd have a little privacy, he was still nervous as hell about she'd say when they were mostly alone. He dropped his backpack and sat on the bench, clutching his hands together to keep from fidgeting. She looked at him for a few seconds, evaluating, and then sighed heavily.

"God, you're a bit of a mess too, aren't you." She ran a hand through her hair, dark magenta for the moment, and Ben wondered if she and Marcus shared hair dye. "Look. I'm going to be really blunt here. Marcus is my person—you get that, right? Just like Ryan is yours." Ben nodded numbly. "You hurt my person."

Ben hadn't thought he could feel any worse, but having Rachel say out loud what he'd been telling himself for the past three days made the tight band around his chest come back. "I know."

"You like him." She stated it like the fact it was. "He likes you too, you know." She tapped an uneven beat on the wooden table. "I probably shouldn't have told you that, but watching you two is just freaking painful." She lowered her voice. "I know you're not out, and I respect that, but you need to tell him what you want." Ben jumped when he felt her fingers smoothing back his hair. "Ryan's your BFF, but if you need someone to talk to, let me know. In fact—" She dug her phone out of her pocket. "—give me your number."

Ben did as instructed and felt his own phone buzz in his pocket a few seconds later.

He felt overwhelmed. It wasn't right that she was being so kind. "Why are you doing this?"

"Doing what?"

"Being nice to me." Ben closed his eyes when she ruffled his hair before smoothing it back again. He couldn't help leaning into the touch just a little bit. He'd been so tense and scared about what she was going to say that it was a relief.

"Because Marcus likes you, and if he likes you then you must be pretty cool." She hopped down off the table and grabbed her messenger bag. "Also, Ryan highly recommends you." Ben laughed softly, feeling a little bit better. "Anyway. I'm going to go and deal with my sad puddle of a best friend"—Ben flinched—"and you're going to promise me that you're going to at least text him tonight."

"I have practice tonight." She raised an eyebrow, and Ben ducked his head. "I mean, of course."

Rachel ruffled his hair again. (He was beginning to wonder if she liked his hair, or if that was just a thing she did.) "It'll be good for you both. Promise." She stepped away from him when the bell rang. "Laters?"

"Sure." Ben felt vaguely like he'd been hit over the head. What had he just promised to do? He looked at his phone and saw the message from Rachel.

Rachel: *do the thing :)*

Ben snorted and saved her number into his contacts.

PRACTICE WASN'T A complete shitshow. At least, Ben was pretty sure it wasn't. Still, he was definitely not at his best. Anxiety about *what* to do about Marcus had his thoughts circling around *how* he was going to do what he'd been told. He'd composed the text in his head about a hundred times and was doing it yet again when he realized something else was off.

He hadn't noticed anything on the ice during practice, but it was definitely quieter in the locker room as he was getting his gear off. There was none of the usual loud catcalls and general obnoxiousness as they hit the showers. Ben looked around, curious, and caught Smithy giving him a definite side-eye.

Huh.

Well, that explained a lot. It had to be because of his outburst yesterday. The thought made his skin crawl. If they were purposefully keeping their distance, what did that mean? Did they wonder about him now, and were just afraid to ask? Well, he wasn't going to play into their curiosity. He'd done what he should have as a person and as their captain, and that was all that should matter. He could handle the quiet.

Ben yanked his shirt over his head and stuffed it in his bag. He wasn't going to allow them to run him out this time without a shower. Ryan was picking him up again and had threatened to leave him there if he didn't at least make an attempt at rinsing off. He felt eyes on him as he stalked off to the showers, towel around his waist, but did his best to ignore them.

After he was dressed and had his gear, he left the locker room and tried to push the weirdness out of his head. Maybe he was just being paranoid.

Ryan was waiting in his usual spot, and Ben smiled at the music coming from the car as he walked toward it. Ryan had gotten sucked into some movie soundtrack and had started listening to seventies rock nonstop. Ben had given Ryan a hard time about it, but it was secretly growing on him. He'd never tell Ryan, though.

He threw his gear bag and backpack in the backseat and got in. Ryan was still singing even as he was buckling his seatbelt.

"I'm hooked on a feeling, I'm high on believing, that you're in love with meeeeee."

Ryan put the car in gear, and Ben reluctantly joined in when the chorus started up again. It wasn't that he was a horrible singer, he just didn't like to sing in front of people. Ryan had told him on more than one occasion that he wasn't "people," so he didn't count.

The song ended, and Ryan hit pause on his phone. "You're in a better mood. Good practice?"

Ben nodded. "Yeah. Well, better than yesterday." Ryan made a noise of understanding, and they rode in silence for a few moments before Ben remembered he hadn't even thought to ask how Ryan's date went. "Oh god, I'm a horrible friend."

"What?"

"I completely forgot to ask you about your date."

Ryan shrugged. "It's okay. You were busy having a crisis."

"Still." Silence again. "So. How did it go?"

Ryan barked out a laugh and grinned. "Pretty good. I think we're going to go out again this weekend."

"Awesome." Ben fiddled with his seatbelt. "She's pretty great."

Ryan smiled dopily. "Yeah, she is." He winced. "I heard she talked to you."

"Gave me orders, more like it."

"You gonna do it?"

Ben snorted. "I'm afraid not to."

"What are you going to do?"

Ben looked out the window. "Text him, I guess. Not that I know what to say. I mean, how do you start that kind of conversation? Sorry for being an idiot? Sorry that I'm a giant dork who doesn't know what the hell he's doing?" He banged his head against the window. "God, I'm pathetic."

"You're not pathetic." Ryan was always so matter of fact. "But you *are* a giant dork."

"Thanks."

"Seriously, though." Ryan turned to look at him when they stopped at a red light. "Just start by saying 'Hey' or something. Be honest. You'll do fine."

"Says you."

"Exactly."

IT WAS ALMOST ten o'clock before Ben quit procrastinating and picked up his phone. He typed several versions of *Hello* before taking Ryan's advice.

Ben: *Hey*

The three dots popped up immediately. Then went away. Then popped up again. Ben thought he was going to hyperventilate. Whoever invented that feature should be...

Marcus: *hey*

Ben blinked at his screen. Now what? He typed, erased, typed, knowing he was causing the same dots of anxiety on the other end that he'd just experienced.

Ben: *I don't know what to say.*

Marcus: *me either*

Ben sat up against the headboard, drawing his knees up to his chest. He had so much he wanted to say, but had no idea where to start. It would be easier in person so he could tell what Marcus was thinking.

Ben: *I don't think I can do this through text.*

Marcus: *ok*

What did that mean? Ben stared at his phone, willing Marcus to say something else. After avoiding him for three days, Ben suddenly wanted to see him.

Ben: *Can you meet me somewhere?*

Three dots. Nothing. Three dots.

Marcus: *now?*

Ben: *Yeah.*

Ben: *If you can.*

Ben got to his feet and paced from the door to his bed and back. What if he said no? He put his phone on top of the dresser and unzipped his backpack. He'd taken Will's dog tag off for practice, and he suddenly missed the feel of it around his neck. He needed some more of Will's bravery. After an eternity, the phone vibrated, and he made himself take a breath before looking.

Marcus: *where?*

That was a good question. He shouldn't have any problem leaving the house, but where could they meet?

Ben: *There's a park in my neighborhood. Just down a few streets from my house.*

Ben held his breath.

Marcus: *be there in twenty*

Ben looked down at himself and realized pants would be a good thing. Going to the park in boxers and a T-shirt was out of the question. He grabbed his favorite hoodie and a pair of track pants, pulled them on, and grabbed his sneakers to carry down and put on outside. He was fairly certain his parents wouldn't give him too much crap for leaving the house that late on a school night, but he really didn't want to get interrogated by Beth. She was ruthless when she thought a secret was being kept from her.

He heard faint music coming from her room as he crept down the stairs, so he was probably safe from that direction. The television was on in the den—through the kitchen and out the back door would be the best route. Biscuit taking that moment to loudly show his displeasure at an empty food dish—and almost derailing the entire plan—had Ben in silent hysterics.

"Shhhhh. Fine. Here." He poured a little bit of dry food in the dish to placate the cat and made his way out the back door.

The moon was full and the sky clear, so he had no problem getting his shoes on and navigating the backyard to the street under the cover of darkness. He pulled his phone out of his pocket as he walked down the sidewalk, the park already in sight.

Ben: *Tell me I'm not a complete idiot.*

Ryan: *not a complete one*

Ben: *jackass*
Ryan: *what are you doing?*
Ben: *Meeting Marcus in the park.*
Ryan: *!!!!!!!!!*
Ryan: *text me after*
Ben: *Fine.*

Ben locked the screen and stuffed the phone back in his pocket. He had ten minutes to kill. He made his way over to the bench and sat on the back of it, feet on the seat. He almost sent a text to Ryan to see if he could meet him there too, but he couldn't keep using him as a crutch.

He had no idea what he was going to say to Marcus. Would Marcus be angry, or hurt, or a mixture of both? And how would that make him feel? He put his head in his hands, leaning his elbows on his knees. Ben didn't *think* he was a bad person. He tried not to be. But somehow he'd managed to hurt someone he'd come to consider a friend. Someone he'd like to have as more than a friend, if he could figure himself out.

Marcus had kissed him. Ben ran the tips of his fingers over his bottom lip. If he closed his eyes, he could still feel the gentle pressure of warm, dry lips. What would it be like to have someone like that? He'd never had a girlfriend, not even in elementary or middle school when it had meant nothing more than sitting together at lunch and holding hands while your friends giggled. It had never interested him, and of course, he knew why now.

Later, he'd had hockey. Ryan had joined the team with him, both of them gangly ten-year-olds still figuring out their skates. Ben had taken to the ice and hockey like he'd been born to it, while Ryan struggled. Ben knew Ryan stuck with it for as long as he did because it was something they could do together, but he hadn't loved it. Not like Ben did.

But now Ben was beginning to wonder if he could have hockey and even entertain the thought of having a boyfriend. *Boyfriend.* Just thinking the word sent a shiver down his spine. What would that be like? He'd seen some of the guys with their girlfriends after a game, all smiles and sneaking kisses. Someone wearing their jersey, someone they could point to and say, "Yeah, I'm with them." It seemed silly, but he thought he'd like that.

What would his teammates think if Marcus, or *someone*, showed up in Ben's jersey, wearing his number? If he kissed him after a game, while still high on a win, or looking for comfort after a loss? The casual slurs that were flung around the locker room were hateful, and he wondered what his teammates would say if they knew that when they used them, they were talking about him.

Would that be enough to make a difference? It wasn't like anyone in the pros was out. There were rumors, of course, but that's all they were. *Rumors.* There wasn't anyone he could point to and say, "See? I'm just like him, and he gets paid millions of dollars to play." There was a reason no one wanted to go first. It would be like painting a giant target on your back for huge guys who smashed people into the boards for a living.

The distant sound of a motorcycle yanked him out of his musing. He still had no idea what he was going to say, but he was about to find out.

Chapter Ten

BEN SCRUBBED HIS clammy palms on his thighs before jumping down from the bench. The motorcycle shut off, and it was so quiet he could hear the ticks of the engine cooling down. He stuffed his hands in his pockets and left the comfortable shelter of the trees behind. It had probably been a mistake to wait at the bench, because he obviously startled Marcus when he walked out of the trees.

"Shit!" Marcus bobbled the helmet in his hands for a second before hanging it off the handlebars. He gave Ben a tight smile. "You scared me."

"Sorry." *You scare me, too.* Ben kicked at the ground with the toe of his shoe, unable to look Marcus in the face. "Um." He heard a big sigh before there was finally a response.

"Yeah." Marcus let out a small laugh, if something that sad could be classified as a laugh. Ben looked up, assessing him. Marcus ran a hand through his hair, and it was his turn to look away. "We're really dramatic, aren't we."

It was Ben's turn to laugh. "Ryan tells me that all the time."

"Same with Rachel."

Ben's lips twitched in a small smile. "She's terrifying."

"God, I know. I wouldn't even be here if I wasn't afraid to tell her I didn't go through with it." They looked up, and their eyes met for a long moment before they both laughed at how ridiculous they were being. The tension eased a bit, and Ben tilted his head toward the bench under the trees.

"Want to go sit down?"

"Sure."

Ben led the way but didn't sit on the bench with Marcus, knowing he'd need to move to get through whatever was coming next.

"Look, I—" He stopped and growled in frustration. "I'm sorry, okay? I'm a mess. Probably someone you don't want to have anything to do with." Marcus acted like he was going to interrupt, but Ben steamrolled over him. If he stopped now, he'd never get it out. At least he could walk home in a few minutes and die a peaceful death. "I'm not out."

"I know that."

Ben stared at him for a few seconds before continuing. "I don't know if I want to *be* out. I don't know if I *can*. Especially at school."

"Because of the team?"

"Yeah. How did you—"

Marcus leaned forward, his hands hanging loosely between his knees. "I might not be involved in sports, but I pay attention. I know how toxic that environment is for guys like us." Ben blinked at the *like us* comment but waited for him to keep going. "But you know that more than I ever could."

"The guys on my team aren't that bad. They say stupid shit, but they're not *bad*." Ben willed Marcus to understand what he was saying. "But that's only my team."

"Would they be willing to have your back?"

"I don't know." Ben was tired. All of the things he'd been too scared to think about were being dredged up and put under a microscope. He sat heavily on the bench, on the other end from Marcus, leaving plenty of space between them. He didn't think either of them were ready to breach that gap just yet. "I won't know unless—"

"I get it." Marcus turned to sit sideways, one leg tucked underneath him. "And, trust me, I'd be the last one to pressure you—"

"But."

Marcus gave him a crooked smile that faded away almost as soon as it appeared. "*But* if not now or this year, when? You're going to Boston University next year on a hockey scholarship, right?"

"Yeah. How do you know that?" Ben wasn't sure what to think. "Why do you even care?"

Ben had never seen Marcus angry before, but that was all the expression on his face could be.

"Why do I *care*? Because I thought we were friends. Or getting there." Marcus stood and paced back and forth, hands flashing as he talked. "I screwed that up, and I'm sorry for that. But—"

"What?" Ben interrupted.

"What what?"

"*You* screwed it up?" Ben was beginning to think he was having a hallucination or something. Marcus's face was clearly visible in the moonlight, and Ben could swear he was blushing.

"I—I kissed you." Marcus continued before Ben could say anything. "And it wasn't what you wanted or what you were ready for or—"

"I kissed you back." Ben couldn't believe what he was hearing. Marcus thought *he* messed everything up? "But then I pushed you away. Rachel said—"

"Rachel is really overprotective. Even when I don't need her to be. And sometimes she takes my side even when I think she shouldn't." Marcus stopped pacing and turned to look at Ben. "I thought you were mad at me."

It was a toss-up as to whether Ben was going to laugh or cry. "I thought you were mad at *me*." Marcus stepped closer, and Ben itched to touch him but still wasn't sure if he should. "We *are* friends." He could feel his face heat, but he was going to get it out there. "And I really like you. I have for—" He stopped. He wasn't about to tell Marcus he'd had a crush on him for years. That was too much.

"For what?" Marcus would pick up on that, of course.

Ben studied his hands. He couldn't look at him.

"For a long time." Ben's face was on fire. "God, this is embarrassing."

He stared at Marcus's boots when he stepped closer, almost between his knees. A gentle hand came to rest on his head, and Ben closed his eyes as fingers stroked through his hair. He was afraid to move. If he moved, Marcus might stop. He didn't want him to stop.

"Hey."

Ben made himself look up and into Marcus's face. Marcus's fingers were at the nape of his neck, still softly moving through the short hair there. The gentleness was almost overwhelming, and he swallowed hard, trying to keep the stupid tears down. He didn't want to cry in front of Marcus. He didn't want to appear weak.

That thought, not wanting to appear *weak*, crashed through his head. It was what he'd been taught his entire life. Or at least while he was on the ice, which seemed to be one in the same. *Man up. There are no tears in hockey. Skate through it.* Gritting his teeth and playing through with a fractured finger, blinking back tears of pain the entire time. It was what he was supposed to do. He looked up at Marcus helplessly, not sure what to do with such an epiphany.

"Jesus, come here." Marcus pulled him forward, and Ben automatically wrapped his arms around his waist, pressing his face to his chest. Marcus's arms were around his shoulders. "Come on. It's okay." Ben shook his head, gripping tighter, his hands sliding up Marcus's back under his jacket.

Marcus made an abortive move, like he was uncertain what to do, and then Ben heard him mutter, "Oh, fuck it," and he was kneeling in front of Ben in the leaves and the dirt and pulling Ben even closer to him.

Ben let him, burying his face in Marcus's shoulder. It wasn't fair. He took a deep breath and said it out loud, hoping he didn't sound like a pouting little kid.

"It's not fair."

Marcus leaned his head against Ben's. "No. It's not."

Ben let out a shaky breath and pulled back a little. They were so close together, their faces just inches apart. This time, Ben took the initiative and leaned in for a kiss. Marcus drew in a sharp breath through his nose in surprise, and for a second, Ben thought he'd made yet another mistake. He broke off to apologize, and Marcus surged forward, kissing him back, hard. In one blink to the next, Ben had his hands in Marcus's hair. Warm fingers snuck under the hem of his hoodie, brushing against his bare skin. For a split second, he thought Marcus was going to climb right into his lap, and if that happened, he might have *died*.

He pulled back, breathing hard, his hands on Marcus's shoulders. A car horn blew somewhere in the distance, and they looked at each other, wide-eyed. They were in a park, barely hidden under the cover of the trees, and he'd been ready to— What? He wasn't sure exactly what he wanted, but it involved pulling Marcus so close there'd be nothing between them.

He slid away until he hit backrest of the bench. "Um."

Marcus sat down beside him, looking equally shocked. "Yeah."

Ben reached over tentatively and took Marcus's hand, lacing their fingers together. "I don't know what to do."

Marcus squeezed his fingers. "I really like you."

"For how long?" Ben blurted out the question before he thought about it.

Marcus huffed out a laugh. "For a while."

"Why didn't *you* ever say anything?" Ben tried not to sound like he was blaming Marcus for not speaking up either, but now he needed to know.

"Well, I—" Marcus looked down before meeting Ben's eyes again. "—I was dating someone for a while—"

"I know." Ben flushed when he said it, but it was true.

Instead of a grin, there was that sigh again. "God, I really like you."

"But?"

Marcus turned to look at him then, a sad smile on his face. "I would never guilt you or pressure you. You're ready when you're ready." He looked down at their joined hands. "But I won't be a secret."

"I wouldn't ask you to do that." Ben wondered, as he said the words, if that was a lie. It sounded so simple. *Say the words. Put them out there for the world to know.* It was anything but simple. "Can I ask you a question?"

"Anything."

"What was it like? Telling your parents?"

Marcus's eyes were on him, and he squeezed Ben's hand. He leaned back, settling beside Ben. They fit so well together, it made Ben's chest tight.

"It was fine, I guess. I mean, I told my mom first because I thought she'd understand. I mean, you know I've dated girls. I like girls." Ben ran his thumb over the back of

Marcus's hand. "But, obviously—" Marcus laughed quietly. "—I like boys too. So, when I realized I liked boys, I told her."

"Just like that?"

Marcus shook his head. "No. I was so nervous. I mean, you think you know someone and how they're going to react, but you never really do for sure. Rachel offered to hold my hand, but I had to do it myself, you know?"

"So how did you do it?" Ben hesitated. "I mean, if you want to—"

"No, it's fine. You should know." Marcus was looking at him again, and Ben couldn't meet his eyes, afraid he might find hope there. He wasn't ready. There was no way. But he was ready to think about what it might be like. "I told her over dinner one night, when Dad was out of town for work. It wasn't long after Rachel and I broke up, and—"

"Wait. You and Rachel?"

"Yeah. For about a month. We're way better as friends." Marcus leaned his head on Ben's shoulder. "Anyway, so we're sitting at dinner, and I just kind of blurted it out." He shrugged. "I said, 'Hey, Mom. I like boys, too.'"

"What did she say?"

"She put down her fork, and I thought, 'Here it comes. She's going to completely freak out.' But she didn't. She asked me what I meant, and I told her that I was bi. She took it pretty well. Asked me if I liked anyone in particular, and we talked about it."

"Did you?"

"Did I what?"

"Like anyone. At the time." Ben could see the faint blush on Marcus's face in the dim light. "You *did*. Who?"

"How do you think I got into hockey?" Ben turned to him, mouth open in shock, and Marcus threw his head back and laughed. "I'm kidding." He nudged Ben in the side with his elbow. "Well, kind of. I did go to some of your home games last year. I thought Rachel was going to kill me."

Ben didn't know what to say to that. So, of course, he said the first mortifying thing that came to mind. "I've had a crush on you since freshman year."

Marcus covered his face with the hand that wasn't still holding Ben's. "Oh my god." His shoulders shook with laughter. "You're freaking adorable."

Adorable? No one had ever called him that before.

"No, I'm not."

"Yeah, you are." Marcus sounded more serious now. "Which is what makes this so much harder." He let go of Ben's hand and stood up. "I've got to go."

Ben felt a desperate impulse to grab on to him again and keep him from leaving. To keep talking to him. "Are we still friends?"

Marcus took a few steps away and put his hands in the pockets of his jeans. "Of course we are." He tilted his head toward where he'd parked his motorcycle. "Walk with me."

Ben got up and followed him, the two of them staying a few feet apart as if by silent agreement. "What did your dad say?"

Marcus turned around and walked backward for a few paces. "He took me to Pride last year."

"So, he was cool with it?"

"Yeah. He was." Marcus turned back around and they made their way to the parking area. They stood next to his motorcycle, and Marcus reached for his helmet, but stopped. He took two steps, and Ben found himself wrapped in a fierce hug. They held on to each other in the parking lot for longer than they probably should have, until Marcus pulled away. He held on to Ben's arms and then darted forward to press one last chaste kiss to his lips. "I'll talk to you later?"

"Yeah. Text me when you get home?" Ben winced. He hadn't meant to say that. It made him sound like his mom.

Marcus chuckled as he buckled on his helmet. "Sure thing."

Ben stepped back as he cranked the bike and then rolled it back far enough to make the turn out of the parking lot.

"Bye, Ben."

Ben raised his hand in return and watched until the sound of the engine faded in the distance.

It wasn't fair. There were a lot of things that weren't fair.

SNEAKING BACK IN was much harder than sneaking out. Ben didn't understand why people actually liked to do stuff like that; it was way too stressful. He'd left the back door unlocked when he left, but now someone had locked it, probably his parents before they went to bed. He crept around to the front door and tried the knob. Also locked.

A light flicked on in the kitchen, and there was no way around it. He tapped lightly on the door, not wanting to wake the entire house up with his stupidity. He tapped again. Ben heard a shuffling behind the door and stepped back just in time for Beth to yank it open, a hockey stick clutched in her hands. She poked him with it, and he smacked it away.

"Ow!"

"What the hell are you doing?" She poked at him again, and this time he took it away from her.

He pushed past her and leaned it next to the door. She must have gotten it from just inside the door to the garage. It was one of his old sticks, but it still hurt when it was applied to his ribs.

"I could say the same thing. Were you going to check a robber to death?"

"No, dumbass. I was going to beat him over the head with it." Beth walked back to the kitchen, Ben trailing behind her. "You're lucky I was the one down here." She shrugged. "Not like they'd ever expect you to sneak out though. What were you doing?" Beth waggled her eyebrows at him. "Meeting a *girl*?"

He should have let her stab him through with that damn stick, because that's what her words felt like. His voice was strangled when he answered. "No. Just went for a walk and forgot my keys."

"Whatever." She went back to spreading peanut butter on toast, her go-to late night snack. Ben snagged the piece she already had on the plate, and she brandished the butter knife at him. "Seriously?"

He grinned at her, his mouth full.

"Ugh. Go put another two pieces in. That way you can have your own." Ben brushed the crumbs off his fingers and did as he was told. He hopped up on the counter to wait for the toaster to pop, and Beth leaned on the other side of him. "So, really. Where were you?"

"Told you. Went for a walk."

Beth made a skeptical face at him and took a bite of her toast. Ben hopped down and got them both a glass of milk. For once, he was grateful for peanut butter: it made it harder for Beth to question him. The toast popped, and he put peanut butter on both slices, handing one to his sister. He took a big bite of the other one and grabbed his glass of milk.

"I'm going to bed. Thanks for the snack."

She made a face when he talked through his mouthful, and he took the opportunity to get the hell out of there before she asked any more questions.

He had a lot to think about.

"SO, YOU NEVER texted me last night." Ryan's voice was overly careful, and for some reason that struck Ben the wrong way.

"Cut it out."

Ben knew he was being unreasonable, but he was tired and cranky. He'd been up half the night, even after Marcus had texted him, letting him know he'd gotten home safely. At least it was a rest day, which meant no practice and no heavy gear bag to lug around. He'd already skipped his morning run because he slept through his alarm, so the day was off to a rough start.

"And someone is cranky this morning." Ryan glanced at him as he drove. "That bad?"

"No." Ben thought for a second. "Yes." He scrubbed a hand over his face in frustration. "Shit. I don't know."

"You want to talk about it? We've got time—we could get Starbucks. My treat." Ryan's voice was still cautious, but Ben knew he wouldn't give up easily. Might as well spill it and get it over with.

He slumped in his seat. "Sure."

"Okay, that was way too easy." Ryan clicked on the blinker to make the turn that would take them to coffee. "Now I'm really worried."

Ben bristled. "What, Rachel didn't give you a full report?" It was playing dirty, and he felt bad as soon as he said it. "Sorry."

"I'm going to let that slide because I love you." Ryan didn't look at him, which made Ben feel worse. "Come on, dude. Talk."

"Okay, fine. God." Ben wanted to bang his head against the window. Maybe saying it all out loud would help. "So I talked to Marcus last night. He met me at the park." Ryan made a noise of approval. "We figured it would be easier to talk face-to-face, you know?" Ben flipped his phone over and over in his hands, just for something to do. "He's not mad. In fact, he thought I was mad at him."

"Really?"

"Evidently Rachel is a little 'overprotective'." Ben made quotes with his fingers. "Sounds like someone else I know."

"Yeah, yeah. Go on."

Ben twisted his fingers in his lap and looked down at his hands. "He likes me, too."

Ryan gave him a big smile. "Awesome!" His smile faded. "It is awesome, right?"

"You're going to miss the turn."

"Shit!" Ryan pulled in, and Ben waited until he'd placed their order before speaking again.

"We talked about some stuff, and now—" Ben hesitated. "—I don't know if I'm doing the right thing or not."

Ryan looked at him for a few seconds before saying anything. "What do you mean?"

"What do you think Mom and Dad would say?" They'd flirted with this conversation before, Ben always talking around the edges, and Ryan waiting for him to say it out loud. "And Beth?"

Of course, that was when Ryan had to pay for their drinks. He wordlessly handed Ben's over and waited until they were back on the road before answering. "You want my opinion?"

"Yeah."

"They love you. And they would want you to be happy. All of them." Ryan eyed him skeptically. "Are you doing this for him?"

"No!" Ryan turned to glare at him. "Well, not all of it. He got me thinking about some stuff and—"

"Did you make out with him again? You did, didn't you."

Ben took a sip of his coffee. It was too hot and burned his tongue, but it bought him some time.

He took a deep breath. "I only want what everyone else has. I mean, it's not—" He stopped himself from saying that again.

"It's *not* fair." Ryan nodded, turning into the school parking lot. "It's so far beyond not fair." He parked and turned to look at Ben, face serious. "You know, whatever you decide, I'm right there with you every step of the way, right?"

"Yeah." Ben smiled. Rachel definitely didn't have the monopoly on overprotective. "I know."

"And—" Ryan reached over and squeezed his shoulder. "—just because you tell your family, it doesn't mean everyone automatically gets to know that information about you. It's no one's business but yours. You have complete control of this. You know Mom and Dad and Bethy would respect that." His hand tightened on Ben's shoulder again before letting go. "You don't have to tell the team, not until you want to."

"But I'd eventually have to."

"Probably." Ryan shrugged. "Especially if you're going to be playing in college."

"God, the season hasn't even started yet. Am I crazy?"

"A little, but not because of all this. Think about it some more, okay?"

Ben nodded, and they got out of the car by unspoken agreement, done with serious conversations for the moment. He looked at Ryan over the top of the car and smirked at him. "So, when are you going out with Rachel again?"

Ryan rolled his eyes. "This weekend. Maybe. If she says yes."

Ben shrugged his backpack onto his shoulders. "She'll say yes."

Chapter Eleven

THE REST OF the week was much better. It was a relief to be talking to Marcus again, even though Ben was no closer to figuring out what he wanted to do than he'd been before. He had to let it go for now. Their first game of the season, an away game, was the next Friday, and Ben had to get his head in the game. Huge life decisions would have to wait until the weekend after.

He was ready as far as practice went. He knew his job, and he knew what to expect from his line and his teammates. They had a pretty good chance of winning, judging from how the other team had done the year before.

On Friday, Ben found himself sitting in a stall in an unfamiliar locker room, taping his stick methodically. The movement was soothing to his whirring brain. *Should he or shouldn't he? Tell or don't? Come out or not?*

He felt like flipping a coin. It probably wasn't the smartest way to make a decision like that, but it had to be easier than driving himself crazy. He put his stick down across his knees and leaned back against the locker. He looked around at everyone doing their own pregame thing, listening to music or whatever Smithy was doing, wearing just his under layers and his helmet. They were all getting ready.

Ben could feel the pressure building inside the locker room as game time approached, slow but inevitable as everyone got dialed in. He needed something to give him a push, something tangible to decide for him. What if they won? If they won, he could ride that energy and talk to his parents, or maybe start with Beth.

The ever-present knot in his stomach eased. It was a stupid way to decide something so important, but it made him feel better.

"You good, Cap?"

Smithy looked ridiculous in his Under Armour and helmet, and it made Ben smile. The weirdness from the previous week had vanished, and it was like it had always been between them again. He hadn't heard anyone say anything that was even close to a slur since, so maybe they'd taken what he'd said at face value. That was good.

"Yup. You?"

Smithy gave him a half-assed salute and went back to his stall to suit up.

It was going to be a good game.

IT WASN'T A good game. At all.

Ben yanked his helmet off, barely restraining himself from hurling it across the room. He sat down in his stall and started pulling off his skates and pads, his movements jerky. Espy, their goalie, stumped by, looking even more dejected than Ben felt. The slumped shoulders with "Espinoza" stretched across them in block letters somehow made Ben feel even worse. He knew Nick was blaming himself for the loss, but it wasn't his fault. They'd all failed to do their jobs, which had made it impossible for him to do his.

It was wildly superstitious, but Ben wondered if losing the game was the world's way of telling him that making stupid bets for *important life decisions* was the worst idea ever. Still in his undershirt, he leaned his head back and closed his eyes. He felt someone sit beside him and cracked open an eye to see who it was. Smithy, of course.

"That was shitty, wasn't it."

Ben sighed. "Yeah, it was."

"We'll do better next time, Cap." Smithy clapped him on the shoulder and wandered off, unabashedly nude, to the showers. Ben shook his head.

He made himself get to his feet and check his phone. There was a message from his parents—they hadn't been able to come and sent their condolences—which he replied to quickly. And one from Gran that was just a sad-face emoji and a frowny face. Well, she tried.

Then there was one from Ryan that made him smile.

Ryan: *to the other guys (.img attached)*

The picture was of Ryan and Rachel, faces mashed together, both flipping the camera off.

Ben: *Thanks guys.*

All he got was a string of heart-eyes emojis after that, so he went to the next message.

Marcus: *sorry man. that sucks*

Ben: *Yeah. We tried.*

Marcus: *nxt time*

Ben: *Hope so.*

The next text was a thumbs-up emoji with an image attached. It was Marcus making a silly face at the camera, eyes crossed. Things were still a little strained between them, but they were both trying hard to act like everything was back to normal. Ben laughed out loud, and he caught people looking at him weirdly. He locked his phone and finished getting undressed. There was only time now for a quick rinse, and then they'd be loading back onto the buses for the ride home.

Ben unzipped his bag to get his towel out and saw Will's dog tag where he'd hastily tucked it away. He suddenly knew exactly what he needed to do.

"CAN I TAKE the car out?"

Ben's mom almost choked on her coffee at the question. He'd never actually driven by himself, but he was pretty sure he'd be okay. He needed to do this on his own, so he was going to have to make it be okay.

"What?" She sounded surprised, and he wasn't sure if he should be offended. "Why?"

He shrugged. "Just want to."

His mom glanced at his dad, and they seemed to be having a silent conversation involving a lot of eyebrow. She finally tilted her head at his dad and nodded.

"Sure. Have it back later this afternoon. I have to go to the store." She was still looking at him like she couldn't quite figure out what he was up to.

Beth wasn't helping matters by glaring at him suspiciously, while methodically eating her breakfast. He narrowed his eyes back at her, and she smirked at him. He didn't think she'd say anything that would get his mom to change his mind. It wasn't like he was known for breaking the rules. But after catching him coming in the other night, Beth had been acting weirder than usual.

"No problem." Ben gathered up his breakfast dishes under his sister's watchful eye and dumped them in the sink. He slipped out of the kitchen to get ready but first sent a text.

Ben: *Can I come over?*

Ben put the phone down and started pulling on his clothes. He was almost completely ready and tying his shoes when the reply to the affirmative pinged his phone. After quickly typing out a response, he grabbed Will's box out of the dresser drawer and headed downstairs.

Pausing at the front door, he looked at the car keys hanging on the hook. He needed to do this on his own, but the thought of being completely alone in the car was daunting. Before he could talk himself out of going, he snatched up the keys and headed out.

The ritual of seatbelt, mirrors, cranking the car was done and then he sat there, staring out the windshield. Ben looked at the wooden box where he'd put it on the passenger seat.

Then he put the car in gear and carefully backed out of the driveway.

BY THE TIME he got to Gran's house, he was a nervous wreck. It felt like his hands were going to be permanently cramped from gripping the steering wheel, but he'd made it there in one piece. He took a few deep breaths and opened the door, reaching over to grab Will's box before getting out.

Gran met him on the front porch with a tight hug and a kiss on his cheek before leading him inside. It wasn't very often he was here without the rest of the family and it felt a little weird and overly quiet.

"How was the drive?"

She was really asking him how *he* was after the drive.

"Good." Ben looked around the living room at the boxes that were starting to dominate the space. "How's the packing?"

"Almost done." She eyed him closely, glancing at the box under his arm curiously. He fidgeted under her scrutiny until she let him off the hook. "So, you finally had time to look at it?"

"Yeah. Sorry it took me so long."

Ben had looked through it again the previous night, even though it had been late by the time he'd gotten home. He hadn't been able to sleep, in equal measures from losing the game and all the other things on his mind. So he'd opened the box and reread the letters, staring for a while at the picture of Will and Eddie. They'd looked so happy together it made him ache inside.

He put the box on the kitchen table, the dark wood a direct contrast to the bright and sunny space. "How much do you actually know about him?"

Gran sat down, pulling the box over in front of her, and waved for him to sit. "I only know what Mum told us." She looked at him with a steady gaze. "I actually knew Eddie. He was Uncle Eddie to us kids." She opened the box and took out the letters. Ben had carefully stacked them in order, the picture sitting on top. He watched as she touched a fingertip to Eddie's face.

"What happened to him?"

She looked at the picture and then put it back down on the table and folded her hands in front of her. "From what Mum said—and I only ever got this secondhand—he was devastated by William's death in the war."

"He never talked about it?"

She shook her head. "He died just after I turned thirty, and in all the time I knew him, he never said a word." She gave him that searching look again. "What did the letters say?"

"That he was glad Eddie didn't have to be there." Ben decided to skip the double-talk. "That he missed him."

Gran smiled at him gently. "You figured it out."

Ben shrugged, but his hands were beginning to shake. "It wasn't that hard, especially once I saw the picture." He reached for it slowly and studied it, though he had it practically memorized. Knowing that the men in the picture never got to see each other again after one of them was sent off to war hit him all over again. He'd watched war movies and documentaries, but nothing brought it home like that faded image. He felt his throat starting to close up. "They look so happy here," he said, his voice almost catching.

Gran smiled sadly. "Mum said they were inseparable. It was something everyone knew, but no one talked about. They were 'roommates' to anyone that wasn't family."

"Did Eddie ever find anyone else?" He could have guessed the answer, but he wanted to hear her say it.

"No one like Will. Though Eddie was actually married for a while." She nodded at his incredulous look. "It was what happened back then. I was very young and had no idea, of course."

"But he never had another—" His voice faltered. "—partner?"

"There were men he'd bring by now and then, a boyfriend here or there, but nothing serious." She patted his hand. "He was destined to be a bachelor in the end, I think."

"Were you close to him?"

He wasn't sure why he was still asking questions. It was a tragic story: two men society had dictated weren't supposed to be a couple when all they wanted was a quiet life together. He'd read about blue tickets. If anyone had seen those letters, Will would have been sent home with a dishonorable discharge, and his life would have been essentially ruined. All for loving Eddie.

"I was." Gran moved the picture to the side and flipped over the top letter, moving them around without reading them. "He was my godfather."

"Even though he wasn't family?"

She cocked her eyebrow at him. "Family isn't always about blood. You know that better than most." She was talking about Ryan, who was as much her grandson as Ben. "Not everyone understood why Mum chose him, but she knew what he meant to her brother and she loved him like one."

Acceptance like what she was talking about had been unheard of back then.

"Eddie was lucky to have Great-Gran, wasn't he."

"I like to think they were both pretty lucky." She straightened the letters. "I'm making tea, want some?"

Ben nodded, and she rose to turn on the electric kettle. Tea had always been Gran's thing, and watching her move around the kitchen was comforting. His eyes fell on the boxes in the corner and it hit him again that she was moving. She wouldn't be a short drive away anymore.

She'd been raised to accept her Uncle Eddie without a second thought. He'd been welcomed into her family—like his family had embraced Ryan. It was what they all did, apparently. Ben looked at his hands, lost in thought for so long he was startled by the clink of the mug Gran placed on the table.

"Are you feeling okay, honey?" She smoothed the hair off his forehead, and Ben felt a little like bursting into tears. His emotional highs and lows had been off the chart lately, and he was exhausted. She was looking at him with such concern. He could do it. Right then and there. Suddenly the decision was easy.

"Yeah." He took a sip of the very hot tea and promptly burned his tongue. "Um, Gran?"

"What is it?"

The words tried to stick in his throat. Ben almost took another sip of scalding tea but stopped himself just in time.

"Um. I'm—" He cleared his throat, holding on to his mug so his hands wouldn't shake. "I'm gay."

He looked into his mug to avoid seeing her reaction. She wasn't saying anything, and what the hell had made him say that, he couldn't take the words back and—

She reached over and took his hand, prying his fingers from their death grip on the mug handle.

"Ben, look at me." He pressed his lips together to keep everything inside and looked up. She had tears in her eyes, but she was smiling that gentle smile. "Ben, honey, it's okay."

"Is it?" His voice broke, and the tears he'd been holding back for days started to fall. She squeezed his hand and rose, pulling him closer to her, her arms around his shoulders. She was petting his hair and saying something he was having a hard time hearing over the pounding of his heart.

"Of course it is. I love you; your mom and dad love you." Gran rested her hand on his head. "Have you told your parents?"

Ben sniffled and sat back down. She kept one hand on his shoulder and reached for a napkin. He blew his nose noisily and shook his head. "No. Not yet." He wiped a hand over his face and sniffled again. "Ryan's known for a while."

"How long?"

"Since we were fourteen?"

Gran patted his shoulder and sat in the chair next to him. She took both of his hands in hers and looked him in the eye. "Thank you for telling me." Ben nodded, not sure how to respond to that. She handed him his tea, and he took a sip, thankful that it had finally started to cool. "Okay?"

"Yeah. I think." He hesitated, taking another sip of tea. "I think I might, possibly, want to be out. I mean, to everyone."

Gran sat back, her face dropping. "You're worried about the team, aren't you."

Ben sighed. That just proved how much was wrong with the sport he loved so much. Gran had followed hockey since she was a little girl, had been the one who got his grandad and dad involved. She knew—*everyone* seemed to know—how bad it was. It was frustrating.

"Should I quit?" Ben shook his head even as he said it, putting his mug down harder than he probably should. "That's a stupid question. I don't *want* to quit."

"You shouldn't have to quit. It's not right." Gran stood and walked to the counter where she kept the container that always had some sort of treat in it. "I think this discussion calls for cookies, don't you?" She put a few on a small plate and brought them back to the table. "What are your teammates like?"

"Loud." Ben smiled when she laughed.

He took a cookie and thought yet again about the guys on the team. A lot of them he'd grown up with and knew pretty well. Most of the guys would probably be okay, but there were two or three who might not. And the freshmen were complete unknowns, but he'd only have to deal with them for the current season anyway.

"I don't know, they're all a pretty good group," he finally said and shrugged. "It could be worse, you know?"

"What about your coach?"

Ben had already thought that one through. "I think he'd be okay." He didn't know that for sure, but the sensitivity training had been Coach Jordan's idea, so all he could do was assume the best.

"That's a lot of people on your side, don't you think?" Gran took a pointed sip of her tea. "And if you think that any of us would stand back and let you suffer alone, you've got another thing coming, my boy."

Ben believed her. One word and she would march down to the school herself, probably with his mom and dad right beside her. "I know. But what about players on other teams? I mean, you know it'll get out, right?"

"Of course it will." She looked over at Will's box that was still sitting on the table. "But sometimes it takes a few to get things started. There are some who will be hateful. But there are also probably others in the exact same situation." Gran rested a hand on the box and gave him a sad smile. "We've come so far, but there's always further to go."

Ben remembered the dog tag that was still around his neck and pulled it out of his shirt. "I wore this— I didn't think you'd mind. I was careful with it." He started to take it off, and she stopped him.

"You keep it." She patted the tag where it rested on his chest, just over his heart. "I think Eddie would have wanted you to have it. He would have liked you."

"You think?"

"Absolutely." She took their mugs and put them in the sink. "So, what are your plans now?"

"For right now, I think all I'm going to do is go see Ryan for a little while and then go home." Ben was tired, but he felt better after their talk. "I don't know when I'll talk to mom and dad, so can you—"

"Keep my mouth shut?" Gran ruffled his hair and put her arm across his shoulders, pulling him in close to her side. "Of course."

"Thanks." He blew out a breath. "I guess I'd better go. Mom said she needed the car later."

Gran walked him to the door and gave him a tight hug. "I'm proud of you, Ben." It was all Ben could do not to get teary again. "So proud."

He hugged her back and walked out, leaving Will and Eddie in her safe hands.

In the car, he looked at himself in the rearview mirror to make sure he didn't look like he'd been crying. He tucked the dog tag back into his shirt and cranked the car.

More decisions could wait.

Chapter Twelve

"YOU DROVE HERE all by yourself?"

Ben nodded and rolled his eyes when Ryan held his hand up for a high five.

"Come on, Benny. Don't leave me hanging here." Ben slapped his hand halfheartedly, and Ryan gave him a big grin. He picked up the box of books at his feet and moved to the next set of shelves. "What'd you do today while I've been working my ass off?"

Ben dropped into one of the squashy armchairs that were scattered throughout the store.

"Went and saw Gran." He reached over and plucked one of the books out of the box and flipped through a few pages, fighting to keep a straight face. "Came out to her."

"What?" There was a *thunk* as Ryan dropped the stack of books he was holding. "Shit." He picked them up and dumped them back in the box before sitting on the ottoman right in front of Ben's chair. He looked around to see where the manager was and then leaned forward attentively. "What happened?"

Ben told him. He told him about Eddie and Will and what had happened to them, and how he hadn't gone to Gran's with the intention of telling her, but it had just happened. And that she was awesome and fantastic.

"I already knew that." Ryan surprised him by pulling him into a hug and almost sitting on him in the process. "I am so fu—freaking proud of you."

"Thanks, now get off me." Ben quickly hugged him tight before pushing him away.

"So, now what?"

Ben picked up the book he'd taken out of the box and started flipping through it again. "I don't know. I asked her not to say anything to Mom or Dad yet."

"Are you going to tell them today?"

Ben shrugged. "Maybe? I don't know."

"I'm not saying that you should run home and do it now, but it should probably be soon." Ryan caught the manager eyeballing him and stood up, reaching for the box. "You want to hang out for a little bit?"

"Yeah. Just let me see if Mom needs the car back." Ben sent the text, and then flipped back to the latest texts from Marcus. He still hadn't told Ryan everything that had happened between them. Maybe he should. His phone pinged a message saying his mom and dad had decided to go out together and to take his time with the car. "I'm good to stay. When do you get off?"

"Another two hours."

"Want me to wait? I don't have anything else to do." Ben thought for a second. "As long as it won't get you in trouble."

Ryan picked up the now empty box. "If you want to. And it'll be fine. I just have to get the rest of these put away." He gestured at the small stack of boxes waiting for him. And then lay a hand on Ben's shoulder. "I really am proud of you."

Ben smiled and settled in to wait.

"YOU KNOW HE'S not going to just randomly show up, right?"

Ben jumped, almost dropping his book. "I don't know what you're talking about." He went back to reading. The book had started to get interesting. He'd never read much urban fantasy, but he was getting into this one.

"Dude." Ryan poked him in the shoulder. Ben looked up to see Ryan giving him a very unimpressed face. "You practically break your neck to look every time the door opens."

As if on cue, the door opened, and Ben couldn't help the glance he gave it. "Am not."

Ryan shook his head. "Pitiful, man." He walked back over to the last box.

"Shhh, I'm reading."

Ben felt something hit the back of his head.

Ryan sighed and picked up the wadded up paper packing material he'd flung at him. "Seriously, though." Ben frowned as Ryan sat on the ottoman again. "I mean, you guys decided that you're not—" Ryan waved a hand around vaguely. "But you're still—" He made a gesture at Ben.

"I'm still what?" Ben wanted to hear him say it out loud, even though he knew where he was going with it. He really was going to have to tell him everything.

"I don't even know. I mean, I know you guys worked it out about, you know, but it's like you're right back where you were." Ryan ran a hand through his hair. "You know, with all the pining and shi—" He looked around. "—stuff."

Ben rolled his head back and groaned. "Seriously?" He scrubbed a hand over his face. "Okay, so you want to know exactly what he said?"

"Only if you want to tell me."

Ben blew out a breath and looked him in the eye. "He told me that he really likes me too—"

"Duh."

Ben glared at Ryan for interrupting. "But that he wouldn't be a secret." Ryan gaped at him, and Ben kept talking. "So, what do I do with that?" He felt like getting up and pacing but knew it would draw too much attention to them. "I mean, I can't blame him, you know?"

"So, what you're telling me"—Ryan was speaking slowly, thinking things through—"is that this hot guy you've been pining over likes you too and would probably most likely be your boyfriend right now if you were out?"

"Pretty much." Ben slumped back down into the chair, but then something occurred to him. "You think Marcus is hot?"

Ryan waved a hand at him. "He's good-looking. I'm not blind. Besides, *you* think he's hot, and that's all that matters." He flicked Ben on the thigh making him jump. "Is he pushing you? Do I need to go talk to him?"

"No. It just gave me a lot to think about."

Ryan lowered his voice. "Okay, so if you came out, what would happen?"

"Everyone would know."

"They would. What else would happen?"

"I could—" Ben swallowed past the sudden lump in his throat. "I could date. I could have a boyfriend."

"Right. And as much as I want you to have that"—Ryan's voice was a little rough, too—"you have to do it on your timetable. I know you. And I know you'll talk yourself out of it again. Telling Gran was an awesome first step, but you have to take the next one."

They both cleared their throats, the conversation far heavier than they could have imagined. Ryan looked up and saw his manager come out of the back. "Look, give me just a few minutes to put the rest of this away, okay?"

Ben sank down in his chair. "Fine." He was grateful they were taking a break from talking. Ryan put the last book on the shelf and then checked his phone before giving Ben a quick glance. Nodding to himself, he typed something that was probably to Rachel.

"Um, Rachel is wondering if we're doing anything tonight. Want to call in reinforcements?"

"You mean for you?"

Ryan snorted. "No, I mean maybe you should talk it out more with Marcus. He gets this in ways I can't."

Ben lay his head back and groaned. "I don't need to discuss this with a committee." Then he realized what Ryan had said. "Wait. Rachel asked what *we're* doing?"

"Yeah. I mean, you know anyone I go out with has to be cool with you too, right?"

Ben blinked at him. He'd never said that before. "What?"

Ryan ignored the question. "Besides, I think she's still trying to get you and Marcus together. I don't know how much he told her about your situation. I haven't told her anything." His gaze flicked up to Ben. "Do you want me to tell her to back off?" Ben looked at him for so long Ryan finally asked, "Is that a no?"

Ben shook his head. "It's a maybe." He didn't know what to do with that revelation. "Thanks."

Ryan gave him a weird look. "For what?"

"For, you know."

"It's not like you wouldn't do the same for me. Anyway—" He tapped something out on his phone, and it buzzed back immediately. "—do you want to hang out with Rachel and Marcus or not?"

Ben sighed. He kind of wanted to go home. But he also wanted to see Marcus, now that that was on the table. "Sure."

"That was very convincing." Ryan put his phone down on a shelf and gave Ben an even look. "Look, if you don't want to, we can always go home and watch a movie or something." He looked down as his phone buzzed with another text. "Again."

"No, it's fine." Ben rolled his eyes when Ryan gave him a look. "Really. What do they want to do?"

"I know you're not into horror movies," Ryan started, and anxiety began to build in Ben. "But they want to go see that new one that just came out. You know, the one with the clown?"

"Um." Ben's voice was faint, even to his own ears. Not into horror movies was an understatement: he actively avoided them. Slasher movies didn't bother him as much since they were obviously fake and a little ridiculous, but anything that had decent jump scares were not his favorite.

"I can ask them if they want to see something else." Ryan's fingers were poised over the screen.

Ben appreciated the gesture, but he'd hate being the person who stopped the fun.

"No, I can do it."

"Really?" Ryan raised his eyebrows in surprise. "Don't you remember the time I brought over *The Ring*, and you—"

"Oh my god, you're never going to forget that, are you?" In Ben's defense, Ryan had tricked him. He hadn't exactly told him it was a horror movie, but that didn't mean he was ever going to let Ben forget how he'd hidden his face in Ryan's shoulder for the majority of the movie.

Ryan put his hand over his heart. "It is one of my most cherished memories."

"You're an ass."

"And you know this, but you love me anyway." Ryan grinned at him, and Ben couldn't help but smile back. "Are you in?"

"I'm in, but I'm probably going to spend the entire movie hiding behind my popcorn."

Ryan snorted and tapped a response, hitting send with a flourish. "I can't wait. I'm going to go clock out."

A few minutes later, they were outside and walking to Ryan's car. Ben had had enough driving for the day and texted his mom to see if they could pick up the car, or if he needed to bring it home first. He was relieved when she told him they'd take care of it and that she was proud of him driving by himself.

He bumped Ryan's shoulder. "You owe me."

Ryan sighed and bumped him back. "I'm going running tomorrow morning, aren't I."

"Yep."

"Fine."

THE LIGHTS WENT down, and Ben was already starting to feel a knot of anxiety tightening in his stomach. They were sitting in a way that had been calculated by at least two of their group—Rachel and Ryan, and then him and Marcus, in that in order—and he still wasn't sure if that was a good or bad thing.

Ryan had, of course, already told them about Ben's humiliating reaction to horror movies. While Ryan thought it was hilarious, Rachel and Marcus had immediately offered to go see something else. They were so nice about it that Ben decided he needed to grit his teeth and get through it.

Ryan had continued teasing him until Rachel glared at him and insisted on buying Ben's ticket. She'd elbowed Ryan until he stopped, and then took his hand. Ben and Marcus glanced at each other at that, and smirked. But it was when she made Ryan buy Ben's popcorn for "being a jackass," that Ben had laughed out loud and hugged her right then and there.

But now, sitting in a mostly empty theater in the dark, he was beginning to think he'd made a mistake. The previews were still on as he settled in his seat, suddenly realizing that Marcus was leaning closer to him, their shoulders pressing together.

"You sure you're okay with this?" Marcus's lowered voice barely reached Ben's ears.

Ben nodded and whispered back. "Yeah."

They quieted as the movie started, and minutes in, Ben had a hand over his face, peeking through his fingers. He put his hands in his lap, clutching his popcorn bucket during a seemingly safe moment, but nearly jumped out of his skin when Marcus's hand touched his and peeled his fingers from their death grip. He looked at Marcus with what had to be an incredulous look on his face. Marcus gave him a small smile and laced their fingers together, squeezing his hand.

Ben couldn't help but glance around the theater to see if anyone had noticed. But when Marcus started to take his hand away, he stopped him, keeping a hold. He tipped his head toward Marcus's and kept his voice low. "No, it's good. Thanks."

Marcus leaned closer and pressed their heads together for just a second before sitting back in his seat. His hand gave Ben something to concentrate on for the rest of the movie, and if he hid his face in Marcus's shoulder now and then, he didn't feel bad about that at all.

They stayed until the very end of the credits because Rachel, Ryan, *and* Marcus insisted, even though Ben didn't see the point. It did mean he got to hold Marcus's hand for a little bit longer, though, so he didn't argue. When the lights started to come up, they let go. Now that it was time to get up and leave, Ben missed Marcus's hand.

Ben and Marcus walked out ahead of the other two, and Ben found himself wondering what it would be like if he could just reach out and take that hand back. Like it was nothing. Like he knew Ryan and Rachel were probably doing right that second. What would that be like?

Marcus bumped his shoulder to get his attention.

"You okay? It wasn't too scary, was it?" Ben shook his head; he couldn't express what he was feeling at that moment. "Then what? You've got that face going again."

Ben laughed despite himself. "What face?"

"It's your 'I'm thinking' face." Marcus scrunched his own face up, his mouth set in a hard line. "I'm guessing that's also your 'face-off face' because it kind of looks like you want to murder someone."

Ben shoved his hands in his pockets and snorted. "Yeah, probably."

"So what's up?"

"I came out to my Gran."

Marcus blinked at him and then smiled cautiously. "How'd it go?"

"Good. It went good. I think I'm going to come out to my parents." He glanced at Marcus to gauge his reaction. He saw several expressions warring on Marcus's face, but the one that stayed was gentle happiness.

"If you feel like it's time, then good for you." Marcus rested his hand on Ben's back and let it linger for a few seconds.

In those few seconds, Ben caught sight of a few of his teammates in the theater lobby—Smithwick with a girl he vaguely recognized and Holt with Jenny. He instinctively took a step away from Marcus and caught Marcus snatching his hand back. Ben's blood ran cold.

Smithy looked up after Jenny elbowed him and pointed Ben out. He caught Ben's eye with a big smile, but then he saw Marcus just behind him, and his expression was...odd. Like he was working something out. Ben was saved from talking to them by their dates pulling them to the concession stand. Smithy shot him one more look over his shoulder, and then Ben was pushing his way out the double doors onto the sidewalk.

"Ben?" Ryan's voice was right behind him as he headed blindly away from the theater, having forgotten in his panic where Ryan had parked. "Jesus Christ, slow down!" A hand wrapped around his bicep, and he jerked away, or tried to, but Ryan dug his fingers into the back of Ben's hoodie and wouldn't let go. "What the hell are you doing?"

Ben whirled around, breaking Ryan's hold. "I—I can't."

"Take a breath and tell me what happened."

"Smithy and Holt. They saw." Ben couldn't explain the intense reaction he was having. After everything they'd talked about and how things had gone with Gran, he'd finally been having fun. But as soon as the real world seeped back in, it was gone in an instant. The reasons why he struggled with his decision had smacked him right in the face.

"Saw what?" Ryan was keeping up with Ben's pace now, allowing him to walk farther and farther away from the theater.

"I don't even—" Ben stopped so suddenly Ryan almost ran into him. "What am I doing?"

"That's what I'm trying to figure out." Ryan's full-blown concerned face was on in force, and Ben knew he wasn't going to be able to shrug him off. Ryan stepped closer, and his voice was low and gentle, like he thought Ben was about to lose it. He probably wasn't too far from the truth. "Can you tell me what's going on?" he asked gently. "You're kind of freaking me out here."

"I don't know. We were walking out and it was—" Ben's voice cracked, and he cleared his throat, determined to get the words out. "—it was *nice*, you know? It was nice and it was like—"

"Like a date." Ryan understood; of course, he did. "And then you saw the guys and panicked."

Ben nodded. He looked past Ryan to where Rachel and Marcus were standing, heads together and talking in low voices. Shame filled him at being so panicked by what those guys would think, when he should be worrying about scaring the shit out of his friends.

"I'm sorry."

"Don't say that. Don't be sorry." Ryan bit his lip. "I've heard what the guys say when they're out on the ice and trying to get under your skin. You don't want to give them any ammunition, right?" Ben nodded. "That's what it is, isn't it? Worrying about what will happen out there or in the locker room?"

"You know it is." Ben felt like sitting down right there on the sidewalk and telling Ryan to just leave him there. "I can't lose my place on the team."

"Do you think all of that depends on who you choose to date?" Before Ben could say anything, Ryan kept on, anger finally apparent. "It doesn't. What you do on the ice has nothing to do with who you like, or whatever." Ben tried to shush him, but now Ryan was on fire. "You're an awesome player and the fucking team captain and you earned that yourself." Ben flinched back from the finger poked into his chest. "You're hurting yourself, and I want you to think about why you're doing it." Ryan sounded like he was closer to tears than he'd been at the bookstore, and Ben almost reached out for him. "I hate watching you tear yourself apart like this. It's something I can't protect you from." Ryan scrubbed a hand across his eyes and took a deep breath, pulling himself together. "Anyway." They stood looking at each other before Ryan finally pulled Ben into a one armed hug. "I love you, you jackass. Okay?"

"I know." Ben hugged him back, and they stepped away from each other. "I am sorry for freaking you out."

"Not the first time, man." Ryan jerked his head toward where the other two stood, obviously trying to look like they weren't watching them. "You ready?"

Ben sighed. "Yeah." Ben followed him and saw when Rachel's eyes went to Ryan, looking for the nod he gave her. Marcus was looking at the ground, not meeting anyone's eyes.

Ben walked over to him and stood in front of him until he looked up. "I'm sorry." Marcus shrugged, and Ben stepped into his space, quivering with how close they were. He lowered his voice. "I'm really sorry." Marcus finally met his eyes and stared at him for a few seconds before nodding slowly.

"Okay." He dropped his eyes and then caught Ben's gaze again. "Are you still going to do it?"

"Do what?"

Marcus dropped his eyes again. "Tell your parents."

"Yes." Ben hadn't been sure before, not totally, but he was now. "I need to."

"Okay." Marcus pressed their foreheads together for a split second, and then stepped back. "Text me if you need me, okay? About anything." He looked over at Rachel and she nodded. "I'm going to the car. See you later, Ben. Bye, Ryan."

Ben watched him walk away, for longer than he probably should have, fighting the wave of what he could only classify as *longing* that coursed through him. He turned around just in time to see Ryan and Rachel part from what had to be a goodnight kiss. Despite his own raging emotions, he smiled to himself and looked away. At least they were happy together.

A hand touched his arm, and then Rachel was pulling him into a tight hug. "You do what you need to do. We're *all* here for you, okay?" She ruffled his hair and then gave Ryan one last wave before heading in the same direction as Marcus.

"Rough night?"

Ben nodded.

"Home?"

"Yeah. Let's go."

Chapter Thirteen

TRUE TO HIS promise, Ryan got up and ran with Ben the next morning. They hardly said a word to each other until they got back to the house, both of them out of breath.

"Do you want me to stay?" Ryan was leaned back on his elbows, sitting on the steps, trying to catch his breath. "The offer to handhold is still out there."

Ben shook his head. "I think I need to do this on my own." He sighed and tried to smile. "Go big or go home, right?"

Ryan held up a fist and Ben bumped it. "Hell yeah, dude. Go get 'em."

Ben got up from the steps and walked toward the door, pausing before going inside. "Just—tell me I can do this."

"You got this, man." Ryan walked backward down the driveway, a reassuring smile on his face. "You're going to be fine."

Ben took a deep breath and opened the door to where everyday life waited for him. Everyday life smelled a lot like breakfast. His stomach growled despite the butterflies in it, and he jogged up the stairs to get cleaned up.

He worried the entire time he was in the shower and then while he was getting dressed. He worried while he sat on his bed and held Biscuit in his arms, letting him go when he started to squirm. Will's tag was in its place in his drawer and he put it on. He needed all the help he could get. He couldn't procrastinate any longer.

As he walked down the stairs, he heard his mom laugh and wondered if she still would if she knew he was about to tip their world on its head. He sat down at the table, Beth already in the prime spot, but he barely noticed. Instead, Ben automatically put food on his plate, and though he was starving, he couldn't bring himself to take a bite. They were all sitting there. His dad was reading something on his tablet, like always. Beth and his mom were talking quietly. And finally, Ben opened his mouth and spoke.

"Um." It wasn't very eloquent, but it made them all look over at him. "I, uh—"

"What is it, kiddo?" His mom glanced at his untouched food, and her expression turned to one of worry. Ben's hands were shaking, just a little bit, and he clenched them under the table so she wouldn't see.

Beth was staring at him like he'd grown a second head. She finally rolled her eyes. "God, Benny, spit it out."

"Beth!" His mom's scolding voice and Beth being Beth jolted him out of his frozen state.

He looked at the table and took a deep breath. "I need to tell you something." His hands were still shaking, and his palms were growing clammy with nerves. He fidgeted, despite himself, before clasping his hands together. "I, um—"

He could feel everyone's eyes on him, and why he'd thought that a breakfast table confession was a good idea, he didn't know. Finally, he looked up at his parents; he had to see their faces, to see the reaction, good or bad. Strangely, he wasn't worried about Beth's reaction at all.

"I'm gay."

Silence. Ben saw the surprise he fully expected, but he hadn't counted on the absolute silence that filled the normally noisy room. It dragged out until he couldn't stand it anymore.

"Oh my god, someone please say *something*." Ben's voice cracked on the last word as he resisted the urge to run and hide. His mom finally spoke.

"Okay, baby." She hadn't called him "baby" in years. "I just— Okay."

"Okay?" Ben said faintly. Beth watched between the two of them, calmly eating a piece of bacon. Ben had worked himself up so much that the word wasn't registering. "What?"

His mom reached over and put her hand on the table, wiggling her fingers when he just sat and stared at it. Ben took her hand, and she gripped his fingers tight for a second.

"Ben, you know we love you, right?" Ben nodded numbly. "And we love you no matter what." He nodded again and glanced at his dad, who had put his tablet down for once.

"Listen to your mom, son." His dad's voice sounded odd, like he was getting choked up. He cleared his throat and took a sip of juice. "She knows what she's talking about."

His mom was leaning toward him with tears in her eyes but a smile on her face. "It's okay."

"Gran knows." He just blurted it out. "I told her yesterday."

"So that's where you went." His mom squeezed his hand and rose, pulling him to her and putting her arms around him. "What did she say?"

"She was okay with it. I took her box back to her. Did you know her uncle was gay?" Ben was fairly certain he wasn't making a whole lot of sense. "I didn't mean to tell her, it just came out."

"She's a good listener." His mom still had her arms around him. "I'm glad you told us."

"Ryan knows too." Ben had lost all control of what he was saying. His mom let him go but kept a hand on his shoulder.

"He does?" That was from his dad. Ben nodded. "For how long?"

"A few years."

"Oh." His dad looked confused for a second. "Why didn't you tell us sooner?"

"I don't know." Ben's mom put her arm back around him. "I was afraid you were going to be disappointed or, I don't know..." He broke off, looking away.

She put a finger under his chin and made him look at her. "We could never be disappointed in you. Do you understand?"

Ben nodded, though he wasn't sure he believed that. "Okay."

When he turned to Beth, she gave him a searching look and then smiled. "Don't cry, Benny. I've got your back."

And somehow, that was what made his mom burst into tears.

Ben: *I told them.*

Ben waited for the group text to blow up. He felt weirdly let down for some reason. His mom had hugged him again before busying herself with clean up that usually fell to him or Beth, and his dad had patted him on the back before wandering off to process. Ben knew he'd be hearing from him later. Beth had just punched him in the arm and gone to her room. Basically, in the course of a few minutes, everything was back to normal except that he had spilled his biggest secret, and they were— They were absolutely fine with it all. His phone buzzed in his hand. And then again.

Ryan: *AND????*

Rachel: *!!!!!*

Marcus: *ARe you ok?*

Ben smiled to himself at the reactions. It was so weird to have the knot of anxiety that had been riding around in his stomach gone, if only for the moment, that he felt like laughing out loud. He lay back on his bed and held the phone above his head to text.

Ben: *It was so weird.*

Ben: *They all said it was fine.*

Ryan: *mom and dad are the best*

Ryan: *little b's okay too i guess*

Rachel: *I'm so proud of you <3*

His phone buzzed again, and this time it was Marcus texting him out of the group.

Marcus: *how do you feel?*

Ben thought for a second. How *did* he feel?

Ben: *Better :)*

There was a tap on his half-open door, and his dad poked his head in. "Mind if I come in?"

It was weirdly formal, but Ben had kind of been expecting something to happen. His dad was one of the smartest and kindest people he knew, but when he needed time to process something, it was best to leave him to it. That was why Ben hadn't been too worried when he'd stayed mostly silent, only giving an encouraging smile or nod.

"Sure." Ben put his phone down and sat up on the edge of the bed. His dad took a seat next to him, and they sat in silence for a few moments before his dad started to speak.

"Can I ask you a question?" Ben blinked at him before nodding, not sure where he was going. "If you didn't play hockey, would you have told us sooner?"

Ben shrugged, looking away. "I don't know. Maybe." He hesitated. "It would have been different, you know?"

"I remember from when I played in high school what gets said in the locker room." His dad's voice was low. "I heard all kinds of crap directed toward teammates and players on the other team, and I did nothing."

"Dad, that's not—" Ben started, but his dad cut him off.

"I just want you to know that when you decide to tell the team—" He glanced at Ben. "Are you going to come out to the team?"

"Eventually?" Ben shook his head. "Gran and I talked about it a little." He looked his dad in the eye. "Honestly, it was nerve-wracking enough telling you guys."

"You had to know we would be fine with—" His dad looked stricken, and Ben rushed to try to explain.

"No, I knew that, in here." Ben put his hand over his heart. "I did. But this—" He tapped a finger to his temple. "—wasn't so sure. I was scared."

"Scared?"

Ben nodded, biting his lip. "Yeah."

"Because?"

"Because you would know and then I would have to tell everybody and it just seemed too big, you know?" Ben sighed. "I don't know. I know it doesn't make sense."

"It makes perfect sense." His dad put his arm around him, and Ben leaned into his side. "I'm glad you told your Gran."

"Me too."

"And we won't say anything unless you say it's okay. You have complete control over this."

"Really?" Ben felt kind of stupid to be that surprised, but he'd built it up in his head that once he opened his mouth and they knew, the floodgates would open. He wouldn't have a choice.

"Really." They sat in comfortable silence for a few seconds before he continued. "So, what do you want to do?"

"I don't think I'm ready to tell the team yet." Ryan thought for a moment. "But maybe soon?"

"Whatever you decide, we're right here to back you up. All right?" His dad squeezed his shoulders one last time and stood. He started to the door but stopped and turned back. "One more thing." Leaning against the doorframe, he folded his arms across his chest. "What made you decide now was the time? I mean, I'm glad you told us. I'm proud of you for that."

Ben looked down at his hands. He'd thought he'd been a coward the entire time, but it was nice to hear.

"Honestly? I was tired of lying. Mom would ask about girls and—" He broke off at the look on his dad's face and backtracked quickly. "I mean, I know she didn't mean anything by it. She didn't know. But, it still felt like lying."

"You know she would never—"

"It's fine, Dad. Seriously."

"Okay." His dad looked down and for the first time seemed a little uncomfortable. "So, um, is there someone that you—" He made a vague gesture with his hand.

Ben fell back on his bed and covered his blushing face. "Oh god. Dad. No."

He heard a soft chuckle and knew that it wasn't over. "There is, isn't there?"

"Kind of." Ben let his hands fall to the bed on either side of his head but kept his eyes fixed on the ceiling. "It's complicated."

"Those are usually the ones who are worth it." Ben glanced at his dad, who was smiling, all signs of discomfort gone. "Was it the guy with the hair? What was his name?" He put a hand to his chin as if thinking hard. "Oh, right. Marcus?"

Ben dragged a pillow over his face. "Oh my god."

"He seemed nice." Ben peeked out from under the pillow to see if he was being made fun of. "You should ask Mr. It's Complicated over again sometime." He rapped on the door and started to pull it shut. "I'm here if you need to talk. About anything. Okay?"

"Okay!" Ben covered his face with the pillow again as he heard the door click.

HE'D SPENT THE rest of the day texting back and forth with Ryan, Rachel, and Marcus. Ryan wanted to come by, but he had to work, and Ben assured him everything was fine. The texts had finally filtered down to just the ones with Marcus alone, and Ben wasn't sure what to make of them. He found himself talking about the box and the letters.

Marcus: *so they never saw each other again?*
Ben: *No. And Eddie never got to read what Will wrote.*
Marcus: *that is the saddest thing*

He was right. Ben put his phone down. Those two had never gotten to live their lives the way they wanted to, but they'd managed to be together in a time when most people hated them for who they were. They probably would have gotten married if they could have. From what Gran said, they'd been completely devoted to one another. It made his situation pale in comparison. He sent one more text.

Ben: *sorry, i'm falling asleep*
Marcus: *it's okay. talk tomorrow?*
Ben: *night :)*

Ben put his phone down, thoughts still whirling in his head. He wanted more. But until he decided to pull the trigger on coming out to the team, it wouldn't be fair to either of them to actually do anything about it. So he tried to push it down. He had to. If he wanted to keep Marcus as a friend while he was figuring his shit out, then he shouldn't think that way. He fell asleep after convincing himself he was doing them both a favor.

However, when he got up, Marcus had sent him a final text, and it dredged up all of those feelings he'd just managed to pack down. It was a selfie, probably taken right before Marcus went to sleep. His hair was falling over one eye and he obviously wasn't wearing a shirt.

Marcus: *night*

It seemed innocent, but the sight of him looking like that made Ben's mouth run dry and caused the butterflies in his stomach to do cartwheels. That one picture undid all of the convincing he'd done the night before.

Before he could think too hard about it, he snapped a quick picture of himself, bedhead in full force against the dark blue of his pillowcase. He was pleasantly surprised that it actually looked pretty good, if he ignored his hair. He sent it along with a text.

Ben: *Morning.*

Ben got up and left his phone on his nightstand to get ready for his run before school.

RYAN JUMPED OUT of his car when he came to pick him up and pulled him into a hug.

Ben squeaked in surprise. "What the hell, man?"

"I'm so damn proud of you." He let Ben go and punched him in the arm. "So, it's still good?"

Ben started to answer but was interrupted by his mom calling from the front porch. "Ryan Davidson, you get your ass up here."

"Oh, yeah." Ben winced as Ryan turned wide eyes to him. "Mom wants to have a word."

"Shit."

Ben shrugged. "I don't think she's mad or anything."

Ryan sighed, but he walked up the front steps while Ben stowed his stuff in the back of the car. He turned around to see his mom hug Ryan tightly and say something too low to hear. Ryan nodded, a faint smile on his lips, and she hugged him tight again before letting him go. Ben gave him a look as he came back to the car, but Ryan just shook his head.

"I'll tell you on the way."

Ben glanced back up at the house where his mom stood watching them both, and then finally got in the car. He waited until Ryan had pulled out into the road before questioning him. "What was that all about?"

"She didn't tell you?"

"No, she just said she wanted to talk to you when you got here."

Ryan watched the road, not saying anything for a long moment.

"She told me thank you for being there for you." He glanced at Ben. "Like I would have done anything else."

Ben blamed the rollercoaster of emotion he'd been riding the past few days for the lump in his throat. He stared out the window, pulling himself together, before he spoke. "I'm glad she wasn't mad at you for not telling her."

"Nah. I didn't really think she would be, but I can't lie, I was a little worried." He gave Ben a smile that eased the rest of the tension he'd been carrying. "How are you doing?"

"Me?" Ben looked at him, eyebrows raised. "Fine, I guess." Ryan gave him an even look that Ben wasn't sure about. "What?"

"You know. Marcus?"

Ben rolled his eyes. "We talked about this."

"The situation has changed." Ben gave him a look. "It has."

"It hasn't changed enough."

Ryan made a frustrated noise. "Maybe you should actually talk to him about that. You could be doing this together."

"I don't know. Maybe." Ben looked away again. "Can we talk about something else?"

Ryan sighed but dropped it, to Ben's relief. "I'm not sure if I'm going to make the game on Saturday. I'm trying to get off early, but I might not be able to." He gave Ben a quick look of remorse. "Rachel and Marcus are planning on going, though."

"Really? I thought Rachel didn't even like hockey."

Ryan shrugged. "Well, she's only going because you're playing."

"What?" Rachel had been nice to him and all, but Ben was still surprised. "Why would she do that?"

"Because you're her friend?" The *dumbass* was unspoken. "Besides, where Marcus goes, she tends to go." Ryan pulled into a parking space and turned off the car. "At least, most of the time."

"How do you know they're coming?"

Ryan gave him a look. "Because we talk about you behind your back?"

"Of course you do." Ben pushed down a sudden urge to tell Ryan about the selfie and see what he thought of it—if he could tell him what it meant. Was Marcus flirting with him again? And if he was, what did that mean? He was confused, but he didn't think he could talk to Ryan about it, not just yet.

"See you after practice." Ben grabbed his gear bag out of the back and looked over at Ryan. "Or are you working?"

"I'm not sure. I'm still trying to swap with someone for Saturday." Ryan locked the car, and they fell into easy step with one another. "I'll let you know, and I'll text Mom and let her know if I can't get you."

"Sounds good." They reached the front door and went their separate ways.

WHEN THEY'D GOTTEN their schedules right before school started, Ben had resigned himself to not having anyone to talk to until possibly lunch and then the Econ class that he, Ryan, and now Marcus, were in. But with Rachel in two of his morning classes and lunch, and the fact that he and Marcus were friends again, it turned out he had someone to sit with after all.

He was still a little baffled by her friendship, but it was nice not to have to find a convenient corner desk to disappear to. And it wasn't as if people didn't say hi to him or anything. He got head nods and small waves and sometimes a smile from one of the girls, but never anyone who wanted to really talk to him, as a person.

Which was why Ben could feel eyes on him when he walked into his first class and Rachel flung herself at him, wrapping her arms around his waist. Startled, he automatically hugged her, glad his backpack was still firmly on his back.

"Rachel?"

Her voice was muffled from where her face was pressed against his shoulder. "I'm so freaking proud of you."

"You are?"

She squeezed him tighter, and he huffed out a laugh, resting his cheek on top of her bright pink head. Her hair was as soft as Marcus's, and he distractedly wondered again if they used the same thing in their hair.

She pulled back and smiled up at him. "Of course I am."

Rachel wrapped a hand around his wrist and tugged him toward the back of the room where they usually sat. Ryan had been right, all those weeks ago; being befriended by Rachel was like being adopted by a small, fiercely protective mama bear with bright pink hair. He was now one of her circle, and Ben could get onboard with that.

Before he knew it—before he could even blink—he was at his desk with Rachel sitting across the aisle, looking at him expectantly.

"Tell me everything." She clasped her hands in her lap and leaned forward eagerly. At his stunned silence, she rolled her eyes and glanced around the room before speaking again. "They're not paying any attention. Give me some credit, I'm not an amateur."

He gaped at her for another second before he finally caught up to what she was after.

"It was surprisingly uneventful."

She motioned for more details, and he found himself telling the entire story from beginning to end while she listened closely. Rachel was easy to talk to. He had no trouble telling her his mom had cried, but when he got to his dad's conversation, he edited some parts out. Just a few.

"And that was it."

She gave him one of her special "friends only" smiles. "Good for you, man." She reached over and patted his knee.

He'd noticed that about her and Marcus—they were very affectionate with each other, always hugging or touching. He didn't mind, but it was something to get used to. Ben also noticed that people had glanced at them more than once, and he could only imagine what the rumor mill would come up with. He almost laughed out loud. If they only knew.

The teacher walked in, and they didn't get another chance to talk, but Rachel gave him a small smile every now and then when he looked her way. Ben grinned to himself and felt happier than he had in what seemed like a long time.

Chapter Fourteen

THEY ATE LUNCH outside at the same table where Rachel had first confronted him, ignoring the chill in the air. She sat on the tabletop like always, boots planted firmly on the bench, and proceeded to steal some of the fries Ben had allowed himself as a rare but well-earned treat. Maybe it was silly to have celebratory fries, but he deserved them.

"So, now what?"

Ben blinked at her and wondered if he'd missed part of the conversation they'd been having. "Now what, what?"

"You going to make a move or not?" She regarded him seriously before snatching the last fry.

Ben groaned and buried his head in his arms on the table. "Not you, too."

Rachel smirked at him. "Let me guess—Ryan?" Ben nodded without sitting up. "You know"—she sounded thoughtful—"you might want to ask Marcus what *he* wants."

"That's what Ryan said."

"Did he?" Rachel nudged him until he looked at her. "Just think about it, okay? I won't say anything else. Promise." She made a zipping motion across her lips, and Ben smiled at her.

"Okay. If you say so."

She pinched her lips even more tightly together and wiggled her eyebrows at him until he laughed out loud. It was almost time for the bell to ring, so they gathered up the rest of their trash and headed inside.

Rachel linked their arms after they'd dumped their trays, walking with him most of the way to his last class. He knew she was walking with him to see Marcus, but he was glad of the company. Just before they got to the classroom, Rachel pulled him to the side.

She still had her hand curved loosely around his elbow, and he glanced down at it in surprise. He stood still when she leaned closer, not sure what she was going to say. Her face was serious.

"You're a good guy, Benny. A *nice* guy. Who *deserves* nice things." He gaped at her as she stepped back and made the same zipping motion across her lips that she'd done earlier, this time miming throwing away a key.

Rachel winked at him and then turned to where Marcus was coming toward them. Rachel slipped an arm around his waist, and he automatically put an arm around her shoulders. They made it look practiced and easy. Marcus gave Ben a smile that put a blush on his face.

"Hey." Ben scuffed the toe of his sneaker on the carpet and saw Rachel look away, trying not to laugh. He found himself grinning back.

"Hi."

Rachel snorted, and Marcus must have poked her in the side because she squeaked and wriggled away. She walked backward and rolled her eyes at both of them. "I'll leave you boys to it, then." She pointed at Marcus. "Later."

Marcus stuck his tongue out at her, and she laughed her way down the hall. "She thinks she's hilarious." He said it with a kind of fond resignation.

Ben shrugged. "She kind of is."

Marcus bumped his shoulder with a grin, and they walked into the classroom. Ryan slipped in behind them at the last second, just before the tardy bell rang. He was flushed, and Ben knew he'd run into Rachel on his way.

They took their seats, and Ben couldn't resist a little gentle chirping. "Cutting it close?"

Ryan grinned at him unabashedly. "Totally worth it."

Ben rolled his eyes, and as he turned to his books, caught Marcus watching them both. His hair had fallen into his face, and it brought back the memory of the picture he'd sent Ben last night. Ben cleared his throat and looked away, cheeks pink. Not a good thing to think about in class, that was for sure.

He wondered if he'd get another picture that night, and the thought left him still a little confused but definitely interested.

PRACTICE WAS THE best it had been in a long time. Ben felt dialed in for the first time in ages, and he was playing better than he had since the season started.

Even Coach Jordan noticed. "Good work, Lewis. Keep it up."

Ben nodded at him, breathing hard but smiling around his mouthguard. He felt good. A small part of the stress he'd been carrying with him for years was gone. His family knew. He'd told them and survived.

Ben's good mood lasted all the way through practice and into the locker room. He didn't think twice before checking his phone right after stripping out of his pads. A text from Ryan: he'd been able to swap shifts with someone at the last minute, so he'd be outside to give Ben a ride home.

And there was a squabble in the group chat about *It*—the book vs. the movie—that made Ben shudder, so he immediately clicked out of it. He'd check back after they finished arguing.

The last text was from Marcus, wondering if Ben wanted to get together on Wednesday night to work on their Econ homework together. Ben almost suggested that Ryan join them, since he was in the same class, but he remembered Ryan was working that night. It would be only him and Marcus. Alone again.

He then remembered what had happened the last time they were alone together.

God, maybe he should take Ryan's and Rachel's advice, and just *ask* Marcus what he wanted.

Ben: *ok*

Ben: *My house?*

Marcus: *Y*

Ben: *Gotta go shower ttyl.*

He got an immediate text back of a wide-eyed emoji and snorted. Ben scrolled back up to the picture from last night for a second before someone spoke into his ear, and he fumbled the phone before managing to lock the screen.

"Get it, Cap!"

Smithy was way too close, and Ben thought for a horrifying second he'd actually seen the picture. He could have kicked himself for forgetting where he was and letting his guard down.

"Shut up, Smithy."

The D-man elbowed him good-naturedly, and Ben did his best not to react. Smithy always seemed to know everyone's business, so it wasn't surprising he was interested. Ben knew his never having dated anyone was a subject of conversation—to this group, anyway. There'd even been a few awkward offers to set him up that had been mortifying. And Smithy had made enough comments that he didn't even acknowledge them anymore. It was annoying.

"Aw, Cap. Don't be like that. Who is she, anyway?"

Ben ignored him and started peeling off his Under Armour. If he was lucky, Smithy would lose interest and go find someone else to gossip to or about.

He wasn't that lucky. Smithy had the stall next to his and wasn't moving on. He could be a patient little shit when he wanted to be; that's what made him such a good D-man. He knew how to wait to make his move.

"I don't know what you're talking about." Ben wrapped a towel around his waist with jerky movements and hoped Smithy would get the hint.

"She goes to another school, doesn't she." Smithy gave him a wide grin. "I bet she does! Did you pick up a puck bunny?"

"Don't be a shit." Ben took his toilet bag out and started toward the showers, shoulders tense. All he wanted to do was rinse the stink off and go home. Why did everything have to revolve around who he was dating or not dating or whatever? What did it matter?

"Sorry." Smithy's voice was quiet, and Ben looked back at him. "You just look happier than usual." He shrugged. "That's all. I didn't mean anything by it."

And now Ben felt like a shit. It didn't change the fact that Smithy would be shocked to know Ben's *whatever* was a guy. Or would he? Smithy gave off a big and dumb vibe, but he was smart and fast, and while he said some stupid things, Ben never heard him be intentionally cruel. Smithy just didn't think before he spoke.

"It's fine." Ben didn't know what else to say. "Don't worry about it." He fled to the showers and stayed until he was fairly certain Smithy would be gone.

In fact, by the time he was done, nearly everyone was gone. He could see Coach Jordan in his office and, for a split second, considered getting it over with and talking to him. Ben got dressed as he mulled it over.

He'd taken three steps toward the office before he stopped himself, went back to his stall, and tugged on his sneakers instead. He didn't think Coach would say anything to the team without Ben's permission, but he wasn't ready. He'd let the knowledge that his family knew sink in for a while before making the next jump.

HE SHOULD HAVE expected Beth to pounce. She hadn't talked to him since his big revelation, and that wasn't like her. He would give her props for waiting until he was tired and not on his guard before her interrogation.

She didn't knock, pushing open the door and flopping down on the bed next to him. He yawned. He'd been trying to stay awake long enough to finish his reading for Lit and hopefully a goodnight from Marcus. Not that he would ever tell her that.

"So. You like boys." Blunt and to the point, that was his Bethy.

He shrugged. "Yeah. So do you." Beth gave him an exasperated look, started to say something, and then stopped. "What?" He rolled his eyes. "Go ahead, get it over with."

"Fine." She thought for a moment. "Have you ever had a boyfriend?"

"No."

"Kissed a boy?"

He hesitated. "No." He didn't want to get into that at the moment.

Beth narrowed her eyes. "You're lying."

Ben sighed. He didn't have to name names or explain. "One boy."

"Who?"

"Not telling."

She chewed on her lip, considering. "Was it Ryan?"

"What? No!" He made a face. "Ryan's my best friend. And *straight*."

She shrugged like that didn't matter. "Kissed anyone else?"

"Yes."

"Who?"

"None of your business."

"No, really. Who?"

"Tracy Martin at her birthday party last year."

"Ew. Why?"

"Someone thought it would be fun and retro to play Spin the Bottle."

"Okay. But no other boys?"

"*No*."

"But you want to?"

"Yeah, I guess."

"Okay." She rolled up to sitting and gave him a look. "This stays in the family, right?"

"For now. I mean, you know that Ryan knows." He didn't mention the other person. Or that person's best friend.

She wrinkled her nose. "Of course Ryan knows. He's *family*." The *duh* was implied. "You can trust me, you know. It's kind of a dick move to out someone. I would never do that. Especially to you."

Ben stared down at the book still in his hands, because if he looked at her, he'd lose it. "Thanks, Bethy."

"Anytime, loser." She patted him on the head and left, closing the door behind her.

Ben leaned back against the headboard and laughed. He could always count on his sister to get right to the point. She'd had questions, and she'd asked them, accepting his answers without a doubt in her mind.

Ben was a little worried about the discussion with his parents that was looming on the horizon. It wouldn't take long for them to realize their birds and the bees talk might need a little revising. And that was going to be mortifying. His mom had tackled the first one a year or so ago, and at the time, he'd been certain he wouldn't survive. She'd handled it like a pro, though, and he wasn't sure if that was amazing or a little worrisome. It was clear exactly where Beth got her bluntness.

He looked back down at his Lit book and sighed. There was no way he was going to get through the rest of the reading without falling asleep. When he checked the time on his phone, he saw a few missed texts on the screen. He must have forgotten to turn it off silent after practice.

Marcus: *hey*

Marcus: *you're prob still at practice*

Marcus: *see you tomorrow*

Marcus: *goodnight*

Another picture. It was similar to the one Ben had taken that morning— Marcus was lying back in his bed, framed by a dark grey pillowcase. He'd dyed his hair again, a deep blue that made his skin glow. He was wearing a shirt this time; Ben could see where the collar of the T-shirt stretched while he'd taken the picture. Ben clicked to save it to his phone and scrolled back to the first one to save as well. He still wasn't sure why Marcus was sending them to him, but if he wanted to keep them, no one needed to know.

ONE MORE DAY of school and one more practice before his study time with Marcus. Ben had sent him another picture that morning, more bedhead and a crooked smile. It felt like they were playing a game, and he didn't quite know the rules. Maybe he was reading way too much into it. Maybe it was just something Marcus did. Ben doubted it, but maybe.

He shook off his obsessing in third period. He needed to concentrate on other things, like school and the line change Coach Jordan wanted to try that night. It wasn't his line, but any changes like that would affect how they played.

He managed to make it through lunch without Rachel noticing anything weird. They talked as usual, which consisted of her chattering to him and his answering when required. She made him laugh, and then looked surprised when he did. After what Smithy had said the night before, Ben was beginning to wonder if everyone saw him as scowling and miserable all the time.

The day was completely normal. And it bothered him because he was so *not* normal. Everything felt like it was too much. He was moving toward something, but he wasn't quite sure what that something was. At least hockey was proving to be the constant at the moment.

Practice was even better than the day before. The team was working together, and it felt great. Their first home game was coming up on Saturday and would be an especially nice one to win. Everyone was coming, even Gran, and Ben was weirdly nervous about that.

And, not to mention, his study *date* with Marcus. He really needed to talk to someone about it, and Ryan would probably be his best bet. He still didn't know Rachel well enough, and she was far too close to Marcus to give him the kind of objective input he needed.

Showered and dressed, Ben shoved his Flyers beanie on instead of worrying over his hair and marched out of the school with his stuff over his shoulder. He was determined to actually talk about what he was feeling for once. When he yanked the back door of the car open, he scared Ryan half to death.

"Shit!" Ryan turned down the music he'd been listening to and stared at Ben as he dropped into the passenger seat, one hand pressed to his chest. "What the hell, dude?"

Ben pulled his phone out of his pocket and looked at the dark screen for a second before deciding what he wanted to say. "What does it mean—" He kept looking down and away from Ryan, not sure if he could get it all out otherwise. "—if someone sends you pictures and tells you goodnight every night?"

"What?" Ryan sounded so confused Ben finally glanced over at him.

Ben sighed. "Promise me you won't make fun of me, because I really need your help right now."

"You know I can't possibly promise that." Ryan still hadn't backed out of the parking space, instead turning toward Ben who was determinedly looking out the window. "I'll do my best, though."

Ben decided he didn't have a choice. He'd have to deal with whatever amount of teasing that came with Ryan's usual surprisingly astute insight.

"Okay." He stopped, the low music coming out of the speakers a backdrop to his uncertainty. And took a deep breath. "I like Marcus. A lot." Ryan snorted, and Ben shot him a glare.

"Sorry, sorry." Ryan held up his hands in surrender. "Go on."

"Anyway." Ben settled back in his seat. "You know what he said about not wanting to be a secret."

"Yeah, I know what he said. And I know that *you* still haven't actually talked to him about that."

"I'm working up to it!"

"Okay, fine. I'm listening."

"I haven't talked to him about anything, but he started sending me these pictures when—"

"Pictures?" Ryan's voice was high-pitched and loud in the confines of the car. "What kind of pictures?" Ryan's face was bright red.

Ben went over what he'd just said in his mind and then almost swallowed his tongue.

"Not those kind of pictures! Oh my god."

Ben covered his burning face with his hands. Ryan started giggling beside him, a little hysterically, and it set Ben off as well. It took them about five minutes to get it back together because every time one of them would stop, they would look at the other and they were off cackling again. Ben had to wipe the tears from his eyes before he could go on. Finally, he opened the texts and scrolled up to the first picture. Ryan sobered as he quickly scanned the texts. He nodded to himself as he read. Ben watched as he got to the picture from last night, and then took the phone back from him.

"Well?"

"Dude, he is so into you." Ryan wasn't smiling. "And either he's changed his mind or he's leading you on." Ben blinked at the anger on his face. "He better not be screwing around with you."

"Do you really think he'd do that?" It was an honest question. Ryan had known Marcus longer than Ben, and Ben would trust his opinion.

"No, I don't think so." Ryan looked very serious for a moment. "I mean, I would hunt him down if I thought he was being a dick and, I don't know, messing with you or something."

Ben was absurdly touched by Ryan's protectiveness. "Thank you for being willing to beat someone up for me. It means a lot."

"Beat him up?" Ryan smirked. "I didn't say anything about beating him up. Of the two of us, you're the one that's used to fighting." Ben made an affronted noise. He wasn't a fighter, even though Coach had recommended he take up boxing or something similar. "Oh, I'm kidding, don't get like that."

"Fine. You'd go tell Rachel on him." Ben pointed a finger at him. "You know that's what you'd do, don't even try to lie."

Ryan shrugged. "Probably. But that doesn't solve the current problem."

"And the current problem is?"

Ben got a smirk that made him more than a little nervous.

"Look, there's definitely something he's trying to tell you. How do I convince you that you're going to have to talk to him about it?"

"But—" Ben didn't have a good follow up. He groaned and banged his head against the window. "What the hell am I supposed to say?"

"Huh." Ryan over exaggeratedly rubbed at his chin. "It's almost like we've had this exact same conversation before."

Ben threw up his hands in exasperation. "You're an ass. I don't know what Rachel sees in you."

Ryan waggled his eyebrows at him. "Wouldn't you like to know."

"Oh my god, that was awful." Ben threw his hat at Ryan, who deftly caught it and jammed it onto his own head. "You're awful."

"Yes, but who else is going to listen to your boy problems?"

Ben squirmed in his seat. "Beth, probably."

"She cornered you and asked you a bunch of questions, didn't she?" Ben nodded, his face burning hot. "Well, do you want to talk about your boy problems with your sister?" Ben shook his head. "See? I'm your only hope."

"That's not Yoda."

"Shh, I'm improvising." The car had been running the entire time they'd been talking, and Ryan put it in gear to back out of the parking space. "Dude, just ask him."

"Ask him how?"

"I don't know. Say 'Hey, you keep sending me hot pictures, and now I'm confused.' How about that?"

"*Hot* pictures?"

"I told you. I know when someone's attractive." Ryan cut his eyes toward Ben, grinning widely. "I mean, you're not unfortunate looking or anything yourself."

"I hate you."

"You *love* me." A pause. "Besides, you gave as good as you got. Pretend I didn't say it like that."

Ben's startled laugh was loud to his own ears. "What are you? Twelve?"

"Sometimes." Ryan stopped at the stop sign just before their street. "Seriously, talk to him. I mean, that's worked okay so far, right?"

Ben cleared his throat. "He's, um, coming over tomorrow night to work on Econ homework."

Ryan arched an eyebrow. "Oh *really*."

"Shut up."

Ryan pulled into Ben's driveway and put the car into park. "Are you going to talk to him, then?"

"I think so."

"What about other stuff?" Ben knew what he was talking about.

"I'm still working on that. I'm going to talk to Mom and Dad before I do anything, though." That was actually a comforting thought. Another little tangle of anxiety fell away. *Huh.*

"Good. You need help with all your shit?"

"Nah. I got it. I'll see you in the morning." Ben rapped his knuckles against Ryan's and got out, dragging his bag out of the back.

"Bye, man. Tell Mom and Dad I said hi."

"You got it." Ben tapped the roof of the car twice and then walked into the house feeling lighter than he would have thought possible.

Chapter Fifteen

IT HAD BEEN on his mind all the next day, but Ben still didn't know what he was going to say to Marcus.

He was quiet enough at lunch that Rachel had poked at him until he smiled, laughing at her being ridiculous to cover up her concern. It took a lot to reassure her that nothing was wrong. He felt a weird urge to show her the last set of pictures, a goodnight from Marcus and a good morning from himself, but it seemed like it was too personal. He didn't know her well enough, though he had a feeling, if things went well, that would change eventually.

It was at Econ where things got interesting, to say the least. It was the first time Ben would see Marcus that day. Ben had been planning to get a ride home with Ryan as usual. But just before class, Marcus found him with another plan.

"Sorry, wanted to catch you before the bell," Marcus was a little breathless and looked somewhat nervous—a feeling Ben sympathized with. "Um, I was wondering if you wanted to ride to your house with me. On my bike?" Ben's mouth ran dry.

"I—"

And then Marcus talked over him, babbling in a way that made Ben feel a little bit better. They were both a mess, and that was weirdly comforting. "I mean, if you even want to. I know it's kind of cold out and not everyone likes to ride them and—"

"It's fine." Ben found himself cutting Marcus off and shrugged, acting much cooler than he felt. "It'll be fun."

Marcus looked relieved. "Cool! I've got an extra helmet stashed in Rachel's car. Well, and my helmet, too." Then it seemed like he was trying to make himself stop talking, and Ben tried not to laugh at him. It was kind of cute. "Anyway."

The bell rang, and they had to take their seats, Ryan quietly grinning at both of them. Between Ryan's smirks and Marcus's little grins, Ben was a bundle of nerves.

Which brought him to his current situation—obsessing about riding on the back of a motorcycle. He'd always liked them. In fact, he and Ryan had gone through a short-lived dirt bike phase, so he'd driven one before. Strangely, they didn't bother him like getting behind the wheel of a car did. But, climbing on the back of Marcus's bike, snugging up close behind him? The mere thought was making his palms sweat.

The end of class came, and they all walked out together, heading toward the parking lot. Ryan peeled off first, digging his keys out of his bag. "Talk to you later?" It sounded casual, but it was definitely a check-in.

Ben nodded. "Yeah, man. I'll text you."

Ryan waved at both of them and made his way to his car, which was parked closer to the school. Ben and Marcus walked farther, toward the back of the lot, before Marcus's bike came into view.

"Hold on a second." Marcus pulled keys out of his messenger bag as they stopped at Rachel's car and unlocked the trunk. He must have noticed Ben's confused look because he explained as he took two helmets out of the back. "Sometimes she has to stay after, and it was easier to give me a key instead of worrying that I was having to wait on her. Not that I mind"—he was quick to clarify—"but she didn't want me to get stuck or anything."

"She's a good friend."

Marcus gave him a small smile as he closed the trunk lid securely. "Yeah, she is." He handed over one of the helmets to Ben. It was a little scuffed up but otherwise looked perfectly sound. "Sorry, it's my old one. Rachel wears it sometimes when we go out."

They stopped next to the bike and Ben put his backpack down next to it. "It looks good." He laughed nervously. "It's been a while since I've been on a bike, and that was only a dirt bike."

"I'm sure you'll do fine. Here, let me—" Marcus's fingers brushed lightly against Ben's chin as he helped him with the chinstrap. "There. It looks good."

They stared at each other for a few seconds before Marcus seemed to shake himself and moved to put his own helmet on. Ben put on his backpack and distracted himself by making sure the straps were tight enough to keep it secure on his back. Marcus swung a leg over the bike, his jacket riding up, and Ben was glad the helmet obscured his flushing cheeks. He moved back when Marcus cranked it and rolled it backward out of the parking space.

"Okay, get on." Marcus planted his feet to steady the bike, and Ben took a deep breath before climbing on behind him. Marcus had pulled his messenger bag in front of him in a practiced move and waited for Ben to get himself settled.

He gingerly put his hands on Marcus's waist, gripping him lightly. "Is this okay?"

"Mmm, no. Hang on." Marcus grabbed his hands and pulled him forward, wrapping Ben's arms more closely around him and forcing Ben to settle up right against his back. Ben felt like the top of his head might pop off and was glad Marcus couldn't see him.

"Hold on tight. It'll be warmer that way, too." Marcus patted Ben's hands where they were pressed into his stomach. He was talking loudly over the sound of the engine. "Just lean with me, okay?"

Ben nodded and then realized Marcus couldn't see him. "Yeah. Okay."

Marcus squeezed his hands one more time, and Ben thought to look around to see if anyone was watching them. That thought flew out of his head when the bike started to move, and he instinctively tightened his grip on Marcus, people in the parking lot be damned.

THE RIDE WAS either far too short or far too long. Ben couldn't decide which, after buzzing with the vibration of the engine and being pressed up against Marcus's back for the past fifteen minutes or so. He slowly let go of Marcus as the engine died and got off the bike on shaky legs, trying his best not to stumble. It was a near thing. He steadied himself before pulling off the helmet and grinning at Marcus. It had been fun. It had been nerve-wracking and exciting and more than a little *stimulating* as well, but fun was at the top of the list.

Marcus pulled off his own helmet, shaking out his dark-blue hair. It was sweaty and sticking to his forehead, but he had an answering smile on his face. Before Ben could think about it, he reached over and smoothed Marcus's hair away, letting his fingertips lightly brush the shell of Marcus's ear. He drew his hand back and looked away, the stupid grin still on his face.

"Fun, huh?"

Ben laughed, heading toward the front porch stairs. "That's just what I was thinking." Marcus caught up with him and bumped his shoulder, following.

For a rare few hours, no one would be home. His mom was working late, and his dad was helping out at Beth's soccer practice. They'd be completely alone. The realization made Ben fumble his key, almost dropping it.

Biscuit met them at the door, meowing loudly. He was so insistent that Ben had to gently move him out of the way. "Don't mind him; he can probably see the bottom of his bowl and thinks he's going to starve to death."

They left the helmets on the bench by the door, and Ben flashed back to the first time Marcus had done that. And how badly it'd ended. Not this time. They were going to talk seriously about what was going on between them if it killed him. Or if he didn't die of embarrassment.

He heard something behind him and turned around to see Marcus with his arms full of fluffy cat. Biscuit was purring contentedly as Marcus rubbed behind his ears. Marcus caught Ben watching and shrugged, looking a little embarrassed. "I like cats."

Ben remembered how much Biscuit had liked him the last time, and grabbed his phone to take a picture. "I have to send this to Ryan, he'll be so jealous."

He snapped the picture, and the screen showed Marcus with a gentle smile on his face, the dumb cat cuddled up to him. It made his chest clench with something he couldn't quite define. He sent the text to Ryan and then cleared his throat, stepping forward to run his fingers over Biscuit's soft fur. "Um, you want something to snack on?"

"Sure."

Marcus carefully put the cat down, and they both wandered into the kitchen. Marcus leaned against the counter as Ben opened the fridge. It was mostly his fault they didn't have normal snack foods, but they always had stuff on hand for sandwiches.

He pulled out what he needed. "Ham or turkey?"

"Turkey." Marcus put his bag down on a chair and started to help, opening cabinets until he found the plates.

They companionably worked together until Biscuit reminded them he was wasting away at their feet.

"Most annoying cat ever." Ben dumped some kibble in his bowl before picking up his own plate and tilting his head toward the stairs. "Want to work in my room?"

"Sounds good."

They carried everything upstairs to Ben's room, and Ben hurried to kick his gear bag into the corner. He'd straightened up a little the night before, but that thing was always in the way. They sat on the floor, plates on their laps, and ate in silence.

After the empty plates were stacked on the dresser and their books were spread out in front of them, Ben found himself waiting for something to happen. He glanced at Marcus, who was flipping through his textbook, hand reaching up unconsciously to swipe his hair out of his face. He wanted to do it for him. Ben must have been staring, because Marcus looked up and caught his eye.

"What?" His lips quirked up in an unsure smile. "Do I have something on my face?"

Ben shook his head. "No." It was now or never. He took a deep breath and jumped. "Look, we're friends, right?"

Marcus blinked at him, book forgotten in his hands. "Yes?"

He'd already kicked off his boots, so he was sitting cross-legged, leaning against the side of Ben's bed. It was almost the exact same spot where they'd kissed for the first time. Ben pushed that from his mind and gathered his courage.

"Is that all we are?" Ben saw Marcus's mouth drop open and hurried to get out what he needed to say. "I mean, I know what you said, and what I said, and what I thought we both thought." He looked down at his hands, suddenly wishing he'd kept his mouth shut. "But, now I'm not sure."

Marcus closed the book and put it aside. "What—"

"We talk all the time. And I like talking to you." Ben was rambling. "But I've—" He stopped. He'd already told Marcus this part, but he was going to have to say it again. "Maybe it's just a dumb crush, I don't know." He let out a harsh laugh. "I'm kind of a mess. You know?"

Ben jumped a little when he felt a hand on his shoulder. He couldn't look, not right then, not if everything was about to go up in flames.

"We're *all* messes," Marcus said quietly. He didn't take his hand away. "And I'm sorry."

That was the rejection Ben had been dreading. He'd said too much, misread what all those texts meant, and now he wouldn't have Marcus as a friend. "It's okay. I understand."

"You understand?"

Ben still couldn't look at him. "That you don't, I mean—" He broke off with a huff. "I'm still not out to my team."

"Right?" Marcus sounded confused. "I know you're afraid of messing that up."

"Yes, but—"

"But nothing." Marcus knee-walked closer to Ben and made him look him in the eye. "I know what I said. And maybe—" He chewed on his bottom lip, and Ben couldn't help but stare helplessly before looking back into his eyes. "Maybe, I wasn't being very, um, I don't know, *fair*." Marcus sat back on his heels and scrubbed a hand over his face. "God, Rachel was right."

"About what?" Ben was doing his best to put on a brave face, but he was feeling more and more like he'd missed something.

"I'm an idiot."

Ben managed a laugh around the disappointment that had risen in his chest. "That does sound like something she would say."

Marcus scooted over to sit next to Ben, their shoulders touching. "I was wrong." He leaned into Ben's side, his head almost resting on his shoulder. Marcus's hand crept into his, and Ben's breath caught in his throat.

"What were you wrong about?" His voice was hoarse, but he needed everything spelled out. It was too important. Silence. "Marcus? Please." He cleared his throat. "What do you mean?"

"You know I really like you too," Marcus said at last, as his thumb drew small circles on the back of Ben's hand. "I meant what I said before. I don't *want* to be a secret, but—"

"I'm going to tell the team." Ben had to speak up. "I'm going to talk to Coach, and then I want to tell the team."

Marcus's hand stilled. "Don't—Ben, don't do that for me."

"I'm not." Ben knew it was true as soon as he said it out loud. "I'm doing it for me."

Marcus pulled away, turning so he was looking Ben in the eye. "A week ago, you were sure it was the wrong thing to do. And now you want to tell the team?" He sounded more than a little exasperated. "Ben, you love hockey. I've seen you play. It's what you do."

Ben shrugged. "Telling Gran and my parents was the best choice I've made in a long time. I shouldn't have to hide to play." Marcus started to argue, Ben could see it in his face, but he stopped him with a look. "I'm not stupid. And I'm not saying I'm not scared." He sighed. "I'm fucking terrified." He reached up and brushed that bit of hair away from Marcus's eye again. "But I want to do it. It has to start somewhere, right?"

Marcus stared at him wide-eyed. "You're serious right now. Are you sure?"

Ben felt like he'd run a gauntlet of emotions. All he needed to do at that moment was kiss the boy he'd wanted since he was fourteen years old, terrified that he wanted him *that way*. He let his fingertips brush the edge of Marcus's jaw. Their eyes met, and he leaned forward, sliding his hand to the back of Marcus's neck, giving him plenty of time to pull away.

They met in the middle.

It was a mirror of their first kiss, almost in the exact same spot. Ben turned, trying to get closer, sliding his fingers into Marcus's hair. It was buzzed close underneath, and he loved the feel of it on his fingertips.

He tilted his head and a wave of *want* crashed over him. Ben had been awkwardly leaning in to the kiss, but suddenly he was being pulled into Marcus's lap, his knees on either side of his hips. It was just on the edge of too much.

"Is this okay?" Marcus gasped. Ben nodded as Marcus's hand slide under the hem of his T-shirt, hot on the skin of his back. It was like his fingertips were leaving trails of heat in their wake.

His shirt was being rucked up, and he'd almost raised his arms so Marcus could take it off, do whatever he wanted to do, when his thoughts finally caught up to what their lips and hands were doing. Ben pulled back, cheeks hot and flushed.

"Wait," Ben said, and Marcus stopped, his hands pressing lightly on Ben's shoulder blades. He didn't pull away but only sat there, waiting like Ben had asked. Ben leaned back a little, moving away so they weren't pressed together below the waist anymore, and took a deep breath. "Just a little too fast."

Marcus didn't take his hands out from under Ben's shirt, only moved them down so he could rest them on either side of his waist. "Whatever you want to do, I want to do. Talk to me."

That was exactly what Ben needed to hear. He wasn't going to let himself overthink or get embarrassed for once. He didn't know what Marcus had done with other people, but it seemed like he knew way more than Ben. Well, Ben knew what he wanted, and apparently all he had to do was ask.

"Can we just kiss for a while?"

Marcus smiled and kissed him on his chin, his cheek, and then his nose, which made Ben laugh.

"That's fine with me."

THEY FINALLY GOT up off the floor after a while and tucked themselves together on the bed. Ben could have stayed right where he was forever, with Marcus's head on his shoulder and their legs tangled together. Just being close to Marcus was the best thing he'd felt in a long time.

"Have you ever?" Marcus's voice was muffled a little by how much his face was pressed against Ben's shirt, but his words were clear. "I mean, you know?"

Ben shook his head, enjoying the softness of Marcus's hair against his cheek. "No. You?"

"Once." Ben felt the huff of breath through his shirt. He tried not to tense up but failed. It was *weird* to think that Marcus had had something with someone else. Was it someone from school? Someone he knew?

Marcus rose up on his elbow, looking down at Ben. "Hey, you okay?"

Ben looked up at him and tried to smile, a little embarrassed for breaking the quiet moment they'd been in. "Sorry."

"Don't be." Marcus lay his head back down, running his fingers up and down Ben's arm. "It was last summer while my family was on vacation."

Ben thought back to that summer. He'd gone to a special training camp and worked his ass off. Boys and sex hadn't been anything he'd given much thought to at the time.

Marcus had gone silent. Ben had to ask. "And?"

Marcus shrugged one shoulder. "It was okay, I guess. I mean, I met the guy at an ice cream stand at the beach, and we kind of hit it off."

Ben felt a hot wave of jealousy run through him. Who had this guy been? Where was he from? Would Marcus see him again? Did they still talk? He swallowed hard, waiting for what Marcus was going to say next.

"It was a summer thing. I don't even talk to him anymore." Ben hadn't realized that he'd tensed up until his muscles relaxed in relief. Marcus noticed and wrapped his arm around Ben's waist. "Okay?"

"Yeah." Ben squirmed when he was poked in the ribs and snorted laughter when Marcus tickled him. As they settled back down, he felt a little better about what Marcus had said. There was a comfortable silence for a few moments before he asked the next question. "Any girls?"

"Not like that. I mean, I like girls, but recently I've been more into guys." Marcus shrugged one shoulder again. "It all depends on the person." His fingers wandered up over Ben's chest until he touched the side of his neck, his jaw. He hooked a finger under the chain that held Will's dog tag and pulled it out from under Ben's shirt, smoothing his hand over it. "I mean, there's been this one guy in particular that I kind of like."

Ben huffed out a laugh, closing his eyes against the gentle touch. "Oh, really?"

"Yeah." Marcus propped himself up on his elbow again so he could look directly at Ben. "I mean, he's kind of a goofball, but he's hot, so that's okay."

Ben covered his face with his hand. "Holy shit, you are the worst."

Marcus pulled his hand away and grinned down at him. Their faces were so close together that Ben raised his head and kissed him, smiling against his lips. He used the hand on Marcus's back to pull him closer. They were so caught up in trading slow kisses neither one of them heard quick footsteps on the stairs.

Beth burst through Ben's open door like she always did, and the strangled sound she made had Ben and Marcus pulling away from each other so quickly Marcus almost fell off the bed.

"Oh my god, I'm so sorry!" Beth had her hand over her eyes, and Ben would have been laughing his ass off if he hadn't been quite so mortified.

He and Marcus scrambled off the bed, tugging their T-shirts back into place. Ben ran his hand through his hair and tried not to panic. It was habit more than anything, the rising panic in his chest. He swallowed it down.

"What are you doing here?" he squeaked. "I thought you had practice."

Beth gingerly took her hand away from her eyes, peeking between her fingers. "I *did*. We're back already." She smiled at Ben in a way he knew was not good. "Guess you were busy, Benny."

Marcus snorted. "*Benny?*" They both looked at Marcus, who'd been silently watching them. He gave them both a wide grin. "That's *awesome*."

Ben groaned. "Oh god. Fine. Marcus, this is my dumb little sister, Beth."

"Hey!"

"Shut up. Beth, this is Marcus, my—" Ben wasn't sure how to finish that sentence. Marcus apparently did.

"Boyfriend."

When Ben whipped around to stare at him, Marcus made an aborted motion toward him and stopped, fidgeting a little where he stood, and added, "I mean, if that's okay."

"Yeah." Ben reached out and Marcus took his hand. "Yeah, that sounds good."

"Ugh." Ben had almost forgotten that Beth was still standing there. "I saw the motorcycle but didn't think—" Her cheeks turned pink. "Just remember to close your door next time, *Benny*." She paused, leaning against the doorframe on her way out. "You're lucky Mom sent me to get you."

"What does she want?" Ben called after her.

"I don't know. Go ask her yourself." He could hear her going back down the steps. "It was nice to meet you, *Marcus*." The last was shouted so his parents would be sure to hear.

"You too!" Marcus called after Beth. He looked at Ben and shrugged. "What? I was being polite?"

Ben rolled his eyes. "We might as well get this over with."

"Sure thing, Benny." Marcus laughed when Ben shot him a betrayed look. "Sorry. It's cute." He pulled Ben closer with their joined hands and pressed a quick kiss to his lips. "I should probably be going anyway."

Ben helped Marcus gather his things, and they walked down the stairs side by side. Just before they reached the bottom, Ben reached over and laced their fingers together.

"You sure?" Marcus asked, searching his face.

Ben nodded. "I'm sure."

Chapter Sixteen

BEN'S PARENTS WERE remarkably *not* embarrassing, at least, while Marcus was still there. Ben was sure that would come later. They said hello and then faded into the living room while Ben walked Marcus out to his motorcycle.

"They seem cool." Marcus nodded toward the house. "You're lucky."

"I think so." Ben really did think that. They hadn't blinked when he'd walked into the kitchen holding another boy's hand. "Do you want me to hang on to the extra helmet for you?"

"Nah. I'll take it." He clipped it somehow to the bike and turned back to Ben as he put the other one on. "You've got practice tomorrow?"

"Yeah, and then the game Saturday." Ben kicked at piece of gravel, weirdly nervous about asking Marcus to come. Even though Ryan had all but promised they were all going to be there. "Are you coming?" he managed, finally.

"Wouldn't miss it for anything." Marcus kissed him then, and Ben hugged him tight. "I'll see you tomorrow."

Ben stood back while Marcus cranked the bike and rode away, staying outside until the sound of the engine faded. He turned and started toward the house, looking up just in time to see someone, or multiple someones, move away from the window. He stopped at the bottom of the steps and considered escaping to Ryan's house, before squaring his shoulders and marching inside.

And now, looking into his bowl of low-fat frozen yogurt, Ben wondered if escape was still an option. The yogurt had been pulled out of the freezer along with chocolate chip cookie dough for his mom and mint chocolate chip for his dad. It was going to be that kind of conversation.

"So, you and Marcus are dating?" His mom got right to the point.

Ben shrugged. "I guess."

"So, he's your..." The question hung in the air. She liked to define things, which was annoying at times, but at least everything would be clear.

"Boyfriend." Ben smiled down at his yogurt before he could stop himself. "But don't make a big deal about it, okay?"

His mom reached over and gave his arm a squeeze. "I'll do my best." Ben took a bite of his frozen yogurt. "Is there anything you want to talk about?" She was smiling, but the question was overly cautious.

Oh god.

Ben put his spoon back in the bowl. He knew what she was hinting at, but he wasn't about to have that kind of conversation in the kitchen. But there was something else he needed to say. He considered his next words carefully.

"I'm thinking about coming out to the team."

The announcement was met with complete silence. Ben looked up to see both of his parents staring at him, his mom worried and his dad thoughtful.

"Kiddo"—her voice was careful, as though she was afraid of saying the wrong thing—"you know we support you, no matter what."

Ben held her eyes, pretty certain what she was going to say. "But?"

She gave him a look. "But. You know how those boys can be. I just—" She broke off, looking helplessly at his dad for help.

His dad sighed and covered her hand with his own. "We worry." He shook his head a little sadly. "The locker room can be an ugly place. Are you sure this is what you want?" He held up a hand before Ben could answer. "Of course, you should do whatever you want, whenever you want. This is completely your choice. I'm only wondering if college might be more accepting."

Ben thought about that.

"I don't know." He hesitated again, thinking about what he wanted to say. "It feels like I've been talking myself into waiting forever. I told Ryan almost by accident. If I hadn't, who knows when I would have." He fiddled with the spoon in his bowl. "It was this big—I don't know—*thing*, and if I hadn't had Ryan, I don't know what I would have done. Maybe I would have told you sooner." His mom flinched and Ben hurried to explain. "It wasn't anything you guys did, please don't think that. It was—"

His mom sniffled, and he realized she was crying, but when he reached over, she waved him off. "It's okay. I'm fine. You keep talking." She grabbed a paper towel and blew her nose, motioning for him to go on.

"Anyway, I don't want to make a big announcement or anything. I don't want to hide anything, you know?"

"All right, then." His dad nodded. "You should probably give Coach a heads-up, so he's aware of the situation." He grimaced. "Wait, no. 'Situation's' a bad word. I mean let him know so he's prepared for any reactions, positive or negative, from the boys." That thoughtful look was back. "I think some of them might surprise you, good or bad."

Ben nodded slowly. "I was planning on it. I can meet with him before practice or something. Maybe I'll do it tomorrow."

"That sounds like a good plan, baby." His mom's eyes were still a little red, but she was smiling again. Ben fidgeted for another few seconds and then got up and hugged her. It was still weird that her head barely reached his chin, but no one gave hugs like she did. And what a relief it was that his parents were backing him up—like he'd just put down a heavy weight. At least if things went horribly wrong, he'd have them on his side.

Ben let himself breathe and hold on to her until it was almost too much. He then cleared his throat and stepped away and sat back down in front of his bowl of rapidly melting frozen yogurt. "Thanks, guys."

"So." His dad had a grin on his face that put Ben immediately on alert. "Boyfriend, huh?"

Ben dropped his head to the counter, but couldn't stop his grin.

"Yeah. Boyfriend."

IT TOOK ALL of Ben's willpower to get out of bed for his run the next morning. He was up and moving on pure muscle memory for the first mile, before he was fully awake. He'd spent half the night texting Ryan, and then Marcus, unable to settle down enough to sleep. All the back and forth over what he was going to do made him feel like his brain was going in circles.

Coming out to the team, the school, everyone, could be the end of hockey for him. Admittedly, that was the worst-case scenario; in his heart, Ben didn't believe that would happen. He *couldn't* believe that, because if he did, then there was no way he'd be able to go through with anything.

He shook his head, pacing around to keep moving while he waited on the light to change. It was his senior year, after all, and he'd only have to make it through until graduation. The next challenge would be playing on the college level *and* being out. He had no idea what that would be like, but he wouldn't have the anxiety of coming out hanging over his head. It would just be one more fact about him.

And then there was the actuality of someone wanting him as a boyfriend. It was something he'd pushed away for so long that it seemed unreal. Marcus was—Marcus was so freaking *cool* and funny, and Ben had no idea why Marcus would waste his time with him. Actually, that was a lie, but insecurity reared its ugly head at the most inopportune times. Like when he was pushing through his tiredness to stick to his routine.

Ben understood why Marcus had said the word 'boyfriend' and declared in front of his sister what they were. Ben hadn't clicked with someone like he had with Marcus, and he guessed Marcus felt the same way. It had been a quick thing, but he felt comfortable with him, like he could tell him anything. He was understanding and nice and his being, God help him, *sweet* was just icing on the cake. Marcus seemed to like Ben an awful lot, at least enough that he liked spending time with him and kissing him and—

Ben suddenly realized he was approaching his own driveway. He'd completely zoned out, jogging on autopilot after making the turn to head home. *Ugh.* He was going to be a basket case all day. Before going inside, he took a minute to get it together, not looking forward to another interrogation session from Beth.

He could hear them talking in the kitchen when he walked inside, but the conversation stopped after he closed the front door behind him. Of course, they were talking about him; he didn't know why they even tried to hide it. Huffing out a laugh, he stomped up the stairs to get ready for school. He was running late as it was and would have to hurry if he wanted breakfast.

The shower helped to shake off his sleepless night, and Ben was feeling almost normal by the time he hauled his gear bag and backpack downstairs. He dropped his stuff by the front door, but stopped at the sight of Ryan in whispered conversation with his mom in the kitchen.

"No problem, Mom." Ryan gave her a hug before turning to Ben, snagging a piece of toast on the way. "You about ready to go?"

"What's going on?"

"Tell you in the car."

Ben grimaced at the spray of toast crumbs and looked at his mom. She waved him away, giving him a watery smile.

"Mom?"

She hesitated for a minute, before finally rounding the counter to hug him tightly. "If I could wrap you in bubble wrap, I would," she whispered as she pulled away and patted him on the shoulder. "I am very proud of you." Ben watched his mom leave the kitchen, sniffling. He wondered if she'd gotten any sleep, either. He looked at his dad questioningly.

His dad shrugged. "We worry."

Beth watched from her perch on a barstool and didn't say a word, which Ben found more disturbing than anything. If Beth didn't have something to say at the moment, it meant she was biding her time for later. She'd probably find him at school or something.

"Come on." Ryan cleared his throat from where he'd been leaning against the counter and jerked his head toward the door. "Grab something to eat and let's go."

Ben did as he was told, hurrying to wrap a few slices of toast in a paper towel and grab a bottle of juice. He'd have to make sure to actually eat all of his lunch today, or he'd never survive practice. Ryan herded him to the front door, picked up his bags, and elbowed open the door.

Ryan looked at him over the roof of the car as he unlocked the doors. "Did you even sleep last night? You look like hell."

"Thanks a lot." Ben's voice was garbled by a bite of toast. They managed to get in the car without incident and were well on their way to school before he asked, "So, what was that all about?"

Ryan didn't answer for a few seconds. "Your mom's just freaking out a little."

"Well, she can join the club." Ben took a long drink of his juice. "I'm freaking out a lot."

Ryan made a hum of agreement. "You still going through with it?"

"Yeah." Ben offered the juice to Ryan, who took a drink without a second thought before handing it back. "No clue what I'm going to say though."

"I can't help you there. It's your story to tell."

Ben sighed. "Just tell me I'm doing the right thing."

"Does it feel like it?"

He thought for a long minute. There were so many things on the pros and cons lists that he'd lost track. It would be nice to have a relationship he didn't have to lie about. The last day or so with Marcus had him convinced it was worth the risk.

"I think so." He hesitated. "What if—What if the guys find out, and they don't want me on the team?"

"Is the team the only thing you're worried about? School includes a lot more people than just the team."

Ryan had a point. A very good one.

"I know, but those people will be gone after this year, most of them anyway. And hockey players are the absolute worst gossips. If the guys decide they're against me, would I have to quit? If I quit then I'll lose my scholarship, and then what will I do?"

"We'll figure it out." They stopped at a red light, and Ryan looked at him. "But I don't think it's going to come to that." He grinned. "Accept you they will."

Ben laughed out loud. "Maybe they will. I still have to actually tell Coach."

"Yeah, you're on your own for that one."

BEN HADN'T ANTICIPATED how he'd feel seeing Marcus after everything that had happened the previous night. They weren't just friends any longer, they were *together*. And he wanted to tell everyone as much as he wanted to keep it to himself, this little secret thing that was making him smile.

Marcus was waiting for them by his bike, and Rachel was keeping him company. But all Ben could see was the small smile on Marcus's face when he saw them coming.

"Wow." Ben jumped at Ryan's voice.

"What?"

"No wonder you want to tell everyone." Ryan put the car in park, and Ben resisted the urge to jump out immediately. "I've never seen heart eyes like that."

"It's not—"

Ryan snorted. "Not like that?" He leaned closer to Ben. "Screw everybody else. Just enjoy this. I haven't seen you light up like that anywhere other than on the ice." He squeezed Ben's shoulder and got out of the car. Ben started to get out so quickly he almost forgot to unfasten his seatbelt.

They hadn't talked about PDA or anything, but Ben shouldn't have worried. Marcus stayed where he was, that wide smile still on his face.

"Hey," he said in an obvious attempt to keep things casual as Ben walked up next to him. There was a muffled giggle from Rachel's direction, and Ben rolled his eyes. She and Ryan were going to be insufferable.

"Hey." Ben used the same measured tone. He wasn't sure what he was supposed to do. He knew what he *wanted* to do, but that wouldn't help him keep his secret. Marcus looked at him for a second and took pity on him, realizing his indecision.

"Come here." Marcus pulled him into a tight, "friendly" hug, but he pressed his face into Ben's neck for a split second and left an unseen kiss there that made Ben shiver. "You know what you're going to say yet?"

Ben was so distracted it took him an embarrassingly long time to figure out what Marcus was talking about. "Um. Not yet."

"It'll come to you. Just be honest, okay?" Marcus ran his fingers down Ben's arm and gave his hand a quick squeeze before stepping away. Ben wanted to follow him and crowd him against the car so he could—

Ben blinked and also took a step away, clumsily covering up the rising flush on his face by turning to drag his gear bag and backpack out of the backseat. "I'll keep that in mind." He meant more than the advice. Turning back, he saw a knowing smirk on Marcus's face that made him blush even more.

Rachel wasn't even attempting to hide her laughter now. She ran up and put an arm around each of them, steering them toward the school. "Thank god you guys worked your shit out. I thought I was going to have to resort to drastic measures."

Ben was almost afraid to ask what that would have entailed.

"That would have been interesting." Ryan's voice floated from where he was following behind them.

Ben could hear the smile in Rachel's voice. "Well, you would have helped."

"Duh."

BEN TRIED TO push his self-imposed deadline out of his mind all day. Rachel did her best to talk him through it during lunch, but while he appreciated her efforts, it hadn't helped that much overall.

At practice, only half of his head was in the game, which was not only bad for the team, it was dangerous. He'd already taken a hard check against the boards, which Smithy apologized for, but it had been totally Ben's fault. He'd been too wrapped up in his own shit.

At the end of practice, they all took a knee to listen to Coach Jordan, and Ben found himself wondering, yet again, if he was doing the right thing. He hadn't had a chance to ask the coach if he could talk to him after practice, but Coach Jordan beat him to the punch.

"Lewis. My office after you change." The entire team hooted like he'd been called to the principal's office, which was exactly what it felt like. "Hit the showers, you heathens."

Ben showered and dressed as quickly as possible, avoiding eye contact with the other guys. He jammed his Flyers hat over his damp hair and made his way to the coach's office. The door was closed and he tapped on it, waiting until he heard Coach's gruff voice telling him to come in.

He took the seat on the other side of the battered desk, gripping his hands together so tightly his knuckles strained. Ben made himself unknot his fingers, pressing them flat against his thighs to keep from clutching them together again, and then glanced up to find Coach giving him an assessing look. He made himself take a deep breath to calm down. He was fine. It would be fine. Coach Jordan was a good guy.

"Relax, Lewis. You look like you're about to jump out of your skin."

Coach got up to close the door, and Ben's shoulders relaxed a little with the click of the latch. No one would be able to overhear anything now, and would probably assume he was getting a dressing down for his performance on the ice. The rolling chair creaked when the coach sat again.

"So, is there something you need to talk about? Because that out there was not you."

"Sorry, Coach." Ben cleared his throat as the other man waited patiently for him to speak. That was what made him a good coach. He was always willing to listen to his players, but he wasn't afraid to tell them what to do and when. "I'm, um—"

"What's going on, son?" Coach's voice was as gentle as it was capable of being, and it helped cut through Ben's nervousness.

"There's something I need to tell you. I don't want to make a big deal or make a formal announcement, but—" Ben squeezed his eyes shut and took a deep breath. He counted one, two, three and then opened them. "I'm gay."

Coach Jordan sat back, his chair creaking in protest, surprise written all over his face. His reply, when it came, was a little unexpected. "Okay." He drew the word out, but it was as decisive as his calls on the ice.

Ben wanted him to say something else, anything to let him know what he was thinking. "Okay?"

Coach tapped his fingers on the desk a few times before speaking.

"I'm guessing you haven't told anyone else on the team, right?" Ben shook his head. "Okay. First, thank you for telling me. I know that couldn't have been easy, but you've always been brave. It's what makes you a good captain. Now—" He paused. "—do you want to tell the rest of the team?" Ben nodded, afraid to speak. "Okay. How can I help?"

Ben blinked at him. He wanted to know how he could help. That was a good thing. Relief flooded through him, and he was very glad he was sitting down. "You'd help?"

"Of course, I would." Coach tapped on the desk again. "This is a pretty big thing you've been carrying around." He leaned forward, as if sharing a secret. "My nephew is younger than you, and he's worried about playing for the same reason. I can't say in all honesty that I blame him. But I promise you I will do my damnedest to make sure your teammates treat you with respect."

"Really?" Ben's voice cracked. He swallowed past the lump in his throat and tried again. It was absurd to be this affected, but this was his coach, after all, not family or friend. He'd expected— Well, he wasn't sure what he'd expected, but it wasn't anything this simple.

"Of course, I will." Coach Jordan sat up straight and folded his hands on his desk. "What do you have in mind?"

"I don't want to make a big deal or have a team meeting or anything." Ben faltered but kept going. "I don't want to hide anymore."

Coach nodded. "All I ask is that you let me know if anyone is less than respectful. And that means *anyone*." The way he was eyeing him had Ben fidgeting in his chair again. "As for the boys, just keep in mind they're a pretty good bunch, even though they don't make the best decisions all the time."

Ben couldn't help but laugh. "That's true." He smiled to himself. "Thanks, Coach."

"Sure." They both got up at the same time, and Ben went to open the door. "But don't think I'm going to let you get away with playing the way you did today. Come back tomorrow and get it together, understand?"

"Yes, Coach." The answer was rote, but Ben meant it just the same. "I promise."

"Good. Now get out of here so that I can go home."

Ben nodded and walked out the door, grabbing his gear bag on the way. Ryan was waiting for him in the car, and they might need to splurge on some celebratory milkshakes.

Chapter Seventeen

"SO YOU'RE OKAY?"

Marcus's worried voice made Ben frown a little. Between his parents, especially his mom, and Ryan, he had so many people checking in on him that it was beginning to get annoying. He sighed and shifted, sitting up against his headboard.

"I'm fine." He rolled his eyes at the skeptical silence on the other end of the call. "Really. Coach was actually very cool about everything." It was the same thing he'd told his mom and dad at dinner. And had repeated it several times before his mom had let him escape to his room.

"You don't have to do this, you know."

"You keep saying that." Ben heard a meow from the floor and absently patted the bed beside him to encourage Biscuit to jump up. He ended up with a face full of fur and a gently purring cat sprawled across his stomach. A thought occurred to him, and his hand stilled where it had been running across the soft fur on Biscuit's back. "Do *you* not want me to?"

"It's not that. It's just—" Marcus broke off. It took him a few seconds to continue. "It's hard, okay? You know I got into a fight with that dickhead Richards. That's what it's like sometimes. Some days, no one notices or says a word. And then—"

"Then you find yourself punching someone in the face." Ben finished for him. He knew all of that, though he hated the idea of it. "But is it worth it?"

He could almost see Marcus's shrug. "Most of the time."

"Then I'm sure." Ben was nervous and more than a little terrified, but he was sure.

"So what's the plan? A banner? Rainbow balloons?" Marcus laughed, and it helped Ben to relax a little. He started petting Biscuit again, the cat's purring a soothing reminder that not everyone was going to judge him.

"Nothing that dramatic." Ben yawned, tired after a long day of worry and then practice. "Maybe I just want to hold your hand, you know?"

Marcus's voice was approving. "I like this plan."

"Good." He yawned again and nudged Biscuit over to the side so he could scoot down a bit. Marcus chuckled in his ear.

"God, go to bed. I'll see you in the morning."

"Bye." Ben pressed END and put the phone on his nightstand to get ready for bed.

By the time he came back from the bathroom, there was a text waiting. He made himself turn out the light and get into bed before checking it, though he had a good idea what it was.

Marcus: *goodnight*

The other pictures had been a little flirty, but could still have been written off as completely innocent. This one, while it didn't show anything, was subtly different. Ben's face flushed as he took in the sight of Marcus, hair a little crazy on the pillow under his head, bottom lip caught between his teeth as he stared at the camera.

Jesus. Ben closed the picture, laid the phone on his chest, and stared at the ceiling. He wasn't coming out to the school and the team and everyone for Marcus, but—he took another peek at the picture before locking the phone and putting it on his nightstand—that was definitely a good source of motivation.

IN THE END, it was both better and worse than Ben had imagined. They'd all met up in the parking lot just like the day before, but instead of only a hug, Ben got a chaste kiss pressed to his lips. He'd fought the urge to look around, to make sure no one saw, but Marcus had simply taken him by the hand to get him moving toward the school. At least he didn't have to haul around his gear bag since it was a rest day. They'd have a light morning practice the next day to prep for the game.

They walked hand in hand to the front doors of the school, and no one said a word. Or even acted like they noticed. He wasn't sure if that was because it was morning and everyone was still half asleep, or because Ryan and Rachel were following behind them like temperamental guard dogs.

They parted ways with a quick squeeze of their hands, and that had been that. Or so he'd thought.

Rachel was waiting for him at what had become their usual table, a frown solidly on her face. She was holding her phone, and her thumbs were flying over the screen. Ben put his tray and backpack down before she looked up at him.

"Well, everyone knows now."

Ben blinked at her. "What? No one was even paying attention." It had been a little bit of a letdown, if he was completely honest.

"Rule number one. They're *always* paying attention." Rachel tapped out something and then put her phone on the table, where the screen continued to light up with messages.

Ben's heart dropped. "Is it bad?"

"Some of it." Rachel gave him a tight, grim smile. "But not all. Your hockey bros are actually helping to squash some of the nasties."

"What?" Ben's voice sounded faint to his own ears. "Who?"

"Taylor Smithwick, Nicky Espinoza, Brandon Holt. Even Jordan Roberts. Who'd have thought that dick had a heart?" She made a face. "He's usually just ugh in general."

God. Ben's heart was about to beat out of his chest. "What are they saying?"

Rachel scrolled up and handed over her phone. It was some sort of giant group text he didn't even know existed. He started reading and quickly realized Rachel knew a lot more people than he did.

It had started with one person saying they saw him and Marcus walking in together, and then steamrolled from there. There were a few people jumping in with the expected "I didn't know he was gay" and "wtf," and some other people saying it was gross. Ben grimaced but kept reading. Pretty soon, other people started piling on the judgy ones, and then the hockey players arrived. It wasn't all of them by a long shot, but a solid number of the guys were sticking up for him. And Marcus.

Ben let go of the phone when Rachel gently tugged on it to take it from him. "They stood up for me." It took a minute to sink in, but then relief washed over him. The knot he'd been carrying around in his chest ever since he'd last seen Marcus loosened, just a little bit.

Rachel flashed him a small, sweet smile. "They did. Screw the haters, dude. It looks like most of the team has your back."

There was a small flash of guilt for having thought the worst of them, but how was he supposed to have known? For all he knew, he could be the first guy that some of them knew to come out. It was a nice surprise.

"Have you heard from Marcus?"

She nodded and flashed the screen at him. There were some screenshots of the text messages from the group, and Marcus had responded with a string of smiley and heart emojis. Ben finally pulled his own phone out and checked it. He didn't usually during the school day, knowing full well he wasn't stealthy enough to use it during class.

Marcus: *ok?*

Ben typed out a quick response.

Ben: *Very okay.*

"This is good, isn't it?" Ben asked, hesitantly but hopefully. Rachel reached over to squeeze his hand, and he gave her a tentative grin. "This is going to be good." He was feeling more confident. He'd been so worried, and now...it was good.

"Enough of it will be, I think." She ruffled his hair and smiled brightly. "We'll set the rest of them on fire, how about that?"

"Rachel, you are a little scary." Ben wasn't sure if he was joking or not, but judging by Rachel's loud laugh, she appreciated it all the same.

BEN HAD STILL been riding the high of the day when they all met in the parking lot, and he suggested they all go out. He'd completely forgotten Ryan had to work that night, and Rachel had already made plans. So it would just be him and Marcus. And, of course, Ben was absurdly nervous. Everything had happened so fast with them.

Marcus had said to surprise him, so Ben immediately decided they should go to the public ice skating rink. Being on the ice would put him at ease, and he thought Marcus would like it.

It was during the drive home to grab his skates that Ryan insisted Ben should change his clothes to go out. And as always, he couldn't help giving out fashion advice. "Wear something decent."

"This *is* decent." Ben plucked at the faded Flyers shirt he'd worn to school, and Ryan snorted. Ben was mostly messing with him, but then did wonder exactly what he should wear. He should probably at least try. "So what do you suggest?"

Ryan thought for a long moment. "You know that grey short-sleeve shirt with the buttons that your mom got you?"

"Why do you even know this?" Ben gaped at him. "Yeah, I think so."

Ryan nodded sagely. "Wear that one. It's…" He made a vague gesture toward his chest. "Clingy."

"Clingy?"

"Yep."

Ben thought about the shirt in question and blushed. The reason he usually didn't wear it was *because* it was clingy. It made him a little self-conscious. "Are you sure? It's a little tight."

Ryan gave him a leering grin. "And that, Benny boy, is the point."

"Why are you like this?"

And Ryan chirped him the rest of the way home.

"OH, THAT SHIRT looks nice, honey." Ben looked up from his phone where he'd planted himself at the kitchen counter to catch his mom coming in from work. "You hardly ever wear it, and I always thought it looked good."

Ben's face was going to just burn off and leave a smoking hole in the world. "Thanks?"

"What are you doing tonight?" The question was asked offhandedly, but he could tell she was curious. It was rare that he went out without Ryan. Or at all.

"I'm going out with Marcus."

"Oh." She leaned against the counter and gave him a careful smile. "Like a date?"

"Yeah." Ben tugged at the hem of his shirt. "We're going skating and then maybe out for dinner. Can I borrow the car?"

She blinked at him, and for a second, Ben thought she was going to cry. "Of course you can. I'm happy for you, kiddo."

He grabbed a hoodie for himself and an extra one for Marcus, just in case, and ran out the door before she got more emotional. It was a short drive to Marcus's house, so he was a little early. And when he trotted up the steps, Marcus met him at the door before he could ring the bell.

Marcus smiled at him and gave him a kiss. "My mom's not home yet. She was kind of disappointed that she wouldn't get to meet you."

"Maybe next time." Marcus smiled at him then, and Ben saw his eyes flick over the shirt. He vowed to never tell Ryan he'd been right.

He grinned back at Marcus and took in his usual skinny jeans and boots, along with a sky-blue T-shirt that took the place of the ratty graphic tees he usually wore. It was a good look, and Ben's fingers itched to see if that shirt felt as soft as it looked. "Hi."

Marcus threw his head back and laughed, smile even wider. "Hi, yourself."

They walked out to the car, and Marcus kissed him again before they both got in. It was a few minutes ride to the rink, during which Ben let Marcus know that he hated to drive.

Their conversation was easy and relaxed. Marcus laughed at him when Ben revealed their plans for the evening. "Is this just you wanting to show off?"

Ben blushed, and a small part of him knew that was exactly why he'd chosen to go to the rink. "Maybe." He shrugged. "Thought it would be fun."

"It sounds fun."

"If you don't want to—" Ben started, but Marcus stopped him with a hand on his arm.

"I want to." Marcus didn't take Ben's hand, but left his close enough so that Ben could take it if he wanted to. "But I warn you that I only skate a little bit better than I bowl."

Ben barked out a laugh and felt the last bits of his nervousness drain away. "Don't worry. I'll teach you."

But as he watched Marcus make his shaky way around the edge of the rink, Ben was beginning to wonder if their first date was going to be their last. Marcus didn't look happy. Ben had offered to help him around, but Marcus had waved him off, wanting to try it for himself first. Finally, Ben couldn't stand it any longer.

"Can I help you? Please?" he asked, and Marcus looked up at him and blew a strand of hair out of his eyes in what looked like frustration. But he nodded, and Ben sighed in relief. "Okay. Just take my hands."

Ben skated backward with Marcus clinging to his hands. Ben was glad he was a strong skater, or Marcus's admittedly adorable awkwardness would have had them both hitting the ice.

"Told you I was bad," Marcus mumbled, staring down at his skates. Ben knew that was part of the problem.

"Hey, try this. Look up at me." Ben was still skating backward, gently pulling Marcus along. Marcus dragged his eyes away from the ice and met Ben's. "You're doing fine. I promise." Ben gave him a reassuring grin. "You know, it feels weird to be out here in regular clothes. Almost like being naked." He blushed as he said it, but it was worth Marcus's laugh.

"Oh, really?" Marcus was smiling at him now, his awkwardness forgotten for the moment.

"I said almost." Ben was still blushing. "At least no one out here is trying to check me."

Marcus laughed again. "Maybe I will. You never know."

Ben smiled at him as they made their way to the back corner of the rink. Marcus's nose was already pink from the cold, and Ben wanted to kiss him. The hoodie that he'd lent him was a little big on him, and it just added to the picture.

He slowed them to a stop and eased Marcus against the boards. Marcus was grinning like he'd had the same thought, and Ben leaned down to press their lips together. Marcus clung to his arms as they kissed, and the cold melted away for a few seconds.

A loud bang on the glass directly behind Marcus made them both jump, and it was only Ben's quick reflexes that kept them from hitting the ice. He looked up and saw someone he vaguely recognized as a player from another team. Ben couldn't remember his name, but he recognized the smirk on his face for what it was.

"What the hell, man?" Ben growled as his heart started to race.

"Didn't know you were *queer*," What's-his-name snarled. He made it sound ugly and hateful in a way that banter in the locker room hadn't.

It was directed at Ben—at both of them, really— and he had to make a choice. He could walk away, or he could stand up for himself. He glanced down at Marcus, who shook his head slightly. He understood why when he saw that the shithead wasn't alone.

He made his choice.

"So what if I am?" Ben said, loudly enough for everyone at that end of the rink to hear. "We're still going to kick your ass next time we play you."

They were drawing attention now, and the asshole player started to back away. "Fuck you, Lewis."

Huh. The asshole knew his name, and Ben still had no idea who he was. The thought that the jerk wasn't someone important enough to be on his radar fueled the bright grin that Ben gave him.

"No, thanks. I have way better taste." He caught Marcus's eye to make sure that he was okay and after his tentative nod, started to lead him across the rink toward the door. Marcus was keeping an eye on what was happening on the other side of the glass, leaving Ben to guide him off the ice. Ben lowered his voice. "Are they following us?"

"No." Marcus's voice was barely audible over the noise of the other people on the ice. "It looks like someone got one of the attendants, and they're getting kicked out."

Ben chanced a look over and saw the jerk and his friends slinking out. He would have to make sure they were truly gone before he and Marcus left. He was surprised at how calm he was. They stepped off the ice, clomped over to one of the benches, and sat.

Ben sighed. "Well, that should do it."

"What do you mean?" Marcus was already untying his skates, and Ben would have laughed at his eagerness to get them off if he hadn't suspected it was related to what had just happened.

Ben reached over and took his hand, squeezing his fingers before slipping them around Marcus's ankle and pulling his foot up on the bench to help. Marcus rolled his eyes, but leaned back and let him.

"It'll get out to other teams now," Ben said quietly as he worked. He was amazed at his own calm. "Guys always have friends at other schools, on other teams. Gossip travels fast." He set the skate to the side and patted the bench for Marcus's other foot. "We all know each other from camps or special leagues. You're around the same group of people so much that everyone kind of knows everyone else's business. I try to stay out of it." He gave Marcus's ankle a squeeze before starting to work on his own skates. "But the truth is, it'll spread faster now than if I'd put it up on a billboard."

"Are you okay with that?" Marcus's hand was on his shoulder, moving up to the back of his neck to play with the thin chain that the dog tag hung from.

Ben nodded. "For some reason, it's not bothering me. It's weird." He was being honest. It might hit him later, but he was fine right now.

Marcus's fingers playing with the chain around his neck reminded him of something. "Speaking of gossip, Beth talks too much. My gran wants to meet you."

"Your gran?" Marcus looked a little nervous at the prospect.

"Yeah. She's moving out of state in a few weeks, and I think she just wants to get to know you before she goes." It occurred to him this was a lot to ask of someone he'd been dating all of one day. "But...I can tell her no if you're not ready for that. It's a bad idea, isn't it. I mean, it's hardly fair..." He started to get his phone out, but Marcus stopped him.

"Ben, I want to meet your gran, okay?"

Ben looked at him for a moment and then put his phone back. "Well, that's good, because I'm pretty sure she's coming to the game tomorrow, and you'd be hard to hide."

Marcus ruffled his hair and grinned at him. "Don't worry. I'm good with grandmothers. They love me."

They both stood, and Ben retrieved his skate bag and their shoes from the locker. After he put his own skates away and returned Marcus's to the desk, he was at a little bit of a loss as to what to do next. They hadn't been there very long, thanks to the jerk and his buddies, but he wasn't ready to go home yet.

"Um, you want to get something to eat? Early supper?"

"Sounds good. The diner?"

Ben nodded, and Marcus took his free hand and gave him a crooked smile. They made their way out the front doors and looked around the parking lot to make sure the jerk had actually left. The coast seemed to be clear, and they walked out to Ben's car.

THE DINER WAS busy as usual. Running into the jerk at the rink had given Ben some small amount of confidence in the moment, but now he was kicking himself because there was a table full of his teammates over in the corner. They hadn't noticed Ben and Marcus yet, but it could happen at any time. He wasn't afraid of what they'd say. Not really. But he hadn't had to talk to them face-to-face yet. Random jerks were one thing, but these were guys on his team. Ben felt Marcus nudge his knee with his own and looked over to see that Marcus had noticed them, too.

"We can go somewhere else if you want."

"Nope." Ben gave him a smile, aiming for reassuring. "It's okay."

"Are you sure?" Marcus leaned in and dropped his voice. "Because here comes Taylor."

"Oh god." Ben only had a few seconds to brace himself before Smithy was squeezing his bulk into the booth beside him. He glanced over at the team's table, and he could see the other guys, and a few girls, looking at them curiously. It made Ben bristle a little.

"Can I help you?" he asked, a little sharpness to his tone.

It came out a little harshly, but Smithy ignored it. "So this is who you've been texting, Cap?" He nodded at Marcus. "You could have said, you know."

Ben blinked at him. "Seriously?"

"Well, yeah." Smithy looked at him like he'd lost his mind. "What did you think we were going to do?"

Ben glanced at Marcus, who looked just as confused as he felt. Luckily, the server had really good timing and showed up to take their drink order. It gave Ben a few seconds to get his thoughts in order. After their run-in at the rink, he was still ready to go on the defensive. After all, this was the same guy who was calling someone a fag *last week*, and now he was giving him a hard time for not speaking up? What the hell?

The server stepped away, and Ben drew in a deep breath.

"What was I supposed to think? Think really hard about that. Think about some of the things you've said in the locker room or, hell, even outside of the locker room, and then answer that question for me. I had no way of knowing how any of you would react."

Ben felt Marcus's hand creep over to his, and he laced their fingers together, right up on the tabletop where everyone could see. Apparently he was incapable of doing things by halves.

"Anyway, you and a few of the other guys might be fine with this, but I know for a fact there's some people on the team who won't be. And those are the people I have to rely on to do the right thing and not let it affect the game. *That's* why I didn't tell you."

Smithy was staring at him now, and he could see out of the corner of his eye that the group of players and their dates were trying very hard not to look like they were listening in. Smithy looked down at the table, his usual smile gone.

"I never thought about it that way," he said, twisting his fingers. "Sorry, Cap."

Ben sighed and put a hand on Smithy's forearm—and was gratified when he didn't jerk away. "Just watch my back on the ice, and we'll call it even, okay?"

Smithy gave him a grateful smile. "No problem. I can do that." He blinked, and suddenly he was the same cocky D-man he'd always been. "Anyway. See you tomorrow." He waved awkwardly at Marcus, who lifted a hand back at him, still looking mystified, and went back to his own table.

"That was..." Marcus looked like he was reaching for words. "Just *bizarre*."

"Welcome to my world." Ben took a quick look at the menu before deciding that he was definitely ordering the cheeseburger. "Hockey players are weird."

"Don't I know it." Marcus bumped his knee and grinned.

Chapter Eighteen

THEY LINGERED OVER dinner, and finally, Marcus suggested they go back to Ben's house and hang out for a little while. But when they pulled up in the driveway, Ben was suddenly nervous again. He turned off the car and sat staring forward, his hands still on the wheel. Ben knew, theoretically, how dates were supposed to work. A nice goodbye kiss beside the car. And it was very likely there was at least someone in his family at home, and possibly watching.

"Um, we're here," Marcus said, nudging him.

Ben looked at the house, trying to gauge where everyone was. The living room flickered with the light from the television, so his parents might not have heard them pull up. Beth's room was toward the front of the house, and its window was completely dark. With luck, she might be out with friends or something. The coast was clear, for the moment. "You still want to watch something? Hang out?"

"Sure." Marcus slipped out of the car after him—Ben wincing at the noise of the car doors slamming—and followed him toward the house. On the way, Marcus reached over to capture Ben's hand, bumping him a little with his elbow as he did so. "Did you have a good time? I mean, all things considered?"

"Yeah." Ben took a chance and brushed his lips over the back of Marcus's hand. "It was really good. Even better than I thought. Despite all the stuff at the rink." He caught a flash of relief as it crossed Marcus's features and wondered how worried he'd been. "Come here."

He pulled Marcus over to the side of the steps, out of the sightline of the door, and kissed him. He finally got to touch that soft shirt as he rested his free hand on Marcus's waist. The kiss only lasted a few seconds, but it felt like the right thing to do. "You good?" Marcus nodded, and he led him up the steps, letting go just as he opened the front door.

"Mom? Dad?" He could hear the TV as he closed the front door behind them. There was a faint mumble in answer, and Ben motioned for Marcus to follow him. As he'd expected, his parents were engrossed in the screen, watching something involving dragons that he hadn't made time for yet. The way Marcus's eyes lit up when he saw what was on the screen made him groan. "I'm going to lose you to *Game of Thrones*, aren't I."

Marcus gave him an incredulous look. "You don't like it?"

Ben shrugged. "Haven't watched it yet. No time."

His dad piped up. "We told him he'd like it."

And that was the perfect excuse to not sit and talk with his parents.

"We could go and watch the first episode. If you want." Ben could have sworn he heard a choked off giggle from his mom's direction.

"There's snacks or whatever in the kitchen," she finally offered after she got herself under control. "Please make yourself at home, Marcus."

Ben took the opportunity to drag Marcus away from his parents and the TV show he was still trying to watch. "You want something to drink or anything?"

"Nah, I'm good. You?"

Ben turned toward the stairs in answer. He was eager to have some time for just the two of them, but he didn't know what that *meant*. They'd been going out for only two days, and it still didn't feel quite real.

He closed the door behind Marcus, kicked his shoes off, and went to set up his laptop. While Marcus wandered around the room, Ben took a quick look to make sure there wasn't any dirty underwear or anything lying about and was relieved everything seemed to have made it into the hamper.

"So you've played hockey for a long time, right?"

Ben looked up from where he was sitting on the bed, and Marcus had a puck in his hand. It had a peeling piece of tape wrapped around the edge with a date written in black marker. It was the puck from his very first goal.

"Yeah. It's kind of the only thing I'm good at." Ben shrugged. "And I love playing."

Marcus put the puck back down on the shelf where he'd found it. "There's more to you than just hockey. You know that, right?" He shook his head. "You're a great player, and it's awesome to see you do your thing, but you? You're *more*." Marcus rubbed the back of his neck, embarrassed. "I just wanted you to know that."

Ben stared at him. He didn't know what to say to all that. So, of course, he blurted out the first thing that came to his mind. "You don't even know me that well."

"Yeah, I do." Marcus stepped closer to him until he was bracketed by Ben's knees, and ran his hand through Ben's hair. "I know you're a nice guy that would do anything for your friends." Ben leaned into the touch. "I know you're one hell of a hockey player because I've seen you play. You give everything out there on the ice, and I think you've got a chance to go places with it." Marcus knelt in front of him so they were eye to eye. "And I know you are one of the bravest people I've ever met."

"I'm not—" Ben started but cut off when Marcus kissed him.

It started out soft and sweet, but quickly grew more heated. He shoved his laptop out of the way and scooted back onto the bed, pulling Marcus up with him with a hand balled in the soft blue of his shirt. He heard two thumps as Marcus's boots hit the floor, and Ben suddenly found himself on his back with Marcus half on top of him.

He lost himself to the moment and let his hands roam, finding warm skin under the back of Marcus's shirt with one hand and burying the other in fading blue hair. Ben's shirt had been pushed up in his rush, and Marcus's hand was flat on his stomach, fingertips hot on his skin. It was fantastic and overwhelming all at the same time. He gentled his mouth on Marcus's, pulling away to press kisses to his jaw. They both broke off at the same time, breathing hard.

Marcus was flushed all the way down his neck, and Ben spared a wild thought as to how far it went. His parents were downstairs, and he just *couldn't*—not like that.

"I, um—"

Marcus kissed him again but smoothed his shirt down at the same time. "Yeah, I know. Not the greatest timing, right?"

"Not really." Ben wondered when it would be the right time. Soon, he hoped, though it was hard to imagine.

Marcus rose up on his elbow and kissed Ben's nose, which made Ben look at him a little cross-eyed. "So, you want to watch that episode or not?"

Ben threw his head back and laughed, wrapping his arms around Marcus again, the moment passed but not forgotten.

BEN GOT TO the rink just before warm up started. Usually, he'd have been the first one there besides Coach and their equipment manager who'd been working with the team since they were freshmen. But he'd waited until the last moment to leave the house, his mom having to uncharacteristically hurry him along, her brow furrowed with the worry he was causing her.

But now, he had to face the team, and he was procrastinating like a boss, avoiding the inevitable first walk into the locker room, where all eyes would turn to him. He was expecting some of the guys to maybe look at him like they didn't trust him anymore, but he hoped against hope he was wrong.

He walked in with his head held high, taking his gear to the stall with LEWIS above it in block letters. The chatter died down when he came in but started up again after a few seconds. That was reassuring.

Smithy, in just his helmet and Under Armour, clapped him on the shoulder as he started taking out his gear. He leaned in to speak in a low voice, which Ben found surprisingly tactful, if not touching.

"Most of the other guys are cool with everything about, well, you know." Ben rolled his eyes, smiling. His smile faded at Smithy's next words. "The ones that aren't"—he shrugged his big shoulders—"know they have to answer to me."

"Shit, you don't have to do that." Ben's stomach knotted, and he made himself not look around to see who was glaring at him in disgust. "Really, you don't—"

"On the ice in five minutes!" Coach Jordan's voice boomed through the locker room, and Ben jumped. He had his under shorts on under his sweats so it was easy enough to strip them off and start pulling skates and pads on. This was all automatic, so it was easy to keep talking to Smithy.

"Smithy," Ben said as he tightened his laces. "Seriously. I don't want you defending my honor or anything. I can take care of myself."

Smithy shook his head. "That's the thing, Cap. With us around, you don't have to. Let us take care of this part. There'll be plenty more for you to do."

It was surprisingly insightful. And Ben couldn't argue with him. Didn't want to, really.

"Thanks, Smithy."

He hurried to finish getting his gear on, finally pulling his jersey over his head while Smithy did the same beside him.

"Anytime, Cap."

THE WARM-UP skate was familiar and grounding. It had taken a little while for him to finally get over trying to figure out who was only there because they didn't want to pick a fight with Smithy and who was there because they didn't mind playing hockey with a guy who had a boyfriend. But he eventually pushed it out of his mind and concentrated on what he was doing.

People started to arrive while they were warming up, and Ben looked around to see where his family was going to sit. They usually sat close enough to the home bench that he could pick out his mom's cheering. She was really loud.

He skated close to the glass, looking up into the seats, and spotted his Gran waving at him. He raised his gloved hand at her and then almost swallowed his tongue when he noticed Marcus next to her. Ryan usually sat with Ben's parents, so Ben wasn't surprised to see him and Rachel there. But *Marcus*. Gran had said she wanted to meet him, but seeing it in person was still a little weird. She tapped

Marcus on the shoulder and pointed toward the ice, and then Marcus waved at him too, a huge smile on his face.

Marcus stood, and if Ben hadn't been in the middle of warming up, he probably would have hopped the boards and gone to him. Marcus was wearing one of Ben's old jerseys: LEWIS and 42 plainly visible on the back as he turned. It was the best thing he'd ever seen and all he'd ever wanted. It felt so much better than he ever thought it would.

Marcus was wearing his name and his number for the whole world to see. There was no way they were going to lose.

THEY WON.

Not only did they win, but Ben managed to pull off his first hat trick of the season. The last goal had been in the last minute of the third period, and he'd put it right over the goalie's right shoulder. The stands went crazy, as they'd run the clock down. Most of the team had practically jumped on top of him, hugs and fist bumps all around. He noticed a few of the guys standing back, but they were definitely the odd men out. It wasn't that hard to ignore them as everyone lined up to shake hands with the other team.

He skated over and bumped helmets with Espy, who grinned at him. "Awesome hatty, Cap."

"Thanks, man."

The other guys followed after, making their way off the ice toward the locker room. Ben was the last one through the gate, and he paused by the side of the stands as Marcus moved through the crowd toward him. Ben held his glove under his arm and took his helmet off one-handed, his sweaty hair matted to his head.

It took a few seconds, but Marcus was finally there and looking up at him, Ben even taller than usual in his skates. His grin matched Ben's own.

"That was awesome. I'm so proud of you." He grabbed a handful of Ben's blue and silver jersey to pull him down and kiss him, messy and fantastic. He didn't seem to mind how sweaty Ben was, which made him damn near perfect.

People were staring at them and Ben didn't care. He was happy and *normal*. He got to have what everyone else had. Still smiling, he stepped back and Marcus let him go. "I've got to—"

"Yeah, go on. I'll see you after."

Ben leaned down and kissed him one more time.

Marcus laughed. "Seriously, go. I'll be here."

"Okay." Ben was giddy and made himself go to the locker room where he was greeted with excited clapping and catcalls. He blushed and made his way to his stall with what felt like a permanent grin on his face. It was so different from how uneasy he'd felt about three or so hours ago, and it hit him, suddenly, that this was going to work. He could have this.

Coach Jordan walked in, and the noise simmered down to a dull roar.

"Good game, boys. It's still early, so don't get too full of yourselves, all right?" They all laughed. "And I've got something for one of you right here." He reached into his pocket, pulled out a puck, and tossed it over to Ben. "Nice hatty, Cap. Keep 'em coming." Ben caught it and flushed as the majority of the locker room erupted into cheers. "Get some rest and be ready to go Monday. Check your crap in and get out of here, you know the drill."

There was another cheer, and everyone started stripping out of their sweaty pads.

Ben hurried to be one of the first in the showers, mostly because he wanted to get the hell out of there and see his family and friends. Marcus especially. And Ryan and Rachel. But he also didn't want to see which guys wouldn't want him in there, the ones who would think he was automatically going to lust after them because he happened to like boys.

He wasn't going to let them bring down his high. Not tonight. He'd deal with that bullshit later. Tonight, he was going to celebrate.

Chapter Nineteen

THINGS CHANGED ONCE the shock wore off that the captain of the hockey team was gay. And had a boyfriend. For the most part, no one bothered them, at least overtly. But he knew some people weren't happy about it. One guy had stopped showing up for practice, and Jordan Roberts had been forced by his parents to quit the team. Jordie made sure to tell him it wasn't his choice, and while Ben appreciated that, he still felt incredibly guilty. The other guy could go screw himself.

John Richards, who'd once found himself on the receiving end of Marcus's fist, had tried to start crap with Marcus again, but this time, it put him on the wrong side of two defensemen. Ben managed to put a stop to it before it got ugly, but he was more than a little pleased that Richards wouldn't even dare be in the same room as Marcus anymore.

It helped that the hockey team had practically adopted Marcus. It was something he found endlessly amusing and a little odd.

"So, I have a question," Marcus said, and Ben glanced over at him, their joined hands swinging between them. Marcus had a perplexed look on his face that Ben found cuter than he probably should. He also had a feeling he might know what Marcus was about to ask.

"Shoot."

They were walking through the parking lot, post-game, after Marcus had waited for Ben to shower and change.

They'd lost, but it had been a close one, both teams fighting hard for the winning goal. Ben had taken a little bit longer than usual to get out of the locker room, taking the time to reassure Espy that he'd done his best—that last goal wasn't his fault.

"What's up with Smithy and his helmet?" Marcus asked, and when Ben laughed, he bumped his shoulder. "Seriously! Why are you laughing?"

Ben was laughing so hard he had to stop in the middle of the parking lot. He took a deep breath to try to get it together but made the mistake of looking at Marcus, which sent him off giggling again. Marcus pulled his hand away and crossed his arms over his chest, a smile at Ben's hysterics attempting to fight its way through the scowl.

Ben stepped over to him and wrapped his arms around Marcus's stiff shoulders, pressing his face into his hair. "Did Smithy put his helmet on you?"

"Yes." The pout was evident in his voice. Marcus relented and unfolded his arms, putting a hand on Ben's hip and playing with the hem of his T-shirt. He hesitated and then pulled back far enough so he could look up into Ben's face. "Why?"

"It means he likes you." The skepticism on Marcus's face was almost enough to set Ben off again. "He's weird about his helmet."

"Weird?"

Ben rolled his eyes. "Trust me, you don't want to know." He hurried to follow up with, "Nothing bad, promise. He means well, and now you won't be able to get rid of him." Ben shrugged, steering them toward the car again, his arm slung around Marcus's neck. "Hockey players are superstitious freaks."

Marcus pressed a quick kiss to Ben's cheek. "What have I gotten myself into?"

Ben's stomach fluttered at the simple fondness in Marcus's voice, and he didn't try to hide the goofy smile that spread across his face.

AS FOR THE other teams, word had gotten around, as expected. Ben was shocked the first time he'd lined up to go out onto the ice at an opposing team's rink, only to have Coach Jordan come storming up to him and say, "Don't look at the stands. I'm taking care of it."

He looked at the stands. At the signs. He looked and immediately wished he hadn't. The worst part was he couldn't tell if they were the work of some dumb kids or if adults had looked at them and thought, *Yeah, that's right. Fags need to just die.*

He stared until Smithy grabbed him by the arm and steered him back toward the locker room. "Let Coach take care of it."

Ben was trying to take the high road. He was the captain and had to set an example. He should have known better.

It was just after the start of the second period when it happened.

He chased the puck where it had been dumped into the corner by Holtsy and was completely focused on beating the other player to it when he was hit by what felt like a small truck. Ben heard Smithy's shout, but it was too late to get out of the way. The other player, a defensemen who probably outweighed him by about thirty pounds, checked him against the boards so hard it knocked the breath out of him.

"Fucking queer" was spat at Ben, low enough for the ref not to hear, and he gave the other boy an elbow to get him to back off. The other boy, his name still a mystery, pushed him again. "You can run but you can't hide."

Smithy got between them, his greater height making the other player back down for the moment, and Ben skated away, head held high. He could do that; he didn't have to stoop to their level.

A few minutes later and it happened again. The player didn't even wait to crush him against the boards. He waited until Ben had the puck and hit him with a low shoulder that was almost a tackle, and very illegal. Ben went down, stunned for a second, when the other player spit on him. That was more than enough.

Ben pulled himself up, and before he knew what was happening, his gloves were on the ice, and he grabbed a double handful of the other player's jersey. His name was Wilson from the letters Ben had in his hands. He'd never, ever gotten into a fight on the ice, or off of it for that matter, but it felt good to spin Wilson around—to see the surprise in his eyes for a split second before he dragged him down onto the ice.

It was more of a wrestling match at that point, but in the end, Ben's helmet was knocked off, and he'd managed to get a hit or two in on Wilson's ribs. Wilson smacked him in the nose in his desperation to get Ben off him, but Ben wasn't going to let up, even as blood ran down his chin.

Smithy got there before the ref and dragged Ben up by the back of his jersey, wrapping his arms around him as soon as he got him up on his feet. "Enough, man. Enough."

Ben had never felt that much rage at another human being before, and it scared him a little. He ended up getting a major penalty, as did Wilson.

Coach raised holy hell about everything from the signs in the stands to his player being spit on and ended up getting most of the opposing team placed under review by the discipline committee. After a few suspensions, and one outright banning, the signs and comments at games stopped.

There were some players who were either too brave or too stupid on the ice for their own good, but the other guys made it a point to make sure they knew it wouldn't be tolerated.

THE NAME-CALLING and dirty hits had been expected. What Ben hadn't expected were the silent indications of "Me too," told to him through eye contact or grim smiles.

It had been a good game. It was the second of two away games, and Ben was exhausted but happy because they'd managed a close win. He'd just finished packing up his gear and was walking out of the visitor's locker room when he almost ran into one of the opposing players.

"Sorry." Ben tugged the strap back onto his shoulder where it had slipped off and started to step around the other guy.

Who shuffled awkwardly in the exact same direction as Ben, effectively blocking his way. They both laughed and Ben tried again. This time, he moved to the side, only to have the other boy stop him with a hand on his elbow. Ben fought the urge to tense up, not wanting to seem like he was afraid. He was definitely on guard. He looked down at where the boy was holding him, and the hand was snatched back as though he hadn't meant to touch him.

"Um." The guy shuffled his feet, not quite making eye contact. He glanced back at Ben, and Ben suddenly realized who he was.

"Kinkaid, right?" Ben recognized the ice-blue eyes that had been glaring at him through a goalie mask all evening. He was tall and deceptively slim without his goalie gear on. He'd been a brick wall the entire game, only letting through two goals.

Kinkaid smiled, a little shyly. "Yeah, Corey." He shuffled his feet again, and Ben looked over to check on where the rest of the team was. He wasn't sure what was going on, and he didn't want to get in trouble for being late for the bus. "You're Ben Lewis."

"That's me." Ben was trying not to seem impatient, but he really needed to get going. "Look, I really need to—"

"That was a sweet wrister."

"Thanks?" Ben hefted his bag onto his shoulder again, the strap starting to cut in a little bit.

Corey glanced around before leaning a little closer. "You want to go out sometime?" It was blurted out all in a rush. Ben barely had time to register what he'd been asked when Corey said, "With me, I mean."

Ben blinked at him. He'd never actually been asked out before, at least by a guy. *Was that flirting?*

He opened his mouth and what came out was "I have a boyfriend."

Corey sighed and studied his shoes. "That's what I thought."

He looked so disappointed Ben couldn't help but feel bad.

"I'm sorry." Ben hesitated. He knew how hard it was, and he wondered if Corey's team knew. From the way he kept looking around, probably not. "I'm not interested, but—"

Faltering for a second as he dug his phone out of the side pocket of his gear bag, he wondered if he was doing the right thing. He unlocked it and clicked on a new contact.

"My boyfriend's the president of the GSA at our school, and if you ever wanted to talk to anyone or whatever." Ben was aware that he sounded awkward as hell. "I mean, if you want."

Corey huffed out a breath, and Ben was sure he was going to say no when he rattled off his phone number.

"Thanks," Ben said, entering it in his phone. Corey ran his hand through his hair, and they were both probably the same shade of red. "I've got to go." Ben turned around and walked off quickly enough that it could be considered fleeing.

As he walked to where the rest of the team was waiting to get on the bus, Ben shot off a quick text to Corey.

Ben: *Hi. It's Ben.*

He waited until he was settled on the bus before texting Marcus.

Ben: *Leaving now.*

Ben: *Got asked out on a date.*

The reply was immediate.

Marcus: *were they cute?*

Ben: *He was kind of shy.*

Marcus: *so I have competition now?*

Ben laughed and sent a text back.

Ben: *It was the other team's goalie.*

Marcus: *i'm going to have to learn how to skate*

Marcus: *j/k he can have you*

Marcus: *no he can't. changed my mind*

Ben: *I gave him my number.*

Ben: *In case he wanted to talk.*

Ben: *I don't think his team knows.*

Marcus: *awwww :)*

Marcus: *but you told him no right?*

Ben snorted so loudly Holtsy turned around and looked at him. He just shook his head.

Ben: *Yes, I told him no.*

Marcus: *good :)*

GRAN HAD MOVED to Florida. It was difficult to see her go, even harder than Ben had expected. But before leaving, Ben and Marcus were able to spend an afternoon with her, so Marcus could read the letters. Ben held him when he cried over the last letter, and Gran hugged him tight to her just like she had Ben.

Will and Eddie had been separated by war and death, but their final resting places were as close together as the family had been able to manage. They all went to see the graves and left flowers, daisies, which were Gran's favorite. It had been a little surreal, the dates on a headstone as final proof that Eddie had lived out his long life without the man he loved. Ben had gripped Marcus's hand tightly, and that time, he'd been the one who had sobbed into Marcus's shoulder.

He still wore Will's dog tag close to his heart.

"YOU GOT THIS." Marcus pressed a kiss to Ben's forehead, chuckling as Ben wrapped himself tighter around him. It had become their ritual over the last few months leading up to the playoffs, Marcus making himself comfortable on Ben's bed, and Ben snuggling in close to him, becoming what Marcus called a "pregame octopus." He was fine with that.

"Maybe."

The team had managed to make it to the finals. It was amazing that they'd made it so far, and if they won the game that was looming over them today, then that would be it. They'd win their regional tournament. It would be a miracle if they won and an even bigger one if they moved on, but Ben was happy with how far they'd gone. It was his senior year, and it had been a wild ride from start to finish.

Ben couldn't help but think he'd survived something special and come out the other side better than he was before. A lot of that was due to the person in his arms. Marcus had been a rock the entire time, including all through the playoffs, and had taught Ben to have a thicker skin.

"What time is it?" Ben was almost too comfortable, but he should probably start getting ready.

"You've got about ten minutes." Marcus ran his fingers through Ben's hair, and that definitely wasn't helping to inspire him to get up. "I've got a surprise for you."

"What kind of surprise?" Ben grinned against Marcus's shoulder and pressed a kiss there, getting a smack on the back of the head for his trouble.

"Not that kind. Hang on a second." Marcus shifted and reached over the side of the bed, digging in his bag. "It was the guys' idea, I just pointed them in the right direction." He produced a roll of rainbow stick tape, holding it front of Ben's face. "Coach Jordan okayed it for tonight, since it might be—"

"Don't jinx it." Ben untangled himself and sat up, taking the roll of brightly colored tape from Marcus's hand. "They're going to use this? All of them?"

Marcus nodded, grinning. "They want to support their Captain. It's kind of sweet."

Ben looked at him, a little bit in awe of how a boy with bright-blue hair had changed his life. Marcus had dyed it that color for the first game of the finals, and it made Ben's day to see it. He told him the whole story. About seeing him and how he felt at that moment.

"There you were." He'd said it quietly, but Marcus had heard him.

"What?"

Ben cleared his throat. "I was just thinking." He brushed his fingers through the soft blue strands of Marcus's hair. "Don't worry about it. Thanks for this." He held up the stick tape. "I can't wait to see the other team's faces." He leaned in and stole a kiss. "How much more time do I have?" He heard beeping and rolled his eyes while Marcus laughed at him.

"Not enough." He was already wearing Ben's jersey, and it was easy to take in how good it looked on him, something Ben never got tired of. He stood and stretched, gathered up his stuff. "I'm riding with Ryan, but I'll come back here after, all right?"

"Sounds good to me." A final lingering kiss and Marcus was gone.

Ben picked up the roll of tape and smiled at it before tucking it away in his bag, the bright colors contrasting against the dark pads.

"There you were."

About the Author

Jennifer has always been a voracious reader and a well-established geek from an early age. She loves comics, movies, and anything that tells a compelling story.

When not writing, she likes knitting, dissecting/arguing about movies with her husband, and enjoying the general chaos that comes with having kids.

Email: jcozwrites@gmail.com

Facebook: www.facebook.com/jcozwrites

Twitter: @jcozwrites

Website: www.jcozwrites.com

Other books by this author

A Boy Worth Knowing

"Coming Home" within *Once Upon a Rainbow, Volume Two*

Also Available from NineStar Press

Connect with NineStar Press

Website: NineStarPress.com

Facebook: NineStarPress

Facebook Reader Group: NineStarNiche

Twitter: @ninestarpress

Tumblr: NineStarPress